REVELATION

NICK PEASE

CRANTHORPE
—MILLNER—
PUBLISHERS

For Julie, Jodie, Joanna, Peter, Toby, Hip and Magoo, with my undying love.

Huge thanks to my wonderful editor, Kirsty Jackson, and to Sian, Shannon, Sue and the team at Cranthorpe Millner for all your great advice, positivity and support.

"There are more things in heaven and earth, Horatio, than are dreamt of in your philosophy."

Hamlet, Act 1, Scene 5

Chapter 1

The sound of someone running frantically through thick undergrowth echoed across the ravine. A cloud of starlings burst in alarm from the soaring pines along the craggy bluffs.

There was an unrelenting, fast, pounding rhythm to the running that did not belong in such tranquil yet rough terrain where one slip could cause serious injury. But the runner did not care. The runner was Marty Robinson and he was determined to die.

Although now in his mid-thirties, Marty was still fresh-faced with boyish good looks, a sportsman's physique and wispy fair hair that had caught many a lady's eye. But now his face was contorted with effort, his mouth half open as his chest gulped for air, while his eyes stared fixedly ahead.

'Marty! Marty, wait up!' The shouts came from behind him and were full of anxiety and fear. But Marty did not wait up. If he had glanced back, he would have seen his work colleague and great friend Jack Taylor desperately trying to catch up with him.

But Jack was struggling to keep Marty in view. Even though he was the same age as Marty and still in good shape, Jack had not shared the same sport-filled college life as Marty. Both brilliant young scientists, Jack was more reserved, unconfident and bookish, whereas Marty had always been exuberant, full of energy and an eternal optimist. Maybe, being such seeming opposites is why they had hit it off so well from the moment they were first brought together on their CIA mission that carried the very highest top secret classification.

'Marty!' Jack was calling now more in desperation than hope. The tears were gently rolling down Marty's cheeks as he ran, but he wasn't sad, he was euphoric.

Reaching the cliff edge above the rock-strewn ravine, Marty did not even break his stride. He jumped to his death with his arms spread wide as if in crucifix. As he jumped, Marty screamed his wife's name with sheer joy, 'JENNY!'

When a body falls from a great height, it makes a sickening sound regardless of the surface below. Marty's neck and spine were broken by the fall and his internal organs savaged. But he didn't suffer, he died upon impact with the jagged rocks along the ravine floor.

Jack reached the edge of the cliff and looked down at his friend's lifeless body, crumpled in an unnatural pose that even the best stage actors could never imitate. Trickles of blood were still finding their uneven way down the exposed rocks beneath Marty's body. Shocked, devastated and distressed, Jack stood frozen to the spot as if hoping this was all just a passing nightmare and Marty would reappear beside him at any moment.

After a few moments, peace was slowly returning to the ravine which lay a little beyond Rock Creek on the outskirts of Washington D.C. It was a beautifully clear early autumn day with rays of bright sunshine casting hazy beams of sunlight through the gaps in the pines. A gentle breeze whispered through the crisp green leaves on the clump of

2

silver birch trees to Jack's right. Some starlings were already settling back in the trees from where they had been so suddenly disturbed.

Jack realised he was shaking, but not with cold. He was in a state of complete shock and had begun to mumble to himself over and over as he stared down at Marty's lifeless body, 'Oh my God, oh my God, what have we done?'

From where he was standing, there was no way down the cliff into the ravine without proper climbing equipment, so Jack would have to return to Marty's log cabin back up in the woods from where they had both come. He must call the police. But he also knew, for reasons he would need to keep to himself for now, that he would have to report Marty's death as an accident. Marty himself had already thought that through and that's why he had dressed in his mountain scrambling gear before taking his own life. He knew the truth of his suicide would eventually come out, but ever thoughtful of his friend even in death, Marty had prepared the way for Jack to handle things his own way in his own time.

Taking one last disbelieving look below, Jack shook his head several times, took a deep breath and slowly turned and started to walk back up towards Marty's cabin. His feet felt like lead weights and his distress was all the more as he found himself following the same freshly flattened tall grass and undergrowth along the way where Marty had just been running. Jack couldn't help but think that just a few minutes earlier his friend had been right here and still very much alive. He felt sick and empty as he reached the wooden cabin that was set in a slight clearing in the woods.

Jack had to use the railings for support as he pulled himself up the few weathered wood steps onto the porch. He and Marty had spent many an evening on the swing settee

3

here, putting the world to rights and coming up with crazy new theories which got ever more outrageous as the measures of bourbon began to outweigh those of cola.

He hadn't even stopped to lock the door after racing after Marty once he realised what might be happening. So Jack turned the latch and walked in to the cosy front room with its low exposed beams, warm furnishings, Native American floor spreads and still fresh ashes in the large open fireplace. Only it didn't feel cosy now. Jack almost expected to find Marty sitting just where he had been only a half hour ago.

But the place was perfectly quiet and still, as if not just Marty but all life had been cruelly sucked from its every corner. Jack went straight through into a back room, grabbing his cellphone that he had left on top of a low bookshelf. On entering the small room which was littered with all manner of tools and equipment, he fixed his eyes on a piece of strange-looking machinery sitting on a low table at about waist height. No-one else in the world, other than Marty, would have recognised it or even guessed its purpose. It was about the size of a small car engine, but there the comparison ended. To a casual observer it looked nondescript, a sort of strange hybrid between a large camera, recording device, crystal cluster and digital telescope all merged into one, yet looking like none of them.

Jack slumped into a straight-backed wooden chair opposite the device and stared hard at it. As he did so, he continued to mumble aloud to himself, 'Oh man, what have we created with you? What in God's name have we started?'

He didn't take his eyes off the device as his trembling fingers tapped out the number 911 on his phone. He spoke in a dazed, distracted voice, 'Police. Yes please, I need to report

4

an accident.'

A few miles away, seated at her desk in the Oval Office, the President of the United States was unaware that something had just happened which would ultimately put the future of the entire world in her hands.

Chapter 2

It was some years earlier when Jack and Marty had first become great friends while working together on various CIA scientific research programmes. The last of these saw them posted to Iraq until American troops were finally pulled out of the country.

Located in a closely guarded area of Joint Base Balad, the United States Air Force stronghold some 40 miles north of Baghdad, Jack and Marty led the covert team working on the highly classified Revelation programme.

The programme had actually been started back in the States, but its urgency was such that it had been felt best to complete it and get it operational in theatre at the earliest opportunity. However, things hadn't progressed as quickly as had been hoped.

The unassuming, single storey, whitewashed building where Jack and Marty worked gave nothing away of its secretive, hidden purpose. Perhaps the only causes for suspicion were the additional security personnel who had orders to destroy everything in the unlikely event that the base ever got overrun.

Inside, all the walls were plain, whitewashed stone and brick, with limited glass to keep out the punishing heat. A narrow corridor with strip lights and nothing other than fire extinguishers led to the large research laboratory specially equipped and set up for those working on the project codenamed Revelation. The walls of the room were hung with all manner of tools, whilst various workbenches groaned with different machinery parts, many of them unrecognisable from any other applications. A couple of operatives were sat at computers working on 3D plans and diagrams.

As if to reinforce their secret, non-military status, everyone in the room was dressed casually, with shorts, t-shirts and trainers the chosen preference.

Jack and Marty were busily working on a strange-looking device no bigger than a small car engine. Their different personalities often caused their workmates great amusement, as Jack would often get frustrated, be more cautious and see problems, whereas Marty always believed they were on the brink of success. This morning had been no exception, with Jack totally fed up whilst Marty remained excited and animated.

Jack slammed down the tool he was working with on the workbench and turned to Marty. 'So, another failure! Will we ever get this darned thing to do anything?'

His question was rhetorical, of course, but Marty couldn't resist coming straight back at him in his usual upbeat way. 'Hey Jack, this is great – one more failure means we're one step closer to making it work! You know it took Thomas Edison over a thousand failed experiments before he eventually…'

Jack cut in before he could finish. 'Marty, I swear, you mention Thomas bloody Edison one more time…'

But Marty wasn't going to diminish his optimism and joked, 'No, come on, don't you realise that means we're still over nine hundred experiments in credit!'

Jack shook his head, as he muttered sarcastically,

'How very encouraging!'

At that moment, Frank Caspari, the CIA station chief entered the room with a fast, efficient manner that demanded attention. Unlike everyone else in the room, Frank was sharply dressed in a tropical cream suit with a light blue linen open-necked shirt. Now in his early fifties, his short, dark, smartly parted hair was grey at the sides, framing a well chiselled face with a somewhat pointed nose and dark brown eyes that would fix piercingly on whoever he was addressing.

He was expert at playing the power game and could be a cunning, ruthless political manipulator who kept his softer side well hidden. People often said he had many colleagues but few friends. A self-confessed workaholic, this had contributed to the breakdown of his childless marriage when his wife, Italia, had found comfort elsewhere. Frank had been devastated. Still deeply in love with Italia, he had never sought the attentions of another woman. Instead, he had pursued his ambitions with even greater fervour, whilst still harbouring a sense of personal failure which he was always at pains to hide.

But today Frank was in a jovial mood. He got on well with the Revelation team, especially Jack and Marty. 'Hey guys, thought I'd just come by and check up on you. So how's it going?'

The two answered in unison, again revealing their different personalities, with Jack saying shit and Marty saying great. 'Great shit! Well I've heard worse,' Frank responded, enjoying their replies. 'Listen, I have every faith in you both, knew you'd make a good team. Just remember, if there's anything you want…'

Marty smiled at Frank, 'Sure thing, Frank. We've already got a bit of a wish-list of gizmos and gadgets on the go.'

'Oh, the highly technical stuff.' Frank laughed at his own joke. 'Well, just let me have it when you're ready. I really need this Revelation thing to work. Say, have you guys been up to the canteen yet?'

'No, we were just finishing here first,' Jack replied.

Frank addressed the room, 'Well I'd skip the cutlets if I were you. If they've ever been near a sheep my name's Scooby Doo.' His comment was greeted by laughter all round.

As Marty assured Frank they would keep his advice in mind, Frank spotted what looked like the beginnings of a replica device in mid-construction on another workbench. He gestured towards it. 'What's this, two for the price of one?'

Jack looked at Frank while turning his eyes to the sky and shaking his head with a slight gesture and nod towards Marty as if to say typical of his friend. Marty just grinned broadly and shrugged, accepting his obsession for always having a back-up.

Frank smiled warmly at them both before starting to walk towards the door, calling out as he left. 'OK fellas, I'm out of here in a couple of hours. Got a flight back to Langley. But should be over here again in a week, so see you then.'

The whole team called out after him, 'See you, Frank.'

As Frank closed the door behind him, Marty clapped his hands together in an excited fashion and exclaimed, 'OK, OK, so this is it. I got it...'

'Someone give me a gun!' Jack muttered half to himself.

But Marty wasn't to be put off. 'No, come on, my friend, this could be it, hear me out. Look, what if we alter the-'

He was interrupted as a very attractive black female orderly entered with some papers which she handed Jack in a busy, efficient way. She wore military uniform and had her long hair tied back, allowing her high cheekbones, beautiful almond eyes and megawatt smile to show why so many men on the base were always trying to chat her up.

'Here Jack, I just need you to sign the bottom sheet,' she said as she sidled nearer to Jack.

'Sure, Tina.' Jack remained business-like, quickly turning over the papers and glancing at their contents.

As he was doing so and unseen by Tina, Marty was nodding and gesturing at Jack and moving his arm as if raising a glass to his mouth, trying hard to encourage Jack to ask Tina to go for a drink with him or something. But Jack just looked embarrassed, signed the bottom sheet and handed everything back to Tina.

'Thanks, see ya guys,' she called out as she left their room.

'Not if we see you first,' Marty called back in a joshing manner.

Jack simply added, 'Bye Tina.'

Marty laughed in a kindly way at Jack's awkwardness and lack of confidence with the opposite sex. He shook his head as he put his arm protectively around Jack's shoulder. 'Come on, my friend, let's go get lunch.'

Chapter 3

A wall of muffled noise and animated chatter combined with a heady mix of different cooking aromas greeted Jack and Marty as they entered the base's canteen.

Laminated wood tables and benches were arranged in neat rows the length of the canteen and, even though now well into the lunch break, were still busy with service personnel in all kinds of uniforms from different branches of the armed forces. Marty even noticed a small team of Brits in desert camouflage uniforms clearly keeping to themselves at a table in one corner. Jack spotted them too and from their rugged, imposing appearance made a mental note they were not the kind of guys you would want to spill your drink on.

The two picked up a tray each and walked over to the food area where a line of chefs stood behind an impressive array of tureens, serving dishes and hotplates. It was one of the compensations of being posted to such an inhospitable place that the food was always plentiful and generally very good – although Frank's advice about the cutlets still echoed in Jack and Marty's ears.

A wall-mounted TV was playing a ball game loudly from back home in the USA, but no-one seemed to be paying it much attention. Various bulletins and posters were displayed on large framed pinboards around the room announcing anything from Sunday worship services to the imminent visits of entertainers and politicians, with the latter attracting inevitable graffiti.

As they made their way to a table, having chosen their dishes, Jack peered at Marty's tray. 'Rather you than me,' he commented at Marty's typically adventurous choice of cuisine.

In turn, Marty looked at Jack's safe choice and teased, 'Don't you like to push the envelope at times?'

'Yeah, well last time I did that was trying to push one of my uncle's campaign envelopes through a rusty mailbox and a pit bull nearly bit my hand off,' Jack replied laconically as the two set their trays down at an empty table.

Marty laughed, enjoying his friend's self-deprecating sense of humour.

As they both began to eat their lunch, an overweight, loud-mouthed but very friendly colleague, Jason, approached their table. In his early twenties, Jason had an engaging naivety about him with a great, outgoing personality and good sense of fun. His tubby appearance and roundish face were topped off by a mop of unkempt, slightly curly light brown hair that clearly hadn't seen a brush or comb for a while.

In his naivety, Jason was chatty with everyone and seemed to inhabit his own world. But he was very popular, although sometimes the butt of friendly, well-meant teasing.

Jason loved his food, as his physique confirmed, and had clearly just eaten well. But he had still just grabbed a chocolate bar from the row of vending machines along one of the canteen walls and was enjoying his munchies. He got on well with Jack and Marty and whilst he didn't know exactly what they did, he knew it was secretive work and that they enjoyed an elevated status amongst the top brass on the base. Reaching their table, Jason spoke with his mouth still full of the last chunk of chocolate he had just bitten into, gesturing to the TV. 'Shit game! So, how're the star laboratorians doing?'

Marty shared in the teasing but came back at Jason in equally joshing manner. 'We're not laboratorians, we're geniuses specially selected by you-know-who to work on a top secret project of infinite importance. Remind me, Jason, how's life in Requisitions?'

Jason enjoyed the banter and accepted the put-down in good humour. 'Yeah, yeah. You both having a ball here at Ice Station Balad?'

This time it was Jack who answered. 'We're good. You?'

'Living the dream!' Jason answered sarcastically. 'Well, see you around, geniuses.'

As he walked off, Marty muttered to Jack but without any malice, 'Schmuck!'

Jack countered, 'Nice schmuck though.'

'Oh the best,' Marty agreed as they both laughed.

As the two of them continued eating, Marty became quite thoughtful and pointed with his fork at his food. 'Jenny used to make spicy black bean enchiladas like this.'

Jack wasn't quite sure what to say, but looked caringly at Marty as his friend continued. 'It'll be two years this Saturday. Why in heck am I not working to find a cure for cancer instead of being part of this circus.'

Jack never knew what to say without sounding trite. He simply said, 'I miss her too.'

Marty nodded, appreciating the sentiment. 'She was my life.'

Again, Jack simply nodded and could see that Marty's

eyes were moist. As the two fell into silence and continued eating, another serviceman got up from his table and pointed at the TV. 'Anyone watching this shit?'

No-one bothered to answer so he walked across the room and switched off the TV. Marty watched with interest, stopped eating for a moment and looked at Jack as if he had been waiting for a chance like this. 'Jack, do you ever wonder about the potential of Revelation?'

Jack didn't pick up on Marty's deeper questioning tone and replied matter-of-factly, 'What d'ya mean? We know its potential, if only we can get the darned thing to work! We're not paid to wonder, just to make it happen.'

But, now that he had his chance, Marty wasn't going to be put off that easily. 'No, I know all that, but hear me out. We're trying to get Revelation to reveal anything and everything in its energetic form, and specifically therefore to reveal IEDs hidden in the ground, right?'

Jack just gave Marty a distracted look, but didn't respond. Undeterred, Marty began to get more animated. 'So look, if it can do that, what else can it reveal?'

Jack finished a mouthful of food before replying in a disinterested way, 'Marty, we haven't even got the darned thing to first base yet.'

'I know, I know,' Marty countered, 'but look at that TV. It's off now but doesn't mean the TV waves aren't still in this room.'

'Where in God's name are you going with all this?' Jack replied, 'you been out in the sun or something? We've got a job to do, end of.'

By now, Marty had become quite excited as he pursued his theme, 'But do you never think what else is out there and around us right now?'

Jack just shook his head in an 'oh boy' way that showed he wasn't taking the bait. At that moment, a couple of other servicemen they knew well walked past their table. As they did so, all four of them saluted one another in an amusingly exaggerated theatrical manner, which was clearly an in-joke amongst them. They all giggled and smirked at each other like naughty schoolboys.

After the two servicemen had passed, Marty tried to resume the conversation, 'Well?'

'Well what?' Jack retorted.

'Got to admit, it's a thought isn't it?' Marty probed.

Jack smiled, shook his head and carried on eating before replying in a sarcastic but very warm way, 'Oh, it's a thought alright. Keep dreaming, Marty, that's what you're good at.'

The two smiled at each other with great affection, but each with very different thoughts.

****

As he stood next to Marty's lifeless body at the foot of the ravine, how Jack wished he could turn back the clock to be the butt of Marty's jokes again and suffer his eternal optimism. But this was now, not back then in Iraq, and he needed to focus,

Together, working on the Revelation device and unknown to anyone else in the world at this stage, the two of them had accidentally made maybe the greatest discovery known to humankind. Jack was still in deep shock as he wiped away a tear and wondered what on earth he should do now.

Chapter 4

Years of practice helped the Washington D.C. Police Chief, Patrick O'Mahoney, take in the appearance of the man in front of him in seconds. What he saw in Jack was what he would later call a kind looking man, with a nice, softly spoken manner. Nothing too remarkable, nothing too ordinary. He couldn't age him exactly, other than anything between early thirties to early forties, although he did notice the first flecks of grey around the temples in Jack's wavy dark brown hair.

Chief O'Mahoney estimated Jack to be about six foot tall, a little thin and gangly perhaps. But then that was compared to his own slightly shorter height and stout bodily presence that was the result of far too many burgers and donuts whilst on endless stakeouts during his rookie years. Combined with his unruly tufts of reddish-brown hair, lunging bent-forward stride and wide swinging arms, it was not for nothing that back in the precinct he was affectionately known as The Bear.

What was very noticeable to him were Jack's gentle, kind eyes that he would describe as brown but were actually hazel. Clean-shaven, with regular features and a self-deprecating, shy manner, Jack would definitely be the kind of guy to attract the attention of Chief O'Mahoney's desk officers – of any sex.

Only now Jack's features were clearly etched with pain, with deep furrows lining his brow. What O'Mahoney couldn't have known is that Jack was no stranger to pain. Born in Pittsburgh, his father had been a cruel, bad-tempered man given to alcohol-fuelled rages. He had treated his English-born mother very badly until one day she had grabbed Jack and his sister Marianne with little more than a suitcase between them all and fled.

Times became very hard as his mother held down two waitressing jobs to try and look after them all and pay the rent on the shabby apartment she had found for them. She had died from a brain tumour whilst Jack and Marianne were still at college. They both blamed it on their father and Marianne spiralled into depression, turning to drugs. Within a year she had died of an overdose. So yes, Jack knew all about pain. It was also what had made him something of a shy introvert who had then thrown himself into his astrophysics studies, excelled in his exams and had gone on to diversify into energetic science – the very reason he and Marty's paths had crossed.

As Jack and Chief O'Mahoney stood at the foot of the ravine, the medics and other police officers were now placing the body bag containing Marty on a stretcher. It would be a bumpy ambulance journey down the rough winding road along the ravine which then snaked and endlessly wound back on itself up and out onto the nearest main road towards the outskirts of Washington, D.C.

O'Mahoney watched his team's final efforts and nodded as one of them told him their work was done. Both officers wore the distinctive emblem of the Washington Metropolitan Police with the District of Columbia motto 'Justitia Omnibus' – Justice for All – proudly displayed towards the top of their right sleeves. O'Mahoney turned his attention to Jack once more. 'So you were kinda best friends and work colleagues then? Was a keen scrambler you say? Tragedy.'

Jack hadn't taken his eyes off the stretcher. 'What? Oh yeah, pretty much why Marty kept his cabin up there in the woods.'

O'Mahoney nodded but continued to probe, although not in any way because he suspected foul play at this stage. 'Hmm – so you were staying up at his place and you found him?'

Jack took his eyes off the stretcher at last and looked distractedly at the Chief. Jack's voice clearly showed signs of genuine shock. 'Yeah, yeah, I'd gone for a walk myself – not much of one for scrambling. But I knew the kind of places Marty liked to scramble so thought I'd catch up with him somewhere. And then I spotted him lying at the bottom of the cliffs.' Jack broke off as he choked back his emotions.

O'Mahoney adopted a sympathetic tone. 'Must have been quite a shock.'

It took a few seconds for Jack to compose himself and reply. 'We were very close. To be honest, yeah, it's a huge shock. He was a good scrambler, but just goes to show…'

O'Mahoney broke in as if to help Jack out, 'Yeah, dangerous hobby. I'm real sorry for your loss.'

Jack heard himself say: 'Yeah, thanks,' but he was already deep in thought about the truth that lay behind what Marty had just done – a truth that would literally change the world if it came to light. He needed to get away and think. But right now his stomach was in knots and he felt totally bereft at losing the man he had shared so many experiences and dangers with and who had become his best friend.

The sound of another police vehicle arriving interrupted their brief silence. O'Mahoney addressed Jack in a comforting tone, 'Well, we'll need you to make a full statement of course, but it can probably wait until tomorrow. We need to finish here first. I'll be in touch. If you want to stick around, it's OK by me.'

Trying to sound as natural as he could, Jack acknowledged the Police Chief's kindness, 'No, it's OK, thanks, but think I'd better head back and call his ma and one or two others.'

Chief O'Mahoney was equally keen to move things on and leave the ravine. 'Understood. Never gets any easier, have had to do enough of that myself, so good luck with it.'

The two men nodded to each other as O'Mahoney turned to walk back towards his deputies. Jack took a last look at the body bag being carried away on the stretcher. How could such an exuberant, full-of-life character end up like that! Jack let out a long breath and then started to walk back up to the cabin. His face still held a tortured expression, his eyes were moist and as he walked, it was as if he carried the weight of the world on his shoulders. And, in many ways, he did.

Chapter 5

Where before the stillness and quiet around Marty's cabin had promised peace and tranquillity, it now felt eerily silent, lifeless and almost menacing to Jack as he sat in the back room. Even the sound of a family of squirrels playfully racing across the roof sounded for the first time like unwelcome intruders.

Still dazed and confused, even though he knew the full truth, Jack sat in shocked silence. He stared straight ahead at the strange-looking yet nondescript machine perched on the tabletop exactly where he and Marty had left it when they had done their last tinkerings only a couple of days before. No-one, other than Jack and Marty, would have possibly had the first clue what it did, how it worked and how to operate it.

Yet this was the device codenamed Revelation and it was about to change the whole world.

Jack sat himself in a corner on the old American-style rocking chair that Marty had been given by his mother and which he stored in the back room for want of anywhere else to put it. The chair had belonged to Marty's father before he passed away and had become too painful a reminder for his mother, even though she had plenty of other keepsakes from their earlier years together. The wood was well-worn and the arms sun-bleached from having been used outside for some time during its many years of existence. But it was comfy and with the addition of a couple of thrift store cushions, very much still fit for purpose.

Slowly and gently, Jack began to rock the chair as he also became a little more animated in his grief, roughing his fingers through his hair and sometimes grabbing at it as if wanting to tear some out. He glanced around the room from side to side, again and again, as if in some kind of stupor.

He suddenly stopped rocking and stared again at the machine whilst musing aloud to himself, repeating his earlier thoughts: 'So, what happens now. What the hell have Marty and I created in you? I wouldn't have done this if I knew it would lead to this!'

Slumping forcibly back into the chair so that it commenced its own rocking motion, Jack began looking around the room again and over towards one of the work surfaces that had always been Marty's station. It was only then that he spotted the envelope. It was propped up against a rusty old empty biscuit tin that had just enough flakes of old paint on it to show that it had once been light blue in colour with a picture of an old ocean liner on the lid. The crisp white envelope stood out in contrast. Jack could see that it had his name on it, handwritten by his friend, now dead.

Jack knew very well why Marty had taken his own life, but perhaps it was inevitable that there should still be some kind of suicide note. So, with a great effort and not sure if his emotions could take much more of a pounding, he stood up heavily, walked over to the work bench and picked up the envelope. For a moment he just stared at his name written in Marty's flowing script and felt a lump in his throat. Many years of working with the CIA had taught Jack to conceal his emotions and inner thoughts as best he could, but he had always been very sensitive from childhood and right now all he wanted to do was curl up in a ball and cry.

Jack steadied himself and carefully opened the envelope, removing the single page that was folded in half and only written on one side. He read the note to himself.

Hey buddy, you know what I've done and why I've done it. Don't be sad, I am so very grateful for what you have given me.
Now go out there and may all the fame and fortune be yours; you deserve it.
And if you wonder where all those spares went, just ask my ma to look in The Alamo as you might get a surprise!
Be happy, Jack. See you when I see you!
Your friend forever, Marty

Tears were rolling down Jack's face. He sat back down, left the opened letter in his lap and slowly put his head in his hands. His gentle sobs continued for some time.

After a while he raised his head and stared ahead as he mumbled out loud to himself in the rambling way of someone totally confused and in deep shock. It was as if he was hoping by some miracle that Marty was still alive and they were talking.

'Oh Marty, you were the best, man. What am I going to tell your mom? I mean, I can't just tell her the truth. Mind you, of all people I reckon she'd understand. And what the hell do you mean about The Alamo? Is this one of your tasteless jokes, man? Oh hell, I'm not sure I can handle this, it's all too big for me. Marty, what on earth should I do now? Shit! Just shit!'

Jack knew the police would want to search the cabin at

some stage, but wasn't worried. After all, the place just looked like a get-away-from-it-all retreat where two crazy scientists liked to experiment. They were probably creating something to look for a new planet or something like that so they could make a name for themselves. And Jack's innocent-like face would be perfect in playing along with such hasty conclusions.

But inside, Jack was in complete turmoil. Every time he thought about what he should do, another contrary thought entered his head to stop him from doing it. He knew he was now caught up in something huge and it scared the hell out of him. He needed help; someone he could trust in completely.

He knew just who to turn to.

Chapter 6

There was nothing particularly special about the panelled lecture hall – just the usual banks of padded theatre-style seats and artificial pine-looking desks that curved in gentle arcs in front of the wooden lectern that stood on a low raised stage from which the lecturer would address the students. In fact, like most lecture halls, it was pretty bland and characterless. But no-one could dispute that the hall offered anything less than state-of-the-art audio visual facilities, including the latest computer and whiteboard technologies.

The light in the hall was dimmed as the lecturer had been using the large screen behind her to show an animated film of a particular scientific demonstration. But now the lecture was drawing to a close and there was the familiar bustling sound as some students were already beginning to pack away their writing pads and books in readiness to head off for their lunch.

As the well-anticipated electronic bell automatically rang out in all the main buildings across the campus, the students were polite enough to wait for their lecturer, Linda Wilson, to dismiss them. As they stood up ready to file out, she called after them, 'And don't forget I need your essays emailed to my inbox by Friday. And yes, that does include you Adam!'

Some students joined in the joke with some friendly,

well-meant banter towards the scruffily dressed Adam as they joined him in leaving the hall. He too smirked as he knew Miss Wilson meant it well and he would genuinely try not to let her down this time.

Popular amongst all the students, Linda Wilson was beautiful, charming and funny. But she was mostly well-liked and respected because she was one of those all too rare science academics who not only have a full command of their subject, but can also communicate it in fascinating, relevant and easily understood ways. It was no surprise that most of her students excelled in their studies.

Now in her mid-thirties, Linda dressed to make the best of herself, although never in a showy way. She often wore what she would call 'killer heels' to make up for her five foot two inches height and was aware of the effect this had on her male colleagues, although she made a point of never being a tease. On campus she tended to wear her light brown hair tied back with a band and wouldn't dream of not being fully made-up, often with a subtle touch of blusher to her cheeks, complemented by a deep shade of pink lipstick. She always wore her stylish tortoiseshell spectacles in the lecture hall, giving her a studious yet undeniably sexy look – one certainly appreciated by her male students. Tennis kept her in good shape and she was a definite head-turner whenever she walked into the staff room.

Like Jack, she too had been born in Pittsburgh and this had become the icebreaker when she first met him. But she had also been a childhood friend of Jenny, Marty's wife, so over the years she had got to know them really well.

An only child, she found out in her early teens that she had been a mistake as her father had never wanted children. Although he ensured the family were always provided for, he never took any great interest in her. After her mother died from a brain aneurysm, it was almost inevitable that she had become estranged from her father once she became an adult and now only exchanged very rare phone calls with him, usually at Christmas, which she never spent with him. They had become comfortable with this. So Linda had learned largely to fend for herself and make her own way in life, developing a fierce independence and great inner strength. She certainly didn't suffer fools and wasn't backward in calling out someone for being condescending or talking bullshit.

She loved her work and had effectively become married to it, having been disappointed too often by men, especially one who had jilted her at the altar at the last minute. It was just as well, as she later discovered he had been unfaithful throughout their romance. That's not to say she had given up on ever meeting Mr Right, but experience had made her wary and she simply wasn't interested in the many suitors amongst the staff, many already married, who clearly just wanted to get her into bed.

As the lecture hall was clearing, one of the more studious looking students with short-cropped hair and heavy dark-rimmed glasses approached her. 'Miss Wilson' he said, using her formal title and struggling against his lack of general confidence.

'Yes Ben, what is it?' Linda replied.

'Could you send me that link sometime to the space wormholes theory you mentioned? I'm really into all that.' He looked plaintively at Linda as she replied, 'Sure Ben, I'll do it tonight.'

Ben beamed, said his thanks and hurried off to catch up with his best friend Alec who was waiting at the open hall double doors which were flooding light from the corridor into the still dimmed hall interior. All the students had now left the hall and Linda busied herself collecting all her teaching materials and cramming them into the well-worn tanned satchel she had used for as long as she could remember.

It was only then that she became aware of a figure in the shadows standing in a side aisle about halfway up the lecture hall. The figure began to descend, slowly making its way towards her.

Linda realised she had forgotten to set the dimmed lighting back to normal and flicked the switch just as the shadowy figure emerged onto the floor in front of her raised stage area.

Linda recognised the man immediately and exclaimed in a mixture of surprise and delight, 'Jack! Jack Taylor! For heaven's sake, it's been a while! Lovely to see you.'

'Hello Linda, great to see you too,' Jack said as he smiled back at her. Great friends from back in their own days at college, Jack had always carried a torch for Linda, but his own lack of confidence coupled with Linda having an on/off boyfriend at the time, meant they had never got it together.

Marty loved to privately tease Jack in a well-meaning way about Jack's fondness for Linda and, in his typically exuberant live-for-today way, had threatened Jack that he would spill the beans to Linda in the hope of bringing them together. Jack would have been mortified had such a thing happened, but knew Marty well enough to know it was his usual joshing.

Jack gave Linda an awkward peck on the cheek and quickly withdrew lest she guess his deeper feelings. But women always know and, truth be told, Linda had always had deeper feelings for Jack than she sometimes let on. A casual observer may well have noticed the sparkle in both their eyes that could not hide their mutual attraction.

But now that Linda could see Jack closer, she noticed the furrows in his brow and that he had something of a pained, troubled expression. His face lacked colour and he seemed nervous.

'Say Jack, you OK? You look like you've seen a ghost!' Linda gave a little laugh as she looked at her dear friend with genuine concern, little knowing just how close to the truth her casual comment had been. 'Anyway, how did you manage to get in here? Not that I'm not really glad to see you.'

Jack forced a smile. 'You forget, Linda, I've been on campus as a visiting lecturer enough times to be recognised and waved through by the gatekeepers. OK, assisted by a little bluffing and fibbing I guess. As to why I'm here, well it's a bit of a story to be honest. Can we go somewhere and talk? Somewhere private?'

Linda could tell by Jack's tone and expression that this wasn't just a social visit and that something very important was on his mind. 'Sure,' she said, stuffing her remaining papers into her satchel and stringing the strap over her head and across her body so that it hung loosely by her side. She led Jack out of the hall and down several corridors. They walked in silence as the corridors were busy and they had to focus on not bumping into students and staff who were mostly going in the other direction towards the cafeterias for their lunch.

All the while Linda exchanged quick, anxious glances towards Jack. She had never seen him like this before; clearly something was wrong. The two eventually reached Linda's tutorial room which she quickly unlocked and closed behind them after they had both entered.

The room was strewn with books, papers and some minor scientific equipment, including an impressive telescope which dominated an area towards the sash window and was pointed towards the heavens. It was a well-used room with old style furniture and bookcases groaning with books and journals, many placed on top of the already stacked shelves where there had no longer been any space. Three stunning large, framed photos of outer space taken by the Hubble telescope adorned the walls and gave the room an uplifting, hopeful atmosphere. It was surprisingly homely for an academic's study and, despite its clutter, still very much displayed a feminine touch.

An old wooden square table and six chairs took up most of the space and was where Linda held her tutorials with those students in her tutor group. Jack hadn't said a word and was looking down as if deep in thought.

Linda cleared a space on the table to lay down her satchel and then turned to Jack. 'So my friend, what brings you to my humble cave?'

Chapter 7

Meanwhile, in the county coroner's laboratory, Marty's naked body was laid out under a crisp white sheet with his head and shoulders protruding at one end and his feet at the other. Although washed and cleaned, his lifeless form was covered in severe gashes and deep purple-hued bruises from his fall.

Police Chief Patrick O'Mahoney, who had seen Marty lying at the foot of the ravine, had kept up an earnest conversation with the coroner and kept shifting his weight from foot to foot in an impatient manner, as if wanting to get finished up and be on his way as quickly as possible.

'So what exactly are you saying?' O'Mahoney asked as the coroner busied herself with tidying instruments away whilst they talked. Tall, thin, with an angular nose, jet black hair, a pale complexion and quite piercing eyes, the coroner was everything the Police Chief expected. She was measured, cautious, highly efficient in her manner and spoke as if addressing a courtroom – which, of course, was often required of her. Some might have called her cold or a bit severe, but in her line of work, even though still only in her thirties, she had seen it all and become quite matter-of-fact about death. No-one except those who knew her extremely well would have guessed that outside of her work, she and her girlfriend were members of a post-punk metal band that was attracting quite a following.

'Well, there were certainly rock and sand particles on his clothes and shoes,' the coroner observed in an almost bored, calm manner, 'just a little strange that his hands were so clean. No grit under the fingernails, that kind of thing. ... what? Yes, over there, Mr Phillips.' The coroner spoke briskly to her assistant; a small, wiry man with thinning hair and a perpetually worried look who had been wordlessly trying to get her attention. He was scurrying about putting boxes and equipment away and was clearly in awe of his boss. O'Mahoney was amused at such formality among work colleagues, even given their different status.

Like most mortuaries, the room was noticeable only for its ultra-modern starkness and clinical fusion of stainless steel, whitewashed walls and bright strip lighting. This was in sharp contrast to the grand old brick building in which it was housed, which dated back to the Civil War era. There was a raised gallery behind glass overlooking the whole lab so that, when necessary – and often in murder cases – vetted officials could overlook procedures and interact with the coroner and her team below via the desktop microphones.

Marty was laid out on one of three mobile stainless steel adjustable tables where most of the coroner's work would have been carried out. But against one wall was a further wide shelf and sinks, along with a steel trolley where particular body parts could be placed whilst under special examination. It was not a place for the squeamish.

Also along one wall were half a dozen waist-high large drawers like those in an oversized filing cabinet. Only these drawers would slide out several feet with heavy duty trays on which bodies could be laid and then closed away in the refrigerated interiors.

O'Mahoney waited a moment and then probed for more. 'You mean you have some doubts that he was scrambling as we were told?'

'No, I wouldn't go that far,' the coroner replied. 'Look, for all we know he may have just started out or whatever and slipped. I'd say it's no more than curious, but nothing that would lead me to put it down as an anomaly. He was certainly dressed for scrambling and at this time of year the rocks can be pretty slippery in the mornings.' She looked up and offered a curt smile to O'Mahoney as if to say *I think we're done here*.

He didn't need any encouragement to try to bring matters to a conclusion. 'Hmmm, so what am I meant to file in my report back at the station? Are you saying there's a chance this might not have been an accident?!'

'No, no, I certainly can't say that at all,' the coroner quickly countered, 'my forensic partner says there was no other DNA on his clothes or anything which we'd expect if there had been contact with anyone else. And there were no other marks on his body other than those caused by his fall, nothing at all to suggest any foul play.'

O'Mahoney was reassured by the coroner's calm demeanour. 'So it looks like we don't need to take this any further and can release his body for the funeral?' His question was largely rhetorical, so he went on, 'Have to tell you, I've already been leant on by some CIA heavy – seems your gentleman here was connected. Think they like to get their people buried before too many people start asking questions about their past.'

The coroner merely nodded. In her line of work this sort of confession was far from unusual, although usually involving organised crime. Very little surprised her anymore.

And in her world, most of life's events could usually be explained.

The coroner could sense the Chief was keen to wrap things up and helpfully said, 'Well, there's not enough here for me to suggest anything other than an accident, so yes, I guess I can release the body.'

'I'm obliged, thank you ma'am,' O'Mahoney responded as much in relief as in deference. He took one last look at Marty's still handsome features even in death and started to put his hat on. He nodded curtly to the coroner and quipped, 'Well I'm off to get some coffee and donuts. Thanks again. My office will be in touch.'

He let himself out while trying hard to pull in his stomach as he said a very cheery goodbye to the very attractive receptionist on his way out. *Strange place to want to work*, he thought before reminding himself that enough of his own officers and good friends had died in the line of duty to make his own career choice a strange one in many people's eyes.

He walked out of the building into the bright sunlight, one-handedly putting on his sunglasses in a well-practiced manner. He strode towards his car with the special insignia proudly emblazoned along its sides, where his driver was patiently waiting. *Job done*, he thought to himself, *that's the CIA off my tail.*

'Harvey,' he called out to his driver.

'Yes Chief?' the lanky, baby-faced, eager young patrolman responded briskly. O'Mahoney was well admired and liked by his officers, mainly because he never shirked putting himself in the front line of danger. This was evidenced by a healed bullet wound on the left side of his abdomen which he delighted in exposing to rookies to let

33

them know exactly what they had signed up for. He was a tough but fair boss.

O'Mahoney peeled a twenty dollar bill from a small wad kept in his back pocket. 'Here, get your lazy butt over there,' he said, gesturing towards the open-fronted café across the road, 'get us both some coffee and donuts.'

'We could wait 'til we're nearer the precinct and go to Joe's,' Harvey humbly suggested, knowing Joe's had the best donuts ever.

'Yeah, we could,' O'Mahoney said patiently and with good humour, 'but I just told you to haul your goddam ass over there before my sugar craving causes me to kick your useless butt halfway down the street instead!'

Harvey smiled as he hurried off. He knew he was one of the Chief's favoured patrolmen, having proved himself in several dangerous situations with him, so he accepted the well-meant abuse in good heart.

O'Mahoney settled into the passenger seat. He was still intrigued by his conversation with the coroner, but hell, he had bigger problems on his plate than to rake around in matters involving CIA personnel. The last thing he needed was to rile up the spooks. *No, I'll just let it all go*, he thought to himself as he rested his arm out of the open car window and started drumming his fingers on the roof to an imaginary tune that clearly had absolutely no rhythm.

Chapter 8

Linda was looking quizzically at Jack whilst he was obviously composing himself to tell her something pretty important. The two had sat down opposite each other at the table, with Jack almost looking as if he was in pain and was clearly struggling with whatever it was he wanted to say.

He kept looking down at the table with his hands clasped together on top, interlocking and then unlocking his fingers with a nervous energy. He spoke in a low monotone, 'It's Marty, Linda. There's no easy way of saying this. Marty's dead.'

The words hit her like a sledgehammer and she recoiled in shock, putting her hands to her mouth as if to stifle any sound. She looked at Jack with disbelief, even though she knew Jack would be telling her the truth. 'Oh my God, oh no, not Marty. How? Why? And after what happened to Jenny. Oh Jack, I'm so sorry.'

'Well that's the thing, in a way Marty's death is linked to Jenny.'

By now tears were gently rolling down Linda's face. 'Oh no, please tell me Marty didn't have cancer too?'

'No, no, he was fine,' Jack was quick to correct her, 'the official line is that Marty fell whilst scrambling on the rocks and cliffs around his cabin up in the hills.' Jack paused and steadied himself. 'But that's not what happened. Linda,

Marty jumped. He wanted to die.'

'Jesus, what?!' Linda exclaimed. She leaned back, held the side of her head with her hands and stared open-mouthed at Jack, who continued, 'He wanted to be with Jenny.'

Linda let the news sink in for a few seconds and wiped away a tear before replying, 'Oh no, poor man. That's just so sad. But Jenny died two years ago, why now? And surely Marty was as sceptical as you and I about there being a heaven or anything like that?'

This was the moment Jack had both dreaded but also knew he needed to share with Linda in order to ultimately get her support and advice. He spoke hesitatingly at first and then eager to divulge his great secret, 'Look…what I'm gonna tell you has to be just between you and me… you must swear to that.'

Linda looked puzzled and slightly alarmed at Jack's words, anxious about what might be coming.

Jack continued, 'I just need to tell someone as I don't know what to do about it and I know I can trust you – and, of course, because you were also Marty's friend. Although, with what I'm about to tell you, you're going to think I'm completely crazy.'

Linda had by now recovered her composure a little whilst she tried to take in the shocking news of Marty's death. She cut in, 'Jack, I think I've known you and Marty long enough to know that nothing my two favourite crazy scientists tell me is going to surprise me.'

She stood up and walked over to a small fridge in one corner of the room, as if needing the distraction. Jack too welcomed the move as he was nervous as hell and got up and started pacing up and down the little area behind his chair, sometimes stopping to grip the top of the backrest as if for support and then moving back and forth again like those trapped bears seen in the zoo.

'Water?' Linda asked.

'What? Oh, sure, thanks,' Jack replied and continued as Linda began to pour two glasses from a metal water flask she kept in the fridge and often took to lectures. 'Thing is, Linda … Marty wanted to be with Jenny because we found out that … well …'

Jack was struggling. Linda put one of the glasses of water down on the table in front of him and asked more out of gentle encouragement than any impatience, 'Come on, Jack, found out what?'

Being in the spotlight was not something that came naturally to Jack, nor something he ever sought. But here he was, about to share something quite extraordinary, something world-changing. He was inwardly thankful that he knew Linda so well as he drew himself up to his full height, looked her in the eyes and spoke, 'Oh shit … OK … here goes. Life after death. Linda, it's true. It's real. There is life after death. Jenny's spirit lives on.'

There was a moment's silence as Linda looked in astonishment at her great friend. She knew it couldn't be some kind of wind-up as Jack was too serious and agitated for that – now Marty, that would have been another matter! Linda's face went from a half smile to disbelief to astonishment. She looked at Jack. 'No way! What? Are you for real? What do you mean? How? Did Marty go see a medium or something?'

Jack held up his hands in the defence gesture as if fighting off the barrage of questions. 'No, no, nothing like that. Look, I know this is going to be hard to believe, but Marty and I have proved it. Scientific, sure fire, one hundred

37

per cent, empirical, categorical truth. We've got the proof. Life after death is a fact. No heaven, no hell, just another dimension, multi-dimensions.'

'My God! What ... but how?' Linda asked as she tried to take in the enormity of what Jack was telling her.

Jack was now gaining in confidence. 'Marty and I created a machine, a device, call it what you will. We call it Revelation. I can explain more, but it all kinda happened accidentally in a way. But the fact is that Revelation can reveal spirit beings. You see and hear them just as certainly as you and I are here now talking to one another.'

Linda looked stunned. She was shaking her head, part perplexed, part in shock and not really knowing how to react. She probed again, 'I mean wow man! That's incredible! You on something Jack? This is quite a thing you're telling me here, but you serious about all this?'

Jack countered immediately, 'Linda, I've never been more sober, more serious in my life. I know it's...look, to be honest, I'm still getting used to the whole idea myself. No-one else knows yet. And that's the thing – I just don't know what to do. I mean this is huge and I don't have Marty's confidence or gift with words. I was the nuts and bolts to Marty's vision. Marty would have known how best to take this forward and break the news – like, how to do it, who with, that kind of thing. But I just see problems ... I just...'

Linda cut in, 'OK, hold up a mo. How do you really know and how can you be certain? And why are you telling me?'

Jack replied softly, 'Because I've known you a long time Linda and I felt you'd understand.'

'Not sure I will,' Linda replied, 'but try me.'

At that moment there was a knock at the door and

without waiting for an invitation to enter, a faculty secretary, Melinda, entered carrying a thin folder of papers which she handed to Linda. The secretary was clearly in a hurry and briefly glanced at Jack inquisitively, half recognising him from when he had given one of his guest lectures.

'Sorry to disturb you,' Melinda addressed Linda, 'but Professor Howard wanted you to see this right away.'

'Sure thing, thanks Melinda,' Linda replied as she accepted the folder. Melinda smiled and hurried out whilst taking another quick glance at Jack. He smiled back politely, despite not appreciating the interruption.

Jack and Linda waited until the departing Melinda had closed the door behind her.

'So, go on.' Linda had composed herself by now and looked directly into Jack's eyes.

He continued, 'Remember how I once confided in you that Marty and I worked on a top secret project for the CIA back in Iraq? Frank Caspari was calling the shots as head of station back then.'

'Take it that's the same Frank Caspari who's now throwing his weight around as White House Chief of Staff?' It was pretty clear by the way she spoke that Linda disapproved of the man.

'The same,' Jack confirmed. 'The project he got Marty and I to work on was called Revelation. It was essentially all about exploring the energetic structure of everything in our universe. But more specifically, Frank and his military overlords at the time got us to focus on the idea of developing a device that could reveal the molecular structure of things in a way that enabled you to see through walls, buildings, steel, underground bunkers, you name it in a far more penetrating, revealing and precise way than any thermal identification devices that just show heat shapes at best. More specifically it was to reveal IEDs and other booby traps and so be able to destroy them.'

'Improvised Explosive Devices,' Linda confirmed unnecessarily, 'hellish things'.

Jack responded, 'Well yeah, and if successful it could be used right around the world to protect people from landmines and the like.'

'Gets my vote,' Linda replied encouragingly. 'We know that everything in existence is just energy and all matter is just billions of sub-atomic particles all vibrating together to create substance. Basic science these days.' She paused for a moment whilst her mind raced with what her friend was telling her. 'So you telling me Revelation was about making this all visible somehow? Impressive! And?'

'And we didn't crack it,' Jack said. They had both sat down again and now sipped their water, quietly studying each other, before Jack resumed in a more earnest tone, 'Marty and I thought we were getting close before Revelation was closed down. But here's the thing. Marty and I didn't close down. We squirrelled away equipment whilst working on other projects and set up a mini laboratory, if you will, in Marty's cabin up in the hills.'

Linda laughed, 'Ha, kitchen chemistry and pirates too, I love it!'

Jack smiled back. 'Yeah, well it was a bit like that and we'd have probably been in a whole lot of trouble if we'd been caught. But we felt we were beginning to make progress. We had come away from all that military bullshit and had begun to focus more on the whole energy thing and basically what connects everything in the universe. And, as our old friend Einstein proved, energy cannot be created or destroyed, it can only be changed from one form to another.'

'That's it, Jack,' Linda joked, 'I can officially take a holiday and you can take my lectures next week.'

'Yeah, sorry for teaching you to suck eggs, I'm just trying to explain,' Jack apologised.

'No, no, you're fine,' Linda quickly reassured him.

'In retrospect, I can now see where Marty was trying to steer us, but I didn't see it at the time. Oh, he'd dropped hints from time to time and he did seem to be taking an unusually keen interest in stories about ghosts and the like. Now it all makes sense. So one evening Marty and I were just sitting on the porch of his cabin setting the world to rights and listening to the radio crackling away whilst we tried to get a better reception in amongst all those pines. And that's when it hit us.'

'Radio frequencies? But there's not much physics in them for much else,' Linda offered.

'No, you're right,' Jack replied, 'but you know how atomic structures vibrate at particular rates and frequencies to create their individual physical form, just like this table.' Jack tapped the table as if to reinforce his point. 'We can pretty much measure everything in the universe as just energy. And these days we can even measure its rate of vibration. So,' Jack was well into his stride by now, 'Marty and I began to experiment with getting Revelation to 'tune in' as it were to different levels of vibration and frequencies just to see what might happen. You could point the machine at a whole area and just see if it revealed anything energetically. Well, it worked. Boy did it work! But what we saw and heard wasn't what we expected.'

Linda was ahead of him, 'You mean…'

'Yeah, ghosts, spirits, the dead.' Jack confirmed as he

watched Linda's mouth involuntarily drop open in that universal way of surprise and fascination. 'We had got Revelation tuned to a very high level of vibrational energetic frequency, at which level it revealed spiritual beings to us right in the same room. You see them, hear them. And here's the funny thing, it was just so natural, not frightening at all. Honestly Linda, it's all just so … normal. Marty and I actually found ourselves laughing and even shedding a few tears with sheer joy. It was only afterwards that the enormity of what we had done began to sink in.'

Jack paused as he could see that Linda was shaking a little as she tried to take in the magnitude of what he was telling her. She was clearly shocked and moved at his words. Linda's reactions made Jack realise even more the scale of what now rested in his hands. He muttered aloud, 'Oh Jesus, this is just too big for me. Wish Marty was here.'

Linda looked reassuringly at Jack. She trusted him implicitly but probed for more. 'Hang on, Jack, I mean how can you be sure it's spirits and you're not just picking up some weird Australian TV station or something?'

'Linda, it's beyond doubt,' Jack insisted, 'they're people you know and recognise – loved ones, friends. And they tell you things only you would know. They look just the same, only happier, in their prime and, I dunno, just less weighed down with physicality is the best way I can describe it. Linda, Marty saw Jenny again!' He paused, noting how shocked Linda looked at his last statement, before carrying on, 'But look, I realise you need to experience it for yourself before you can fully accept it. Revelation's still up at Marty's cabin and I'll give you a demonstration if you like.'

Linda nodded. 'Wow! Lucky I've known you so long or I would definitely think you're crazy! If what you're saying really is true, this is seismic. I mean this is huge Jack. To be honest, I'm struggling to get my head round it at the moment, but sure thing, you can give me a demo. Sorry, but once a scientist…'

'Sure, of course,' Jack cut in, 'you're going to need proof, I wouldn't expect anything less and I'd be the same. I know this must all seem pretty mad right now, but don't worry, I'll prove it to you.'

Linda was thinking out loud, 'Revelation – good name indeed. Well, I guess I could probably do tomorrow if that fits in with you? Morning would be best as I've got some free lectures.' Linda had a far-away look on her face as she reminisced. 'Poor Marty, He and Jenny were so in love, so perfect together. She was so ditzy. My God how we laughed when she used to innocently come out with things without realising their double meaning! And remember the time when Marty nearly blew up his research lab while experimenting with liquid hydrogen or something!'

'Was lucky he didn't flatten half the State,' Jack chipped in with a smile. They both sat in silence for a moment, enjoying their fond memories. 'Look, tomorrow suits me fine. I'll pick you up around ten and take you up to the cabin. But please don't say anything to anyone for now.'

Linda shook her head as she replied, 'No, of course. But what are you going to do? You going to be OK?'

'Yeah, yeah.' Jack waved away her concern, trying to appear casual, whilst he felt as if his whole insides were tied in knots. 'I'm fine, just need time to think. I'll probably stay up at Marty's cabin tonight.'

Linda spoke sweetly and reassuringly, 'OK, but call me if you need me. And I'm so sorry about Marty, one of life's truly nice guys.'

Jack looked at her and took just a second to think to himself how beautiful she looked. 'Yeah. He was very fond of you too.'

'Nice to know,' Linda smiled.

A few minutes later Jack was walking across the quadrangle outside Linda's tutorial room. He laughed to himself remembering one of Marty's pithy statements that *a problem shared is a problem halved*. Only right now Jack didn't feel that way at all. He needed to walk and think.

Chapter 9

Jack walked along the streets deep in thought, distracted and as if without any real direction. The streets were bustling with people and he couldn't help but brush into one or two of them as he was so lost in his thoughts.

It was a bright autumnal day with a slight breeze that gently caressed Jack's cheeks. The outstretched branches of the occasional trees planted along the sidewalk reached up into the piercingly blue sky, their golden and reddish brown crisping leaves basking in the sunshine before taking their final dance of glory towards the ground.

Jack crossed a road and turned into a narrower side road full of small cafés, bars and individual shops, many with an artistic, bohemian flavour selling hand-made clothing, curios and similar.

The street was very busy with an eclectic mix of all kinds of people, mostly very different to the sort of business and professional types Jack had just been passing on the previous main street.

A couple of hippies were chatting and laughing in a doorway, whilst snippets of different languages briefly caught Jack's ears from people dressed in Middle Eastern or Asian clothing.

Jack noticed a street preacher standing on a corner beside a billboard. He was holding forth in loud, pompous tones whilst his two plainly attired female accomplices with pudding bowl hairstyles handed out leaflets: '…for truly my friends, it is written in Revelation that the unbelieving and the sexually immoral shall be consigned to Hell's fiery lake of sulphur…'

Jack shook his head dismissively as he walked on. A small group of Hare Krishna singers passed him clashing their cymbals and chanting, 'Hare Rama, Hare Rama, Rama, Hare Hare.' The street preacher tried in vain to compete with the singers for attention, but temporarily gave up as they passed him.

As Jack continued along the street, he was fascinated at the kaleidoscope of sounds, smells and sights. He thought to himself how this whole world, its cultures, traditions, religions, philosophies and ways of life, was all about to be challenged by the discovery of Revelation.

Jack passed a young student busking. She was not playing any instruments, but singing through a microphone on a stand linked to an amplifier. She was singing in an angelic contralto voice. Not many would have recognised the song, but Jack was something of a fan of progressive rock and knew it to be Jon Anderson's *Change We Must*. The girl had a full backing track playing, including the choir. Her beautiful ethereal singing echoed along the street.

Change we must indeed, Jack thought to himself. He was familiar with the song and found himself humming along to its catchy chorus.

As Jack walked on, his attention was drawn to one particular New Age type shop with a striking window display full of mystical paraphernalia like dreamcatchers, crystal pendants and the like. To say that this wasn't Jack's territory at all would be an understatement. A sceptical scientist through and through, he had little time for such fairytale myths, as he would call them. Having said that, it was in his nature to live and let live, so he certainly wasn't hostile towards any of it and it mildly fascinated him that so many millions of people could be such devotees of so many unproven practices and beliefs. But then again, hadn't he and Marty just gone and proved the very biggest of them all!

Jack's eyes were drawn to a flamboyantly calligraphed sign in the window: *Private spiritual sittings with renowned international clairvoyant Maria Gonzales. Enquire within.*

He smiled to himself, if only she knew! And what was so special about the *'international,'* so she had been abroad, big deal.

'Hola señor,' the cheery effervescent greeting came from his left. 'A very good afternoon to you good sir.' The Hispanic lady addressing him was indeed the clairvoyant, Maria Gonzales, and owner of the shop. She was very colourfully and eccentrically dressed, with a long flowing layered dress, multiple outsized costume jewellery and large hooped ear-rings. Her ample dark hair had been back-brushed before cascading down over her shoulders just like those pictures of Flamenco dancers Jack had admired in the Spanish bar he and Marty used to frequent. The effect was accentuated by bright green colouring in the wisps of hair around her ears. Fuller figured and proudly displaying her ample cleavage, she was what most would definitely describe as voluptuous and very striking in appearance. Her voice carried a strong unmistakably Hispanic accent. She had come out to stick another notice on the glass pane of her shop door – something about meditation classes as far as Jack could make out from his quick glance.

She continued to greet Jack as if he were a long lost

friend. 'How are you today? Enjoying the sunshine?'

'I'm good thanks,' Jack replied, feeling a little uneasy. This was way out of his comfort zone.

The clairvoyant was eyeing Jack up, not quite knowing what to make of him. She tried to engage him in conversation, 'Got some lovely fresh incense just delivered.'

'Thanks, not really my thing,' Jack replied. 'Like your window display though, very colourful,' he offered lamely as a prelude to making his escape.

'Thanks,' Maria replied, 'all my own work. You know, just so happens this could be your lucky day. I've had a cancellation if you want to come in and let me try and communicate with your departed loved ones.'

Jack shuffled his feet awkwardly away from Maria. 'Lady, you're very kind, truly, but think I'll pass. And I hate to tell you, but you're going to have to find yourself a whole new career.'

Maria was more intrigued than offended by the stranger's suggestion, 'Huh? How do you figure that?'

Jack smiled kindly. 'Oh, nothing.'

Puzzled and somewhat confused, Maria called after him, 'Don't be a stranger.'

As she went back inside her shop she was still talking out loud, but this time it was clear she was in animated conversation with someone unseen who only she could hear, 'What's that you say? Oh, I know, well you get 'em don't you, the cheeky so-and-so, but seemed like a nice guy. What's that you say darling, you were best of friends huh? Say hun, what's your name? Marty, that's nice.'

Chapter 10

It was early morning and Police Chief O'Mahoney emerged from Marty's cabin with one of his deputies, closely followed by Jack.

'Thanking you, Mr Taylor.' O'Mahoney nodded towards Jack. 'I'll be able to report that there's nothing untoward here. Say, did they let you know the coroner released your friend's body?'

'Yes, yes I heard, thank you,' Jack replied. 'He didn't have much family but I'll be helping his mother with the funeral arrangements.'

'Sure.' O'Mahoney looked down as if in respect. 'Well you look after yourself and hey, good luck with getting that weird telescope thing in there to discover that planet you're looking for and make a name for yourself,' he laughed. 'Look forward to seeing you in National Geographic,' he added with a further laugh.

'Well you never know,' replied Jack and then quieter to himself as the Police Chief and his deputy got into their car, 'you never know.'

Jack looked at his watch. 'Shit!' he exclaimed. He had promised to pick up Linda and it was already well past nine. He ran back into the cabin to grab his car keys, quickly locked the cabin door after him and strode quickly over to the two Chevrolets parked in the horseshoe of bare dusty ground out front. He hated being late for anything, but reckoned he would just make it in time.

Anyone who knew Jack and Marty at all well would have instantly identified which car belonged to each. Marty's classic, sleek-styled, metallic grey Corvette still stood where he had last left it, the passenger seat littered with CDs by his favourite West Coast rock bands old and new. A few feet away stood Jack's deep blue Cruze Hatchback, a more modest choice as befitted its owner's personality.

It was only now as Jack hurried to his own car that he briefly noted how for once Marty had actually bothered to park neatly over to one side. If he had taken any notice at the time, Jack might have found it out of character for Marty and might have joshed him about it. Now he knew full well it was all a part of his friend's preparations for what he was about to do.

As if to clear his mind, Jack immediately punched the CD button on his car stereo as soon as he had closed the door. The cascading, crazy opening piano bars of *Awaken* by YES filled the car's interior. Much to Marty's amusement when he had accompanied Jack to buy the car, all his friend had seemed to be interested in was the power of the car stereo and the fact that it had a sunroof and parking sensor.

'Of course, the beauty of this little baby is the clock,' the car salesman had told Jack. Whereupon Jack had peered in a somewhat confused fashion at the digital timepiece on the dashboard, wondering what was so special about it but gesturing his agreement anyway, if only to please the guy. 'No, not that, I mean the clock – see it's only done just over 6,000 miles.' The salesman corrected Jack's gaze to the mileometer. It was too late; Marty was already laughing hysterically. How could his friend, who wouldn't be out of place in a NASA rocket-building team, take so little interest in an automobile!

But all that was now sadly in the past. Right now, Jack was allowing himself to be bathed in the pomp and majesty of prog rock gold as he drove down the hill, trying desperately to clear his mind of the worries that had plagued his fitful sleep.

He reached Linda's apartment block in downtown Washington just before 10am, but had to park a couple of blocks away. So he was a little late anyway by the time he rang the bell simply marked 'Wilson' in the bank of 14 buttons. 'I'll be right down,' Linda's voice came through the doorphone, having already seen it was Jack from the discreet camera mounted above the block's main entrance.

As she emerged from the building a couple of minutes later and greeted Jack with a beautiful smile, he felt those familiar butterflies in his stomach that he always got when he saw her. He now wished he had made more of an effort to dress better – then again, he would have hated to seem too obvious. For her part, Linda was smartly dressed for her later lectures.

'How you feeling, Jack?' she asked softly with genuine concern.

'I was about to ask you the same,' Jack replied. 'Car's this way.'

As they walked towards the parked Cruze, Linda admitted, 'Can't deny I'm not a little nervous. But kinda excited too. I mean it's not like we're just going to the movies or something.'

They both laughed nervously as Jack opened the car door for Linda and made sure she was comfortable. 'Ever the gentleman,' she mused and flashed him another heart-melting smile. Jack had safely stowed the YES album in the glove compartment, although the initial silence made him nervous as he had never been good at small talk.

****

Some 240 miles away in Bronxville, just 15 miles north from midtown Manhattan, Martha Robinson, Marty's mother, was busying herself around her bungalow.

She was pleased that Jack Taylor had been the one to call her with the news of Marty's death a few days ago. She was extremely fond of Jack and had appreciated what a good friend he had been to her Marty over the years. But the news had felt like an arrow through her heart and with her husband Burt also long gone, the pain had been all the more acute. She and Jack had talked on the phone for a good half hour. She had promised Jack that she would tell her neighbours the news so they could perhaps pop over, keep her company and generally keep an eye on her in the coming days before Jack could visit. But once she had put the phone down, Martha collapsed in an armchair and wept like a baby.

Now, Martha was sorting through her clothes to check she would be ready to do Marty proud at the funeral that no parent should ever have to endure.

Chapter 11

The woods around Marty's cabin were particularly beautiful for the time of year. With the many shades of green slowly turning to every hue of gold, red and brown, the Fall had always been Marty's favourite season and one of the main reasons that had attracted him to the location of his cabin. Squirrels scampered about stockpiling nuts for the winter ahead, while the sound of a woodpecker hard at work echoed through the trees.

None of this really registered with either Jack or Linda as they stepped out of the Cruze in front of the cabin. Both were too preoccupied by the reason for their visit.

'Did you come up here often?' Linda asked.

'More so latterly,' Jack responded. 'Once we felt we were making progress on Revelation, I'd come up here of an evening to work on it with Marty. I can vouch for how comfortable the couch is,' he added, alluding to the many times the two friends had worked into the early hours before Jack would crash out of the couch.

There was in fact a tiny second bedroom at the back of the cabin, but a family of squirrels had clearly nested just above it in the roof and the noise at dawn would wake even the heaviest sleeper.

Jack held out a hand to gesture Linda towards the wooden steps leading up to the cabin's door. He had closed all the outer shutters on the windows in advance, to ensure no prying eyes could be privy to what was to come.

Linda seemed a little nervous, but that was understandable. He boldly but reassuringly put his hand on her back as he unlocked the door and gently steered her inside and flicked on the lights.

'Coffee?' Jack asked.

'Oh no, no thanks,' Linda answered as she scanned the cabin's interior. 'Perhaps a glass of water if that's OK.'

'Sure thing,' Jack smiled. Linda's eyes were moist as she took in the very lived-in, cosy atmosphere of the cabin's interior. There were still books on tables and coats hung up as if Marty was still there – perhaps he was, she thought to herself, in anticipation of what Jack supposedly had in store for her.

She tried to break her nerves by joking to Jack in a slightly coquettish way, 'You have brought me up here to show me Revelation and not for anything else, Jack?' but she immediately regretted it as she saw Jack's cheeks turn all shades of red as he walked over with two glasses of water. 'Oh God, no Linda, I…'

'Jack, Jack,' she interrupted him whilst taking one of the glasses and gently touching his arm with her other hand, 'it's OK, I'm sorry, I was only joking.'

But in that moment, the two of them made eye contact in a way that spoke volumes.

'Well,' said Jack, gathering his composure, 'no time like the present and all that, shall we?' He gestured Linda to follow him into the room where the device codenamed Revelation was casually hidden under an old blanket.

Outside the cabin, the beautiful autumn cycle of nature continued undisturbed for what must have been the best part of an hour whilst Jack and Linda were inside. The freshening autumnal breeze played with falling golden leaves as they spiralled and tumbled towards the ground like a graceful ballet that only nature could perform. The rustling of the lighter birch and fir branches emitted an almost mystical whispering sound, while the woodpecker's industry continued to echo intermittently from somewhere deeper in the forest shadows.

The idyllic scene was suddenly disturbed as the cabin door opened abruptly and a weeping Linda emerged followed closely by a concerned looking Jack.

She needed the handrail to guide her uncertain steps until she stood on the bare ground and held her head in her hands. She was weeping so hard that she could hardly breathe and her voice came in staggered gulps and loud, breathless exclamations, 'Oh my God, oh my God!'

Jack kept a few steps away from her as he knew she needed some space just then to let what she had experienced begin to sink in. He stood awkwardly, his brow furrowed, as if unsure about whether he had done the right thing in bringing Linda to the cabin. At the same time, he had been desperate to share his secret and get her advice.

Linda spoke breathlessly in loud stops and starts in-between her sobs, 'What the...oh Jack, thank you, thank you so much...mom, my mom! Oh wow, Mom! I was just with my mom again and it was like she was alive – she *is* alive! Oh my God, this will change the whole fucking world!'

'That's what scares me,' Jack responded with clear concern.

Linda turned to him, her cheeks wet with tears. 'Are you kidding?' she said, gathering some of her composure, 'this is totally mind-blowing, beyond incredible! I mean it's….it will change the way everyone thinks, behaves, feels. Jack, you've just gone and changed the whole bloody world! It could lead to no more wars, no more hatred, I mean the total love that was coming through back in there…'

Jack was nodding but cut in, 'Yeah, but look what it made Marty do. And what about all the religious and political implications. I've spent sleepless nights over this, Linda. I just can't figure what's the best way to make this public knowledge without causing all kinds of potentially far-reaching issues. Yeah, of course, I'm with you, I think it's life-changing, incredibly uplifting and reassuring, but I can also see it being just too big for many people to handle. I can do the science, but Marty was the vision, he would've known what to do.'

Linda had closed the gap between them and gently put a reassuring hand on Jack's arm. She could see how troubled her friend was by his extraordinary discovery and she wanted him to know she would stand by him. She gestured with her head towards the cabin and Revelation. 'Well why don't you ask them?'

Jack raised a weak smile and gave an even weaker laugh, 'Yeah, don't worry I already have. But they don't tell you what to do. Seems we have free will to go our own way and cock things up – and don't we just!'

'Amen to that,' Linda agreed. 'Oh man Jack, this is just huge. I mean, wow!' The two stood in silence for a few seconds until Linda continued, 'Look Jack, if Revelation started with Frank Caspari, why not go to him? After all, he's now the President's right hand man and, as grand as he now thinks he is, he must know you well enough to grant you access. Let them deal with it. At least that will give it some authority and control. Could get out of hand if you just go to the media.'

Jack nodded and was feeling more reassured by Linda's sound advice. 'Maybe you're right. And my thoughts exactly about going to the media. Frank and anyone who was anyone in the CIA on the Revelation project will be at Marty's funeral. Perhaps I'll try and grab a moment with him then. This is too big for me to handle on my own.'

'Jack, I'd like to be at the funeral,' Linda said solemnly, reminding them both of the great personal loss that Revelation had caused them both.

'Sure,' Jack replied, 'I'd like that and Marty would too – and I can prove it to you!' They both laughed somewhat self-consciously.

Linda now held both Jack's hands as she stood opposite him, looked into his eyes and spoke reassuringly, 'It'll be alright, Jack, you won't be on your own, I'll support you. My mom! The sheer love I felt back in there was overwhelming, I didn't have a care in the world. And it all felt so normal, I wasn't frightened at all – in fact, I've never felt so happy, so inspired. Jack this is amazing, you crazy, mad, wonderful scientist, you're going to turn the whole world upside down!'

Jack tried to sound grateful for Linda's gushing praise, but was still clearly troubled, 'Thanks Linda, but that just frightens the shit out of me. But I think you're right, let the authorities handle it. It'll sure be a whole weight off my shoulders. I'll drop you off at your college and then I think I'll stay up here for a couple of days until the funeral.'

'OK, that's fine,' Linda replied, 'you can count on me to stand beside you. I won't let you face this alone.'

'Thanks Linda.' Jack stared at her deeply, again thinking how beautiful she looked. 'You don't know how much that means right now.'

Linda smiled warmly as she joshed, 'Hey, I'm best mates with the greatest scientist that ever lived, how cool is that!'

He laughed. 'Well, I wouldn't say that.'

Linda was now looking at Jack with more than just professional admiration as she said, 'I know you wouldn't, Jack, that's what makes you you.' She leaned forward and tenderly gave him a brief kiss on the cheek. They looked into each other's eyes, but something told them the moment wasn't quite right and they did no more than hold each other with both hands. Linda squeezed Jack's tight as she said, 'Well, you'd best get ready because you have no idea what's coming your way.'

'And that just scares me all the more,' Jack replied honestly.

Linda laughed as she looked hard at Jack and gently shook her head as if in disbelief but also in deep admiration. 'Jack Taylor, who'd have known.'

Chapter 12

Some 3,700 miles away in an unassuming gabled Victorian-style building just a stone's throw from Battersea Park in London, a demonstration of clairvoyance was taking place at The Spiritualist Association of Great Britain.

Spiritualism itself had long fallen out of fashion from its dizzy heights in the 1980's when the Association had been headquartered in the much grander premises of 33 Belgrave Square, surrounded by embassies and billionaire property developers' empty unfinished projects. In those heady days the building had been a hive of activity, with people from all around the world visiting for talks, demonstrations, private sittings, development circles and more. And many mediums of the day were often featured prominently in the media.

But today, one could say that most spiritual matters of all kinds had faded from the public consciousness, with congregations of most faiths and church denominations dwindling significantly while the young espoused the new religion of social media instead. The subject of life after death seldom gained any attention, while the peace, love and truth-seeking torchbearers who had emerged from the Vietnam War generation, had been usurped by a more brutal and selfish politics and materialism.

So it was hardly surprising that there were those in the audience that evening who were pretty unforgiving as the medium struggled to give her demonstration. Her long pauses and pinched features that betrayed her increasing anxiety, fell under the watchful gaze of a mounted bronze bust of Sir Arthur Conan Doyle, the celebrated Sherlock Holmes author who had once written a two-volume set about spiritualism.

There were enough plain hard wooden seats laid out in rows in the hall to seat up to 100 people. But the place was barely a third full, even though the medium, Margaret Gray, enjoyed a reasonable reputation. Now well into her seventies, frail of frame and slightly bent over from her back problems, she peered out at the audience through her dark-rimmed glasses, while holding on to the lectern she was stood behind with her bony, arthritic hands. But no-one could deny that she had the kindest of faces with a sweet smile, just like everyone's favourite granny.

A group of four very casually dressed friends barely into their twenties and sitting in a row together, sniggered amongst each other as the medium tried hard to form a connection to a lady she had picked out in the fifth row of the audience. It had not been going particularly well, with Margaret failing to give any real evidence her recipient could place.

'I'm getting a lady in spirit who tells me she's your sister.' Margaret was determined to carry on. Mediumship had never been a precise science and she had experienced evenings like this before.

'That's right, I have a sister who died,' replied the lady in the audience.

At last, Margaret thought to herself.

'Can you understand that she has a son who's still alive? That would make him your nephew,' she continued.

'Yes, but I rarely see him,' the lady replied in an

unimpressed way, causing the group of young friends to snigger some more.

But Margaret pressed on undeterred. 'That's OK, that doesn't matter. She's showing me the American flag for some reason. I don't usually do this when I get this kind of thing, but I can't ignore it. I need to tell you to get an urgent message to him. I'm seeing crossed arrows and a black car; it's a warning to your nephew that he needs to take great care. I'm sensing real danger. Is this making any sense to you?'

The lady in the fifth row just shook her head in a somewhat bewildered way. Others in the audience exchanged glances with each other and shuffled their feet awkwardly under their chairs. Margaret Gray still had the link to the lady's sister, but shortly decided that retreat was the better part of valour, sent the lady love and moved on to an elderly gentleman who seemed perhaps too ready to accept the evidence she gave him. So all was not lost, although later, as the hall emptied after the demonstration, whispered exchanges of 'disappointing' and 'what a shame' could be overheard.

The lady from the fifth row had reached the glazed oak doors leading outside and noticed a light shower was falling. Always prepared, she took out a small extendible umbrella from her handbag, unfurled it and stepped out onto the wide street.

What a strange message, she thought to herself as she walked towards the underground station. It was true, her sister had married an American and they had had a son who was now in his thirties. Distance had meant the aunt and nephew only enjoyed rare video calls and hadn't actually met in person for a few years. *Well I can't very well just call him out of the blue and tell him his life may be in danger, can I,* she mused to herself. What would he think of her, especially if she told him the source of the warning. He would think her a crazy old bat – probably already did. Still, perhaps in the morning she would send him an email and just see how her nephew Jack was doing.

Chapter 13

It was much later in the evening and Jack was sitting on the swing bench on the balustraded balcony of the cabin. He used his toes to gently rock the bench to and fro; lost in his thoughts.

Although now autumn, it was still relatively mild enough to be sitting outside and, in any event, Jack had wrapped himself in a cosy fleece jacket to keep out any chill. It was a reasonably clear night and Jack was looking up at the fabulous night sky full of stars and planets. Astrophysics had always been his main love as a scientist and Jack enjoyed picking out all the constellations that he first became familiar with as a young boy.

It was his father who had helped him identify his first constellation, The Big Dipper, also known as Ursa Major. Sadly, it was one of the few positive things his father had ever done for him. Wherever he had subsequently been in his life, Jack always looked up at night for The Big Dipper almost as an escape and his own private security blanket.

A naturally shy and introverted child, he had withdrawn even more into his shell as the alcohol had increasingly taken over his father's temper and made the man more and more violent. After his mother had walked out, taking Jack and his sister Marianne with her, she had often struggled to put food on the table and spent most of her time working to see Jack and Marianne through their schooling. Jack had been a good pupil and excelled at his studies. But he never had the confidence through his teens to make much of his social life, especially when it came to girls. After his mother died and losing his sister too whilst still in his college years hadn't helped, as he had lacked any close female influence or advice during his most important early adult years.

Jack smiled to himself, recalling his own gaucheness in those days while blotting out the pain, as he gently rocked himself on the bench. But now as he looked up at the stars following what he and Marty had discovered with Revelation, his curiosity was heightened all the more. He wondered to himself about the whole meaning of life and exactly what else might be out there in the universe waiting to be discovered.

He took his cellphone from his pocket and dialled Linda. 'Linda, it's Jack, sorry to trouble you, you still up?' he enquired in the superfluous way people do when their call would have disturbed the person anyway.

'Yeah, had some marking of essays to do,' Linda fibbed whilst propping herself up against her bed pillows, having just turned in for the night. Her bedroom, like the rest of her apartment was tastefully decorated in pastel colours with minimalist modern furniture and thick-piled rugs covering part of the natural wood floors. In marked contrast the walls were hung with bold, striking and exuberant expressions of modern art.

'Look, I've been thinking. I mean what if after all I go straight to the media and talk to one of the more respected mainstream newspapers or something?' Part of him wanted Linda to say yes just do it, so he could unload the burden off his shoulders. But she was naturally wary of the press and reminded Jack of the possible dangers.

'Well, as we said, it's an option. But they might just sensationalise it, there'll be no control and, I don't know, could all get out of hand. This is your life's work and the most important thing you've ever done. And you yourself have recognised that it's not without its potential problems. You need people on your side who you know are going to take it seriously and handle it responsibly.'

'I know but…oh look, I'm just having doubts, you know me! Really nervous about taking this thing higher.'

Jack loved the way Linda was so calming and reassuring. 'That's very understandable,' she said, 'but you can't just sit on it. Don't forget, Marty entrusted Revelation's future to you.'

Jack almost wished she hadn't said that as he replied, 'I know, that's what makes it worse. Marty only ever saw the good in people and situations. He would've just thought that Revelation would be a ride in the park and bring me fame and fortune.' He laughed awkwardly.

'And so it should,' Linda interjected.

Jack continued, 'Yeah but Marty wouldn't have foreseen any major problems and would assume I'd have enough strength and vision to know what to do, who to go to and so on, but truth is I don't. I can't see beyond Frank Caspari.'

'Well, being able to confide in the White House Chief of Staff ain't exactly a bad place to start!' Linda offered reassuringly. 'And besides, don't put yourself down; you can do this. Look, I'm on a tight schedule this week so I'll have to see you there at the funeral. You'll be fine and I'll be there to support you. And I promise not to sneer at that rodent

Caspari too much!' They both laughed. Neither wanted to hang up on the other.

Jack looked up at the stars again. 'Man the stars are bright tonight!'

Linda smiled to herself and snuggled down further into her pillows while gently stroking her quilt with one arm as if in her mind she was stroking Jack. 'Wish I was there with you to see that.'

This was a moment Jack knew he should have taken, but was too shy and nervous to go for it. Instead all he could manage was 'yeah'. To mask his gaucheness he quickly changed tack, 'My mom always told me if I made a wish while looking at the North Star, it'd come true'.

'That's so cute,' Linda giggled coquettishly. 'So…what are you wishing for?'

Jack tried to hide his embarrassment. 'Oh…um…well, good things.'

Linda quickly replied in a suggestive tone, 'Well then, here's to good things coming true.'

Both laughed gently together, as if sealing their wish.

'Guess we'd better get some rest,' Jack said after a further brief pause.

'Yeah,' Linda agreed, 'and don't beat yourself up and lie awake all night!'

'Yeah, I'll be fine, goodnight.'

'Goodnight Jack,' she replied sweetly.

Reluctantly both put down their phones, each having romantic thoughts about the other.

Jack sat back in silence, staring up at the sky once more. Just what did the future hold and how would he cope with what was to come?

Chapter 14

There was a light drizzle falling like a cloak of sadness at the Oak Hill Cemetery in Washington's Georgetown district. It's one of Washington's oldest cemeteries dating back before the Civil War and occupies 22 acres of landscaped gardens, with well-planned paths and terraces that lead down into Rock Creek Valley.

Marty and Jenny had rented a small house in Georgetown and spent many happy years there before Jenny's death. They had often gone for walks through the cemetery's pretty grounds, stopping to look at some of the famous names on the headstones. Both had said what a lovely place to be buried and Marty had pulled some strings to ensure his beloved wife got her wish. Now he would be joining her in an adjoining grave.

The cemetery's Gothic-style chapel was built on a high ridge in a striking black granite and red sandstone style that had got it listed in the National Register of Historic Places. Its circular emblem of 12 crosses above the arched doorway looked more like a tribute to the European knights of old, yet somehow blended perfectly with the distinctively sharp-roofed architecture of the chapel and its pretty surrounds.

The funeral service had been a relatively simple one, with many of the official-looking attendees having to stand at the back due to the lack of enough seating.

Some had drifted off after the service, whilst a good many now gathered beside Marty's graveside right next to that of his wife. The drizzle was enough for some to have black umbrellas up, adding to the sea of solemnity. One figure stood out. Ever the hippie with non-conformist views, Marty's mother Martha was smartly but colourfully dressed in a bright royal blue raincoat which she had removed in the chapel to reveal a beautiful maxi dress with an anarchic rainbow splash of colours above a pair of calf-length black leather boots. Martha had her own funeral etiquette and no-one would persuade her otherwise. She was there to celebrate her Marty's life, not wallow in sadness at his death.

Jack had managed to catch Martha for a brief chat on their short walk between the chapel and Marty's grave. She had embraced him as if he were her own and it was only then that she allowed a tear to roll gently down her cheek. Jack desperately wanted to talk to her about Marty and especially about what he had meant with his reference to The Alamo. But with so many CIA and other officials attending the service, he thought it better done elsewhere. Besides this was a mother who had come to bury her son, it could wait – but not for long. So he had suggested to Martha that he drive up to see her sometime in the next few days just to see how she was getting on, to which she had happily agreed, although she insisted she was fine and would be OK.

Flanked by his security detail of Secret Service heavies, Frank Caspari had nodded warmly at Jack as they took their places on opposite sides of the grave. Linda had been running late, having had to drop off some important papers at college, but she now stood next to Jack and placed a reassuring arm across his back – something that didn't go unnoticed by two of his work colleagues, Jermaine and Alexis, who were also alongside them. Jermaine and Alexis exchanged knowing smiles. Nothing would have pleased them more than to see Jack find some happiness after losing his best friend and long-standing work partner.

As the pastor went through the usual graveside protocol in his well-practised sing-song tone, it was all a blur to Jack as his mind was racing. Once it was over, this would be his moment to approach Frank, but he was nervous as hell and his mouth had gone completely dry. Equally, he knew he couldn't let this moment go.

And then it was all over and people were already walking briskly towards their cars to find shelter from the unrelenting drizzle. Linda knew this was Jack's moment, squeezed his hand and nodded her encouragement. With his face screwed up slightly against the drizzle and a somewhat haunted look, Jack set off in pursuit of Frank and his team, who hadn't wasted any time in marching swiftly back across the grounds.

As Jack had nearly caught up with them enough for one member of the security detail to glance round, the man turned full face towards him to check him out. Jack noticed the man's overcoat was unbuttoned and could only guess at the weaponry that could be aimed at him in one brief, well-practiced moment. Undeterred, he called out, 'Frank, Frank, I need a word with you.'

Frank stopped to turn around as did the other Secret Service men alongside him. Frank had always liked Jack and greeted him with what seemed like genuine warmth. 'Jack! Good to see you again. Shame about the circumstances. You keeping OK?'

Jack was a little breathless, partly with the effort of

catching up with Frank's team, but also with nerves. He heard himself splutter, 'Yeah, yeah, thanks. Look Frank, I really need to talk to you.'

'Sure,' Frank replied, 'tell you what, call my secretary Fiona and we'll have lunch. I'll tell her to expect your call.'

Jack was gaining in confidence, 'No Frank, we need to talk now.' He hesitated as he cast a quick glance at the Secret Service men, one of whom was scowling furiously and had made no pretence at allowing his raincoat to billow open revealing a leather strap running diagonally across his pristine white shirt and down under his left shoulder. But Jack could not allow himself to be distracted, as he continued, 'It concerns Revelation.'

Frank had been fidgeting, transferring his weight from leg to leg in the way people do when they are keen to get away. But at the mention of the highly classified Revelation, he stopped dead in his tracks.

Frank tried to appear nonchalant. 'What about it? We canned all that.'

'Frank, please just spare me a few minutes. Believe me, what I need to tell you is huge and you won't regret it. It's a matter of national importance – world importance.'

Frank eyed Jack carefully with his conspiratorial eyes that hid a razor-sharp mind and, as many could testify, a Machiavellian political nous second to none. But, at the same time, he had always known Jack to be an honest, straight-as-a-dye kind of guy, so he nodded as he said, 'OK Jack, got to admit you've got me intrigued pulling that old name out of the hat.'

He gestured to his accompanying security detail. 'It's OK fellas, I'll just be a few minutes, we'll only be over there.' He motioned to Jack to walk with him until they were alone amongst some of the older graves. Frank appeared to be taking a casual interest in the names and dates on the gravestones. After all, many famous politicians, military top brass and high level diplomats had been buried in this cemetery.

Frank now turned full face to Jack, looked straight into his eyes and adopted his deathly serious, measured tone that would often turn many of his subordinates to jelly, 'Revelation. World importance. Well, I'm listening. What is it?'

Normally Jack would have been intimidated by Frank's grand inquisitor showboating, but he also knew that Frank respected people who stood up to him and besides, it was too late now to pull back. 'Frank, you remember what Revelation set out to do?'

'Of course, I sanctioned it. Sorry we had to pull the plug,' Frank replied.

Jack countered, 'Well that's just it, Marty and I didn't pull the plug. Look, I won't go into the how's and why's as you'll probably want my scalp, but we kept on with it on our own.'

Frank had softened and actually found what Jack had told him quite amusing. He started making teasing tut-tutting noises, 'Mavericks working for the CIA,' he said, enjoying his own ironic flippancy, 'whatever next! Hang on a minute, don't tell me you actually got it to work?'

'Not exactly,' Jack replied. 'We did get Revelation working, but not in the way we expected, not in the way we all set out to. We got it to see and hear things using energetic high vibrational frequencies, but not substance as we know it.'

No scientist himself, Frank looked quizzically at Jack,

'Not sure I'm following you, what do you mean?'

Jack took a deep intake of breath, 'Oh man…OK…well, thing is, Revelation works. We accidentally got it tuned to the same high level of vibrational frequency as spirit existence. Revelation reveals ghosts, spirit beings, people who have died. You see and hear them almost just like you and me standing here. Frank, Revelation proves scientifically that life after death is a reality, it's a nailed-on truth.'

Frank interrupted him, now looking a little confused, 'What? You for real? Hope you're not wasting my time by pulling some kind of practical joke.'

Jack shook his head vigorously and raised his voice as much as he dared, 'No way. Frank, I'm totally serious and on the level here. This isn't fantasy, it's scientific fact. I can prove it to you – dead people aren't dead!'

Frank looked stunned as he glanced around at all the surrounding graves before replying ruefully. 'One helluva place to tell me! Look, I dunno, I'm gonna need more than a lot of convincing on this one, Jack – and I mean a lot! That's quite a claim you're making there. Anyway, why come to me?'

'I've given this so much thought, Frank,' Jack replied, 'and think it can only be handled at the highest level, especially when you start to consider the many possible consequences once something like this becomes public knowledge. And Revelation was your bag back then. It's such a massive breakthrough – well I guess for humankind – that it will need careful managing so that it's given due authority, doesn't get sensationalised or become some kind of circus.'

The two paused, both deep in thought, before Frank replied, 'Hmm, I take your point. I really hope you're sure about this Jack and can prove it as otherwise…wow, I mean, if true, this is big, this is huge. Not sure I can quite get my head round it yet. What and where is this Revelation thing? Is it very different to when I last saw it?'

'Actually it hasn't changed much at all,' Jack replied, 'turns out Marty and I weren't that far away from making some kind of breakthrough, we just didn't expect it to be this. Remember Marty's cabin retreat up in the hills beyond Rock Creek?'

'Sure,' Frank nodded, 'we used it as a safe house a couple of times.'

Jack continued, 'Revelation is up there. The cabin's locked up and only I have a key, but in any event, anyone breaking in wouldn't have a clue what the device is or how to make it work. I'll be happy to give you a personal demonstration so you can experience it for yourself and have your own proof.'

Frank was already thinking ahead, 'You told anyone else about this?'

Jack lied to protect Linda, although at that point he couldn't imagine why she might need protecting, 'No, no-one. I can see the wider implications. After all, it's what made Marty want to kill himself.'

'What the…!' Frank exclaimed in genuine shock. 'You mean it wasn't an accident? He took his own life?'

Jack nodded. 'Once Marty knew for sure about spirit existence, that we live on, he just wanted to be with his wife Jenny.' Jack paused for a moment. 'Only she isn't dead in the way we normally think about it.'

'My God, Jack, this is some heavy shit!' Frank's face had changed completely to one of shock, surprise and growing concern. If this was all true, he too was beginning to anticipate the potential consequences.

It was Jack who was now more in control. 'I know. That's why it's got to go to the very top.'

Frank was hesitant. 'You mean the President? I can see your thinking but I'm not sure I would want to approach her just yet. Think it's best if we keep this just between you and me for now, pending the demo of course. If this thing really is what you say then we'll take it from there. I assume my office people still have your cellphone and address on file?'

'Yeah, I keep all my agency details up-to-date, although I'm staying up at the cabin for now for obvious reasons,' Jack confirmed.

Frank was now back to his business-like self. 'Good. Don't tell a soul and I'll be in touch in the next day or two. Oh, and so sorry about Marty.'

'Yeah, thanks Frank,' Jack replied. The two shook hands and Jack watched as Frank rejoined his security detail, pausing to look back very briefly at Jack in a very ambiguous way. Jack watched them all walk through the tall black iron gates flanked by ornate high red sandstone pillars as he heard the sound of car engines being started.

There were soft footsteps approaching from behind and Jack turned as Linda rejoined him. She noticed that Jack looked thoughtful and somewhat troubled rather than happy to have offloaded his great secret.

'So?' she asked. 'How did it go?'

'I dunno,' Jack replied truthfully. 'I told him everything, but...' he trailed off.

'Problem?' asked Linda.

Jack looked down at the ground as if trying to hide his inner doubts from Linda as she had been such a strength. 'Says he'll be in touch in the next couple of days or so to arrange a demo.'

'That's good isn't it?' Linda could sense Jack's unease and was trying to encourage him.

Jack sighed. 'Guess so. I didn't tell him about Marty's note or his reference to The Alamo though.'

Linda tried to make light of it even though she shared Jack's feelings. 'Maybe wise, seeing as you don't trust your own shadow! Mind you, subterfuge is probably Frank Caspari's middle name! Anyway, you really had no option than to take it to someone high up.'

Jack nodded but wasn't convincing in his reply. 'Yeah, yeah you're right. And it's done now. Told him I'll stay at the cabin until I hear from him.'

Linda patted Jack on the back. 'Good idea. Look, I've got to get back to college. Listen, call me, ok?'

'Sure.' Jack smiled at her. 'Thanks Linda, your support means a great deal.'

'I'm here for you, Jack,' she replied, 'take care.' And with that, she pulled the see-through hood tighter round her head and hurried off.

Jack watched her go. It was only then that he realised how wet his hair had become standing in the drizzle without an umbrella. He must have looked a right mess. He walked quickly back to his car.

He drove aimlessly and deep in thought, although thankfully his subconscious was on autopilot and guided him to take the right turns in the right order to get back to his apartment in the Watergate complex next to the infamous Watergate Centre in the Foggy Bottom neighbourhood of one of Washington D.C.'s oldest areas. Yes, it was expensive to have an apartment there, but Jack was well paid and single, so it was a luxury he could well afford. Jack's apartment was in Watergate West on Virginia Avenue and the complex was indeed impressive, complete with its seven gardens and open shopping area with ornate fountains. There were boutiques, restaurants, a heated pool and 24-hour concierge service. Jack was well known to the doormen and they exchanged friendly greetings as Jack made his way across the beautifully tiled lobby towards the elevator.

Still deep in thought, Jack silently moved around his minimalist apartment with its clean white walls, discreet lighting and occasional pieces of modern art. These included some striking, provocative artworks by a supposed up-and-coming artist who Jack had never heard of. They had been chosen for him by a friend as Jack didn't have too much time for the art world, just knew he should have some pieces to add character to his apartment. But when your apartment has large windows offering panoramic views across the Potomac River, what else do you need – or at least that had been Jack's thinking.

His furniture was simple, with mostly light pastel coloured shades of wood of a highly practical high-end Scandinavian design, complemented by thick carpeting in a whiteish hue of cream that says no kids live here. But Jack preferred the simple life. He moved across his bedroom, opening drawers and wardrobes and loosely throwing a few things into a well-worn dark brown leather holdall, adding to them with some bathroom essentials. He already had stuff up at Marty's cabin, but this would tide him over until after Frank had made his agreed visit.

He was soon back in his car heading out towards the cabin. He needed a distraction and flipped open the glove compartment, reaching for the YES CD.

Chapter 15

As White House Chief of Staff, Frank Caspari's office was down the pristine, white-painted corridor from the Oval Office in a discreet corner of the building. It was a long spacious room, decorated and furnished in a traditional conservative style. The clean white walls were hung with a host of paintings ranging from schooners and sailing ships to black and white Civil War photos, as well as some historic documents which no visitor to the office had ever bothered to read. But no-one could deny they looked impressive all the same.

The large floor to ceiling windows had full length dark yellow brocade curtains neatly tied back with thick bands of the same material, allowing daylight to flood the room from the gardens and well-trimmed lawns outside. The innocuous light brown carpet led the full length of the room where, over to one side, was Frank's L-shaped heavy oak desk and large padded black leather chair. As befits men of status, the desk was empty save for two computers, a memo pad and the White House secure phone system with its large display screen and range of pre-programmed buttons.

The high ceiling and size of the room meant that the long solid mahogany table with its ten matching Chippendale chairs did not in any way dominate the room. The table was also towards the end of the office behind Frank's desk and with only windows and outside walls to the other two sides that did not give onto the room itself. The walls were thick anyway, but it meant that top secret conversations could and did take place at the table without anyone overhearing.

Which was just as well. Because that morning, an increasingly animated discussion was taking place between three of the most powerful people in the country. They were Frank Caspari, White House Chief of Staff, Bob Howard, head of the CIA, and General Sam Collins, Chief of Staff and head of the U.S. Military. Also present was Reverend Walter Cunningham, the White House resident pastor whom Frank had invited to the meeting purely for an ecumenical perspective on what was to be discussed.

The meeting had already been in progress for some 20 minutes going over and over the various ramifications of what Jack had told Frank about Revelation. As the discussion developed, things were getting pretty heated.

It was the Reverend in particular who was leading the charge. 'Don't get sidetracked by all that science horseshit Frank, this Revelation thing has to be stopped now!'

The Reverend was known for his firebrand evangelical no-nonsense approach, albeit that he had what could generously be called a fairly blinkered, one-sided approach to religion. However, he was always outwardly friendly and welcoming when meeting religious leaders from other faiths on their occasional visits to the White House. He had struck up a good friendship with a local Imam, having discovered their mutual interest in ancient Middle Eastern art. But the two were careful never to let their conversations stray into the differences between their strongly held faiths.

The Reverend was not to the President's more liberal

tastes, but she had inherited him from the previous administration and had learned to tolerate him or, more to the point, ignore him. A thin, weedy man with a sharp pointed nose and hollow cheeks that gave him a Dickensian appearance, Walter Cunningham made up for his slight frame with a fiery temperament. Now in his sixties, he had suffered a number of bronchial health problems which had wracked his body and left him with a permanently gaunt expression and a slight wheeze to his voice.

Frank was quite taken aback by the strength of the Reverend's feelings and the implied venom in his voice. In fact, the whole meeting wasn't exactly going as Frank had expected – although later he would admit to himself that he hadn't quite known what to expect in the first place.

Brought up in a staunchly Catholic family that would have viewed Revelation as sinful and dangerous, Frank's life experiences had long ago made him loosen his bonds with orthodoxy. This had particularly been so after his painful separation from his wife Italia. He had spent many lonely hours agonising over the reasons that had led up to the split and knew he was mostly to blame. As a result, he was generally now more open-minded and tolerant, although it still came as a bit of an effort to acknowledge someone else's point of view when Frank felt he had right on his side.

He tried to calm the Reverend down. 'Look Walter, no-one's saying this whole thing doesn't come with potentially big problems, but what if it's true, what if…'

'To hell with it being true, Frank!' the Reverend cut in angrily. 'You seriously propose to overturn every religion on the planet and the entire world order without knowing the consequences?' He turned pleadingly towards Bob Howard, 'Bob, come on, back me on this.'

But it was Frank who persevered instead, 'But surely, Walter, life after death is a cornerstone of what yours and most religions believe in?'

'Not like this!' Walter barked back, whilst also noting the disowning use of 'yours' in Frank's question, 'it's about having faith, the word of God is enough. It's…'

'Listen guys,' it was Bob Howard who interrupted them with his calm, deep voice whose measured, relaxed tone confirmed how he had seen it all and done it all – most of which he would of course deny. His half rolled-up sleeves on his badly ironed shirt, no tie and laid-back demeanour hid one of the shrewdest, most astute minds that would be willing to sacrifice anyone and anything to protect the State.

But away from the office, he was very much a family man with no less than seven grandchildren whom he doted on. He made great efforts to always find time for them, taking them fishing and being most generous at birthdays and Christmas. Having been one himself, Bob cared deeply for his field agents. His wife, Carol, had often been woken in the middle of the night to hear him on his phone personally making extraordinary arrangements to extract an agent from a life-threatening situation.

Bob slowly ran his hands over his balding crown that had earned him the nickname 'egghead' amongst his subordinates, although none would dare mention it within his earshot. What little hair he still had at the sides was now grey and framed a sharp-featured face. His bony arms and bodily frame were still reasonably lean, more through stress than having the time or inclination to exercise. He continued at the same measured pace, 'Let's take it away from all that for a moment. Frank, didn't you say that one of these guys, Marty whatever, killed himself in the belief that this would get him to some other life? And that, although I never met the guy myself, he was one of us and presumably a highly intelligent man?'

'The best,' Frank immediately retorted.

Bob continued, 'Well, what if millions of other people felt the same way? I mean this life ain't exactly a bed of roses for a whole lot of people. Could cause a worldwide epidemic of suicides – a stampede to get to the other side!'

No-one laughed, although Frank gave him a half smile. Instead it was the general's turn to chip in, 'This is precisely what my boys have to put up with all the time – fanatics wanting to blow themselves up to get to a supposedly better life. If this Revelation stuff is true and gets out, we're about to give every raving nutcase the perfect excuse!'

'Ignorant fools,' muttered the Reverend, failing completely in self-awareness to recognise the irony between his own brand of religious fundamentalism and that of others.

The general nodded. Sam Collins was as good a caricature as you could get of a rather overweight, redneck 'shoot first and ask questions later' kind of military man who probably should have retired by now. In his prime he had been a Special Forces sniper in Vietnam before being invalided out after being bitten by a Pit Viper whilst lying doggo in some godforsaken swamp waiting to get his shot away at a North Vietnamese Colonel. 'A goddam son-of-a-bitch slippery serpent,' he would bellow when recounting the tale to anyone who would listen whilst rolling up his left arm sleeve to reveal the now hardly visible two little pinprick scars from where the snake had bitten him on his forearm. He had later returned to action and distinguished himself as a three-star lieutenant-general in both Iraq wars and so his rise to the very top had not surprised anyone. Always in full uniform and never shy to wear a full display of his impressive medals, he was bullish and not to say a little belligerent. But he was definitely a man you would want on your side when the going got tough, although perhaps not as a dinner companion.

His outward demeanour belied the fact that he and his childhood sweetheart wife, Betty, regularly helped out by fundraising and attending events for various military and other charities. This was partly because they themselves had experienced the agony of losing a son in conflict. Pragmatic to a fault, the general was used to making fast, difficult decisions, preferring to deal only with what was in front of him rather than worrying about looking too far ahead.

Frank was desperately trying to bring some balance to the discussion. 'Hold up, hold up a minute. Look fellas, wouldn't it actually make people more hopeful about life in general, more peaceful and tolerant, more – I dunno…'

'Oh come on, Frank!' Bob cut in sharply. 'Have some of the President's pseudo hippy ramblings rubbed off on you and made you go soft or something?'

It was rhetorical, but Frank calmly answered it anyway, 'No, I'm just thinking that if it's managed carefully, maybe…'

Sam wasn't going to let him go any further down that road. 'True or not, unleash this on the world and God knows what might happen.'

'Thank you, General, my point exactly,' the Reverend said supportively, 'sometimes it's better to believe in something than to get sidetracked by all that science baloney.'

It was clear that Frank was on his own as Bob added, 'Frank, with all our ongoing problems in so many areas of the Middle East with people who are already willing to have one foot in the grave, it would be like poking a stick in a hornets' nest.'

Sam was quick to follow up, 'And my boys will bear the brunt of it. Don't forget, we're about to launch the Scorpion programme.'

'Sam, that's highly classified,' Bob chided, 'I don't think the Reverend...'

'It's OK, I'm a man of God, you can trust me,' the Reverend said with a sorry attempt at a smile.

Frank doggedly pursued his theme, 'Yes, of course I'm aware of how close we are to launching Scorpion. But who knows, maybe Revelation means we can avoid it. Maybe it'll make people want to live in peace and look for a greater meaning to life.'

'They've already got that, if only they'd see it,' the Reverend quickly countered.

Sam Collins was shaking his head, 'Frank, you know that Scorpion will clean up the whole fucking Middle East mess.'

'And add billions to the economy,' Bob added.

'Guys, guys, time out,' Frank was not giving up, 'I mean this Revelation thing – Jack Taylor's due to give me a demo in the next day or two and let's just say it works and really does prove life after death is true, let's face it, it's got to be the greatest discovery ever made in the history of humankind. We can't just hide it under the carpet or whatever you're suggesting.'

'Destroy it. Jack Taylor too. There's no other way.'

Frank looked genuinely shocked by the words he had just heard the Reverend utter. He spoke to him gently but firmly, using his title rather than his name to emphasise his point, 'Reverend, I asked you in on this to get an ecumenical perspective on the whole thing. With respect, it's not your position to be making those kinds of suggestions.'

'But he's right,' the confirmation unsurprisingly had come from the general.

Frank wasn't going to let the Reverend off the hook, but addressed him again, this time by his name, 'Well, if I remember my history correctly, Walter, it was your holy inquisition heavies who threatened Galileo just some 400 years ago for daring to adopt the Copernican theory, something we now know as fact – this is even bigger than that!'

But the Reverend was on the attack, 'And that's exactly why it must be stopped. It's dangerous, the world's just not ready.'

'So would the world be ready for a second coming?' Frank demanded with mounting frustration and some hidden anger.

'That's different,' the Reverend said, without feeling the need to explain why.

There was an awkward pause before Sam took up the cudgel again. 'I'm afraid I tend to agree with the Reverend here, the world's just not ready for something like this. And with Scorpion and the way things are, the timing's all wrong. No-one's saying if this Revelation thing really does work it's not pretty amazing to say the least, but I repeat, the world just isn't ready yet. Sorry, but the bottom line is we need to act before the cat's well and truly out the bag.'

'Agreed,' Bob and Walter said almost in unison.

Frank let silence reign for a moment and then said as calmly as he could, as if trying to take some of the tension out of the room, 'Look guys, how about this – why can't we just park it up, put it on ice somewhere. Christ, if I have to I can hide Jack away in luxury on some paradise island somewhere for as long as it takes until we think the timing's better.'

As head of the CIA, Bob was certainly no stranger to these kinds of arrangements. He currently had several successfully turned foreign agents literally eating into his budget whilst being closeted away at great expense and in great secrecy hidden from the pursuing hoods from whichever intelligence service happened to be on their tail. But that's why Bob also knew how many people had to be involved in such operations and this had led to a couple of recent security compromises that had put lives in danger. So he counselled against this approach, 'Too risky, Frank. What if he talks, something leaks, too many people would need to be involved. And then the timing could be even worse and we'd have no control. We can't risk any delay to even see a demo of the damn thing. You've already said you trust Jack Taylor's word completely and look what it made this Marty guy do. That's enough for me – we've got to assume this is the real deal and act now. Look, if this Revelation thing can be invented once, it can be done again, just not now, not on our watch.'

Sam nodded, 'Bob's right, it's unfortunate…'

'Unfortunate!' Frank interjected. 'Hell, Sam, can you hear yourself! This is a man's life we're talking about. And discoveries like this don't just happen every day!'

The general was unmoved, referring instead to Frank's previous incarnation in the CIA. 'Yeah well, I'm sure it won't be the first time you CIA boys have burned one good guy 'pro bono publico', shall we say.'

'This is on a different level and you know it,' Frank hit back.

Bob spoke in a matter-of-fact way as if discussing a shopping trip, 'Make the appointment with Jack and I can have a wet team up at that cabin within four hours. We'll make it a TPA – Terrorist Preventative Action. Destroy, burn, leave no trace. A rogue scientist discovered to be in league with whoever and planning some imminent atrocity. Leave the back story and all that to my guys, we can make it look watertight.'

'My God!' Frank was reeling with it all, 'Jack's a good man. This is crazy, dangerous territory. I don't like it.'

Bob had been in his position far longer than Frank had been in his and spoke firmly, 'Frank, believe me, I do understand your concern, I do. But we just need to do this and get it done – fast. Don't rock the boat.'

It was three against one as Sam looked solemnly at Frank and said, 'I agree. Today, without fail. Think of Scorpion – nothing can compromise it.'

The room fell into silence. Frank had got up from his chair and was pacing anxiously around the room deep in thought. He sat down again and had another try at a compromise solution, 'So why don't I have a quiet word with the President? I mean we're all agreed that this is a major scientific breakthrough, it's history in the making. Who knows, despite what you say, Bob, if we put a stop to Revelation now, what if it can never be replicated?'

'Good,' commented the Reverend. 'The world already has all the proof it needs.'

Sam glanced at Bob and Walter before addressing Frank, 'Think about it, Frank, this just isn't the time and there are too many ifs and buts with any alternative. There's too much at stake – it's taken us years to get Scorpion ready. We can't put all that at risk now.'

Frank was looking exasperated but was beginning to see things more from his colleagues' point of view. They all sat in silence for a moment before Frank finally exclaimed, 'Shit, shit, shit!' He paused, looking up at one of the Civil War photos on the wall as if looking for some kind of inspiration. Finally he looked around slowly at all three other people seated at the table before sighing heavily as he heard himself say, 'Fuck! Alright, OK. But no-one and I mean no-one outside these walls gets to know the real story behind all this. We keep this tight and Bob, I don't need to tell you, your wet team need to be totally on message here. And let's keep the Feds well out of this, they leak like a sieve. Make no mistake, our butts are on the line here like never before. The official story will be it's a terrorist preventative action, end of.' He slumped back in his chair, not quite believing what he had just agreed to.

Bob had assumed a business-like manner as if this kind of thing happened every day. In his world, it often did! 'Absolutely, Frank.' He tried to sound reassuring. 'Although I'll have to file a formal report with the Feds once it's all done, just to keep the lid on it. But don't worry, it'll have the highest black classification. In the extremely unlikely event that something does leak, we'll stick to the TPA story and slap a total gag on all media. Do you think Jack's told anyone?'

'Says he hasn't,' Frank replied wearily, 'and frankly he seems quite shaken by it all, a little frightened even. Revelation was mostly just his and Marty's baby and certainly what happened subsequent to the programme being pulled was definitely just between the two of them, so no, I'm almost certain he hasn't. Not yet at least. But we can't bug his phone in case the listeners hear anything that could cause us problems.'

Bob nodded, 'I don't like that, but we'll just have to trust he's true to his word and has kept quiet so far.'

The Reverend looked self-satisfied as he said emphatically, 'Let's just get it done fast.'

The keenest are always the ones who don't have to do the dirty work themselves, Sam thought to himself, but kept his peace for once.

All of them began to rise from the table as Bob said, 'OK gentlemen, I've got work to do.'

'Oh God,' Frank said out loud, but mostly to himself whilst looking down at the floor.

As the other three filed out of Frank's office, the Reverend was last to leave and turned to call back, 'Don't worry Frank, I will pray for you.'

Chapter 16

Linda Wilson loved her work as a lecturer. She was originally from Pittsburgh, but had completed her Master of Science degree at the George Washington University in Washington D.C. where she had first become friends with Jack and Marty. She liked the buzz of the city so much that she stayed, having also gained a lecturer's post at the Washington College of Science and Technology. This enabled her to pursue her research interests alongside teaching her students.

Ever since Jack's demonstration she had thought of nothing else. In her apartment and even out and about when she thought no-one was in earshot, she would talk out loud to her mother. She heard nothing back, but that didn't deter her, as she was comforted to know that her beloved mom would have heard and was keeping an eye on her.

Right now she had to remind herself to focus, as she was in the middle of addressing her lecture hall where around 40 students were listening attentively. That's the good thing about higher education, she mused to herself, the kids actually want to learn! Surprising even herself, she had also begun to seek out and read articles and stories which appeared daily in the press and on the internet about ordinary people who claimed to have experienced seeing or hearing spirit beings.

She switched off her laptop which had been connected

to the big screen behind her where she had been running through a pre-prepared presentation. There were still a few minutes to go before the official end of the lecture, so she looked up at the banked benches of students and smiled as she said, 'OK, listen up, guys. Time to have a bit of fun. I'm going to set you something a little out of the ordinary for your essay this week and you're going to have to use your imagination.' She said the last bit as if it was a challenge and some of the students smiled at each other as she continued, 'Well, you know how I'm always telling you to push the boundaries, don't accept the accepted, challenge everything. Go your own way, find your individual path. So here you go, I want you to imagine what would be the most amazing scientific discovery if it were to happen tomorrow.'

She paused and allowed herself an inner smile, knowing she was already privy to just such a thing. *If only I could tell them*, she thought to herself. Instead, she carried on with her theme, 'I'm talking about something huge, something life-changing, but based firmly on possible scientific proof. Like alien existence, another Earth-like planet, teleportation, a plant extract that cures all disease, life after death, whatever. But I want you to substantiate it as best you can.'

'Miss Wilson?' the question had come from a female student in the second row back. She had a shock of dark brown curly hair that tumbled down the sides of her roundish attractive features. She had an unmistakably New York accent.

'Yes, Nettye,' Linda replied.

'When you say substantiate, do you mean based on facts as we know them today?'

'Not entirely,' Linda replied, 'let your imagination run

90

free. But whilst I'm not placing any restrictions on your thinking, I definitely don't just want science fantasy. It's got to be credible, something that you think could really happen based on scientific principles. A small step but one which represents a giant leap, to paraphrase Mr Armstrong.'

Jackson, another student, now had his hand raised. He could hardly be missed at six foot six inches tall, muscular and a linchpin of the college basketball team. His afro hairstyle must have added at least a further six inches to his height, which delighted his coach when he saw the reaction of opposing teams when Jackson stepped onto the court.

'Yes Jackson,' she said, pointing at him.

He cleared his throat nervously. 'My dad says we've already had visits from aliens but that it's all been covered up.'

Some students sniggered before Linda replied, 'Yeah, well I can't comment on that as nothing's been made public yet if there is any truth in it. But OK, if you're going that route, what's the most likely way this could happen? What science are you going to base your discovery on? We'll worry later about how things would pan out. I just want you to give free rein to your imagination – maybe something you'd like to see happen. I mean what if someone could prove energetically that there is life after death?'

'Is anybody there?' one of the students towards the back cheekily called out in his best séance impression. A number of the students laughed. But Linda welcomed it, 'Good, you're laughing. But just remember, there can't be a great scientist in history who wasn't laughed at when they first came up with their theory. Quite a thought, isn't it. So come on, give me your best shot. What, how, where – don't worry too much about the detail as long as you make it scientifically credible in a way that can back your argument. Let me see if I've got an Isaac Newton or a Marie Curie in my class!'

The students grinned back at her as the bell sounded and they gathered their books and papers in readiness to leave the lecture hall. Linda had to raise her voice to be heard above the general chatter, shuffling and rustling, 'OK, usual drill, essays emailed to me by 10am Friday. Have fun!'

Chapter 17

It was one of those idyllic mornings that make being surrounded by nature during Fall so magical. The early dew still nourished the ground, whilst down in the valley the final wisps of an early mist were gently evaporating like ghostly reeds of steam under the warming rays of the sun.

Suddenly a deer was startled and bolted into the woods as two black Jeeps with darkened windows came roaring up the track, spewing dust and small rocks in all directions. The window of one of the Jeeps was wound down displaying a man's bronzed muscular arm resting on the door. Clearly visible above his elbow was a tattoo of the crossed arrows insignia of the U.S. Special Forces. The Jeeps were on their way to Marty's cabin.

Meanwhile, an unsuspecting Jack was sitting with a mug of coffee on the swing bench on the porch. The morning birdsong was in full chorus. He loved nature and sat in silence whilst admiring the beautiful sights, sounds and smells that soothed his senses and would normally have made him feel completely at peace.

Only Jack's mind was far from peaceful. Given to catastrophising at the best of times, his thoughts raced with the potential problems that could lie ahead. And the last thing he wanted was to be the centre of all the attention when his and Marty's discovery became public knowledge.

At other times he felt elated to know there was greater meaning to everyday life. But he was puzzled as to why Marty hadn't yet shown himself, despite the couple of occasions when Jack had operated Revelation since Marty's funeral. He had found the various 'visitations' during those sessions quite emotional, especially from his father, even though they hadn't been at all close during his life. In fact, quite the opposite. So to have his father come through to him with love, humility and understanding – things he never showed Jack during his lifetime – had an even greater impact on him. He wondered to himself whether newly passed individuals took time to adjust to being 'on the other side' and what happened to them to make them more enlightened. *We're just at the very beginning of finding out what really happens when we die*, he thought.

He'd finished his coffee and walked down the cabin steps. A tame squirrel that had been scurrying around in front of the cabin stopped in its tracks momentarily and then, as if recognising Jack, continued about its business searching for nuts. Jack squatted down as he spoke gently to the animal, 'Hey little fella, it's you again. You're a bit late today – bit of a lie-in? Don't blame you.'

The cellphone in Jack's pocket rang. He wandered aimlessly around the yard as he heard Linda's voice. 'Hey Jack, you OK? Anything yet?'

'Nothing so far, thought this might be him,' Jack replied.

'OK, keep me posted?' Linda's voice expressed genuine concern and care which touched Jack. They both said goodbye as Jack walked back towards where he had seen the squirrel.

Now where did he go, Jack thought to himself looking

around for the squirrel. The fact that it was a bright sunny morning was about to save Jack's life. He spotted a beautiful bird feather on the ground and as he bent down to inspect it, a reflected sharp glint of sunlight on metal flashed briefly across his eyes. It was fortunate that he didn't react in any obvious way as that would have given away the fact that out of the corner of his eye he had just caught the most fleeting sight of one member of the SWAT team crouched in the woods about 200 yards away.

As Jack was stooped down, he pretended to pick up the feather whilst he very furtively took the quickest of glances towards the woods. The team had temporarily stopped amongst the trees, perhaps sensing that Jack might be aware of them. But Jack's glance was enough to spot the muzzle of an M16 assault rifle just protruding from behind a large pine. Jack had seen enough of these rifles in Iraq not to need a second look.

His heart pounding in his chest, Jack was trying to make sense of what he had just seen. The human brain is indeed extraordinary in how quickly it can process and assimilate information. Jack had quickly ascertained this wasn't a social call. Frank would have been driven up to his door as if nothing was the matter. No, this could only mean trouble and for whatever reasons which he would try to figure out later, Jack knew his life was in danger.

In an explosion of movement an Olympic sprinter would have been proud of at the sound of the starter gun, Jack was suddenly up and running and weaving at full speed towards the cabin, just at the same time as the first silenced shots whizzed past his ears.

Jack raced up the cabin steps taking them two at a time and burst through the door as more silenced shots whistled and fizzed past, only just missing him and slamming into the cabin's wooden walls. Jack threw himself to the floor and fast-crawled towards the back room. He scraped his hands and knuckles in his race to get away. Raising himself to a low crouching position, he ran into the back room, slamming the door behind him and raising himself up to standing position. As he ran past Revelation he glanced at it with a look of horror as the realisation of what might happen to it began to dawn on him. He ran to the back window, opened it and jumped the four foot drop onto the ground behind the cabin. He slipped slightly as he could hear shouting behind him.

Just as he raced like someone possessed into the woods behind the cabin, he heard the first incendiary ordnance hit the cabin, blowing it apart and engulfing everything in fierce flames. He glanced back in terror and disbelief as he kept running and weaving, thankful that he knew these woods so well.

However, being in such a hurry and under such stress, he still ran into low-lying branches, one of which hit his face and caused a slight gash on his temple.

He could hear the sound of pursuers struggling through the undergrowth behind him and the occasional shout, but he was already well ahead of them.

The team leader sent four men into the woods to find Jack but he was long gone and they had instructions not to pursue him more than a couple of hundred yards in case of being discovered.

Just before Jack had jumped from the back window of the cabin, he had heard the sound of boots running across the yard behind him, accompanied by the clipped, controlled voices of what could only be a military or specially trained unit.

But even the best trained units struggle against an enemy familiar with their own territory – they had learned that in Vietnam. Jack kept running until he reached the cave he had been aiming for, whose tiny, concealed entrance was mostly hidden by bushes. Marty and Jack had once joked that only a timber rattlesnake would try and hide in such a dank, dark place. But right now Jack prayed any snakes were out basking in the last of the autumn sun before hibernating for the winter.

Jack squeezed into the cave, with both sides of his body brushing heavily against the rock on either side as he did so. The space was tiny and Jack had to forcibly kneel whilst he tried to control his out-of-breath panting so that he wouldn't give himself away. He peered towards the sliver of daylight at the entrance to the cave as he took some comfort in the fact that he hadn't heard any dogs barking amongst his pursuers, as otherwise they would surely not take long to find him. *The arrogant bastards hadn't thought about having to end up in a chase*, Jack thought to himself, so they hadn't brought dogs with them.

His mind raced in the way it does when people are under great stress, as he tried to think who might be trying to kill him and why. But he knew Frank would have to be behind this and that it was all because of Revelation. He could join all the dots together later, right now he just had to focus on staying alive.

For what seemed an eternity, Jack crouched stock still until his muscles and bones began to ache. Several times he thought he heard heavy footsteps very close until they were replaced by the sound of a number of footsteps crunching dead twigs and leaves underfoot and coming to rest no more than a few feet from the entrance to the cave.

Jack braced himself as he thought of Linda and just hoped it would be quick. Then he heard the impatient drawl of an elderly sounding man from the Southern states, 'Come on Mabel, we're nearly at the top.' *Thank God, hikers*, he thought to himself.

After they had passed, Jack knew this was his moment. Whoever his pursuers were, they weren't going to start a shooting match with civilians potentially in the way. Jack squeezed back out of the cave, unknowingly treading on a rattlesnake's discarded skin as he gave a quick glance back in the direction of the cabin before racing on down the hill, grasping at trees and saplings to steady himself as he went. He passed a small pond and threw his cellphone into the middle of it. He knew only too well the sort of people who were after him.

In that brief glance back, Jack had noticed heavy palls of smoke rising from the direction of the cabin. *Shit, the bastards are destroying Revelation*, he thought to himself. He had also been right, the pursuers had noticed the hikers and called off their pursuit. Right now, they were busy torching the cabin and everything in it, without stopping to wonder what the strange looking device in the back room might be.

Standing in almost the same spot where Jack had stooped to pick up the feather, the team leader held a special phone to his ear as he called in to someone, 'Zoo to keeper; cage and contents destroyed. However, bird on the loose, repeat, bird on the loose.'

Chapter 18

Even with the thickness of the walls, the room still shook from the force with which Frank slammed shut his office door. As he strode furiously towards the long table where Bob Howard, Sam Collins and the Reverend Cunningham were seating themselves, Frank was already at full throttle 'Just fucking unbelievable! One simple fucking operation!' With his face red with anger and jagged veins standing out on his temples, he sat down heavily and turned sharply to Bob. 'What kind of fucking monkeys you got working for you these days?!'

'Hold up, Frank, calm down a little,' Bob deliberately spoke slowly and quietly to try to help diffuse the situation. 'We're on his tail, we'll find him and sort it.'

'What if he talks?' The Reverend asked with clear concern. He enjoyed a very comfortable existence as the White House pastor and could now see both it and his freedom at risk.

Bob cut him off, 'Even if he talks, what can he say. There's no longer any proof, people will think he's delusional, some kind of mad scientist – a view we'll naturally reinforce through our media contacts. And as soon as he breaks cover, he's ours.' There was a chilling finality in the way he uttered the sentence.

Bob was also at pains to explain why his team had been

instructed to go for a sniper's shot rather than engage with Jack in the cabin and kill him there. Bob hadn't wanted any possible interaction with Jack with the chance of him saying anything about Revelation to his men that could go against the back story and might later get out. His team had also been told that Jack was very dangerous and could not be approached at close quarters.

Sam nodded. 'I can mobilise some more special forces if you need back up. But I imagine your current unit should have it covered.'

Bob nodded appreciatively for Sam's vote of confidence. But the Reverend persisted, 'We can't just leave him out there, this needs to be finalised – Frank?'

Frank couldn't hide the tension in his voice, 'Don't you think I know that, Walter! Bob, your guys need to find him and find him fast. And need I say, with the utmost discretion.'

Bob remained calm, 'Already got my best men on it. Story is that Jack's a nuclear scientist who's sold out to a foreign power. Don't worry, they'll deal with him.'

Everyone nodded with approval, although Frank was clearly the most perturbed by how events were unfolding. He addressed Bob with a strange concern, given what he was sanctioning, 'Keep it clean; Jack's a good man.'

Sam gave Frank an understanding look but said, 'Frank, we just need to get the job done, whatever it takes.' The Reverend was even more emphatic, 'This man needs to be neutralised!'

It was clear from Frank's expression that he didn't appreciate the Reverend's hard-line input on the matter. Nor did he like his use of the word neutralised as if that somehow softened or sanitised what he was calling for. But, having first asked him to join the initial meeting about Revelation for ecumenical advice which Frank had never imagined would lead to this situation, he just had to accept it and couldn't exclude him now.

He turned to Bob and there was a hint of desperation in his voice, knowing the stakes could not be higher for all those present in his office. 'Bob, you call me the minute it's over, you hear?'

Bob's voice was much calmer, reflecting the fact that putting his head on the block with dark operations like this were his stock-in-trade. 'Of course – and rest assured, my team didn't leave so much as a wing nut up at the cabin to suggest Revelation or anything else for that matter had been there. If anyone chances across it, all they'll find is a heap of ash. And if we get wind of any snooping, I've already got a back story prepared about how Marty left the cabin to go scrambling and must have forgotten he'd left a fire on or somesuch. Don't worry, Frank, I'm across it all.'

The meeting broke up and Sam, Walter and Bob filed silently out of Frank's office. Frank stood in the middle of his office deep in thought. This was like a bad dream and he had always liked Jack. Frank had spent his career chasing after power, but right now he wished he was still an up-and-coming attorney back in Baltimore. He walked slowly over to his desk as if the weight of the world was on his shoulders.

At that moment, Daniella, the White House Press Secretary, knocked and entered. A tall black woman in her early thirties, she had excelled at Harvard and brought a fierce intelligence combined with great efficiency to her role. Her charming manner also often helped to diffuse difficult press conferences when the news-hungry, unforgiving journalists were at pains to put the administration under fierce scrutiny.

As she entered, the Reverend had been first out of the door, but Bob and Sam brushed past her without a word. Daniella gave them a look as if to say rude bastards, but could see they were both preoccupied and seemed angry about something.

She approached Frank and could see that he too was looking harassed. 'Tough day, eh?' she asked in a caring way.

'Understatement,' Frank replied laconically.

Daniella smiled engagingly, 'Well, I could say it can wait, but it can't. President's issuing a statement later about the situation in Kazakhstan and I need your OK on the final draft.'

Frank liked Daniella and admired her efficiency. 'Sure,' he replied, 'can you leave it with me for ten minutes? Got a couple of urgent calls to make.'

'You got it,' Daniella answered, as she handed Frank a couple of sheets of typed paper. As she turned and started to leave, she called back cheerily, 'Hope your day gets better.'

Frank struggled to raise a smile in return. He had worked all his life and pulled every trick in the book to get where he was today and he wasn't going to give it up lightly. He sat back in his chair and wondered what he would do now if he was in Jack's shoes.

Chapter 19

Dishevelled and very scared, Jack flitted amongst the shadows and alleys of the city streets. As with anyone trying to hide, every car that passed seemed like a potential threat and every person who happened to glance in his direction could be an enemy who knew exactly who he was.

He had half run and half walked as fast as he could for a few hours to get to the heart of the city, whilst trying to look like a man in a hurry rather than someone on the run. But his legs ached from the effort and his heart pounded against his chest through exhaustion and fear.

Having found a quiet alley, he had lain low waiting for dark, sometimes striding up and down the alley to keep warm as the temperature began to drop, as he had run away without a coat. Thankfully no-one paid him any undue attention.

As soon as it was dark enough, he moved out of the alley and strode purposefully along the sidewalks, his head bowed and never looking up, as the whole city would be saturated with CCTV cameras. He knew time was not on his side, as whoever was chasing him meant business and would no doubt be pulling out all the stops to find him. And he had no doubt that they were powerful enough to commandeer the use of the city's CCTV and anything else to trace him. Hell, they were probably right now redirecting satellites to scour the whole city and surroundings!

Every now and then Jack stopped, feigning to take an interest in a shop window, but in reality to check if he was being followed. The off-duty banter and chat in the canteen with the spooks who regularly passed through Joint Base Balad en route to some highly classified secret mission, was paying dividends now as Jack checked for any tell-tale signs of a classic diamond formation of followers, front, back and sides. Remembering how, after a few beers and knowing Jack was assigned to the CIA, the spooks sometimes forgot themselves and tried to top each other by swapping stories of playing a tramp, a drunk, a pimp and more, Jack checked again for anyone like that or appearing to loiter. But all seemed to be clear.

Jack noticed a bargain clothes shop that seemed to sell everything else too and headed inside. 'Closing in five minutes, sir,' the Chinese proprietor called out to him cheerily whilst his wife and teenage son helped him tidy away.

'Oh, I'll be quick, don't worry,' replied Jack. This was not the time to worry about fashion, so Jack hastily chose a coat, shirt, underwear, wide-brimmed hat and some overnight essentials. He said a quiet prayer of thanks to his dead mother for always telling him to have enough cash in his wallet for emergencies – and boy was this an emergency! He could have used his debit or credit cards, but that was a sure short-cut to being discovered. At least by paying cash, he might have bought himself some precious extra time to get away before anyone paid the storekeeper a visit.

The store owner thanked Jack profusely, as it wasn't often someone bought nearly three hundred dollars of goods in cash, especially at closing time. Jack waved goodbye and with the collar of his coat turned up and the brim of his hat pulled down, he headed back out into the night, carrying his shopping. It felt better to look more like a normal shopper on his way home.

If he had left the shop thirty seconds earlier, he might have been spotted from a Jeep with blacked-out windows that had slowly cruised past and whose occupants were busy scouring the sidewalks. But for now, lady luck was on Jack's side.

Bob Howard's most trusted CIA desk team were working into the night, but still hadn't cross-checked every detail about Jack's past, his friends and known associates by the time Jack had followed a couple of commuters into Linda's apartment block. He had smiled at them as if he knew them and of course he was a fellow resident, how could they possibly think otherwise!

He knocked frantically at Linda's apartment door. Having checked through the spyhole in her door, Linda opened it to find Jack looking tired and distressed. Uncharacteristically, he strode into the apartment without waiting for an invitation.

'Jack, you look terrible, what the hell's up?' Linda asked as she hurriedly closed and locked the door, noticing as she did so the gash on Jack's forehead. Jack was still a little breathless as he replied, 'They're trying to kill me, the bastards are actually trying to kill me!'

Linda had been working at her laptop computer and took off her glasses as she looked at Jack in shock at what he had just told her. 'What? What d'ya mean? Who's trying to kill you? What's going on?'

'I dunno, Frank's men I assume, CIA, Feds whatever. But they're pros alright, a SWAT team or something, seen enough of them in my time.' Jack was almost gasping as he tried to get all his words out at once. 'They had guns, shot at me, destroyed the cabin, Revelation, everything. I was damn lucky to escape.'

'Oh my God, Jack! What? That's just terrible. Why? Look, you're hurt,' she gently touched his forehead and could see that he had also scraped his knuckles. 'Here, come and get cleaned up while we talk.' She led Jack to her bathroom, 'I'll get you something for your cuts.'

Jack started to take off his coat and shirt as he replied, 'Thanks, I'm OK – was about to say I'll live, but not too sure about that! Now I'm on the run. Just needed to warn you first in case they come here asking questions. You haven't seen me since the funeral and you've never heard of Revelation.'

'Sure…but…think you were followed?' Linda asked, still trying to come to terms with her shock at what Jack had told her.

'Don't think so,' Jack answered. 'Used all the tradecraft I know and pretty sure I've given them the slip for now. But I need to keep moving.' He turned the taps in the basin and began to wash away the smears of blood on his hands and forehead.

As they talked, Linda went into the open-plan kitchen area and took a First Aid kit from a cupboard. At one point she stopped briefly, gripped the work surface tightly with both hands and looked up at the ceiling deep in thought and clearly making a decision.

She took some ointment and pads and walked into the bathroom where Jack was standing bare-chested and drying himself. She gave his body an admiring glance as she handed him the items. As she did so, their hands touched. Jack put down the items next to the sink and held both Linda's hands. They looked deeply into each other's eyes and both were excited by the intimacy, but it was Jack who thought better of taking things further at this time and entwining Linda with his fate.

Linda left Jack to finish in the bathroom, but unseen by him, she began to pack a holdall for herself as well as some snacks from her fridge and a water bottle for the two of them. She had clearly decided to go with him.

Jack spoke loudly to her from the bathroom, expressing a mixture of shock and real anger, 'Just can't believe Revelation's gone. All that work. What we achieved. Shit! I mean how in God's name can they do this!'

Linda called back as she hurriedly continued to finish packing, 'They must see Revelation as a threat or something. Bloody Neanderthals.'

'Yeah, I'm mad as hell!' Jack agreed and smacked the palms of his hands against the tiled bathroom wall.

'That snake Caspari must be behind this,' Linda said.

'Yeah,' Jack confirmed, 'but he's utilising the CIA or military to mount an attack like that. Why is Revelation scaring them so much?'

'Dunno,' Linda shrugged, 'maybe Revelation threatens their power base, the status quo, that's all I can think.'

'So why didn't they just talk to me?' Jack asked with genuine innocence.

Linda countered, 'Because people like that shoot first and talk later. Watched too many movies! All we know is they came to kill you – and that won't have changed just 'cos they destroyed Revelation. You're a threat to them now.'

'Oh I sure intend to be!' he answered, trying to convince himself as much as Linda, whilst muttering to himself. 'Shit, why didn't I just stick to astrophysics!'

107

She liked his fighting response, 'Look, you and Marty have made an incredible discovery – maybe the most brilliant in the history of humankind. Most scientists spend their whole lives dreaming of something like that. You've got to make sure the world gets to know about it.'

Jack nodded. 'Have to stay alive first! Then I'll have to figure what to do without any proof.' He emerged from the bathroom and noticed Linda finishing her packing, 'What's this?'

'Coming with you' she replied with a matter-of-fact finality. 'And don't even try to talk me out of it!' she said firmly. 'Think about it. They'll check up on everyone who attended the funeral. They'll find out you came to my college, that we're long-standing friends. If I were them, I'd reckon you'd've told me about Revelation too. If these brain-deads want a fight, we'll give them one!'

Jack let the truth of what Linda said sink in for a couple of seconds. He realised that what she was saying was the truth and that she may well now be a target too. He looked at her with immense admiration and deep affection. He knew it would be useless to try and talk her out of it. *What a woman*, he thought to himself.

Linda walked over to her laptop. 'Right, we need to get going. I'll just close down my computer. Been working on a new pet theory of mine. Guess that will have to wait a while now!'

'Hold up, why don't you email it to yourself? Always a good safeguard that.'

'Oh yeah, thanks for the reminder,' Linda replied and quickly emailed the file to herself.

Jack watched and continued, 'Marty was always on at me about that. He'd always say, Jack you gotta make a back-up.'

Jack froze. He stared at Linda in shocked silence as the word 'back-up' echoed in his head and the realisation hit him like a sledgehammer.

'Holy shit! A back-up! Oh man! That's what Marty must have meant when he said if I ever need any spares I might get quite a surprise! Oh my dear God!'

'What the hell!' Linda exclaimed as she beamed excitedly at Jack.

He looked skywards as he cried, 'Marty Robinson, a back-up, trust you my beautiful friend!' They both laughed out loud.

Linda picked up her holdall while handing Jack the carrier bag of snacks. She also picked up her cellphone, but Jack told her they would need to throw it down a drain as soon as they could. As she handed him her bag, their hands touched again and they looked at each other in a way that needed no explanation. This time they put down their bags and let their lips gently touch each other before kissing and holding each other with a quiet intensity that held the promise of so much more. After a quiet moment while they just looked into each other's eyes and without another word, they then picked up their bags and walked to the door. As they exited, Linda turned out the lights and closed the door behind them.

****

Just a few blocks away, a blacked out Jeep was cruising the streets. Inside, the attack team leader was on a secure radio phone talking to other members of his unit in similar Jeeps criss-crossing the city. 'We've had a credible possible sighting in this area so stay focused. If he's here and we lose him, it'll be like looking for a needle in a haystack in this city, so I'm counting on you all. Out.'

Chapter 20

Linda drove her Chevrolet Aveo fast into the night. She could see how nervous Jack was in the passenger seat by the way he kept checking the car's side mirror for any signs that they were being followed. It was a nailed-on certainty that it wouldn't be too long before Linda's make of car and licence plate, as well as her description, would soon be on an APB to every cop in the State, so time was not on their side.

They had decided to drive through the night, stopping in a remote spot en route for a few hours' sleep in the car before aiming to get to Martha Robinson's old bungalow in Bronxville, a village in Westchester County, New York State, by early morning. Linda had enough fuel in the tank not to need to stop at a filling station until they were clear of D.C. – anything that might buy them more time before they were picked up by cameras somewhere.

Linda had asked Jack why they needed to go to Marty's mother's home. Whilst she drove, Jack explained that after Jenny's death which happened quite soon after Marty's father had also died, Marty had spent a lot of his weekends at his mother's. Jack had always thought it went beyond being a dutiful son, but now it was all beginning to make sense. A back-up, a Revelation copy just like Marty had been assembling in Iraq, it had to be.

Jack made Linda laugh when he said he used to be

grateful to Marty for always taking away seemingly surplus spares, bits and parts to keep the workplace tidy. Jack had never questioned Marty about it but had just assumed that Marty knew a good place where to dump stuff. Just goes to show – never assume, he told Linda.

They drove on in silence, although the conversation had clearly prompted a train of thought for Jack.

'Come to think of it, Linda, he did drop some hints, but maybe he thought I would object or something as I was always one for teasing him about his obsession with having back-ups. And it was kinda strange in a way as I was the more cautious one and you'd have thought it would be me if anyone to think like that. But Marty was always clear about it – jeez I can hear him now: "Jack you gotta have a back-up", ha! Boy, will I be glad if this turns out to be true.'

Linda gave him a quick smile as they hit a stretch of open road that seemed to be drawing them deeper into the darkness. Both tried to hide their nerves from each other, but both also knew their lives were in danger and they needed to be very careful about their next moves, whatever the outcome of their visit to Marty's mother. Linda was already playing around with some thoughts in her head about where they could go and trying to second guess the possible outcomes, like playing a game of chess in her mind. The only priority right now was to stay alive.

Jack was talking again, as if externalising his own thoughts as to why Marty hadn't told him if indeed he had made a back-up copy of Revelation. The way Jack figured it was that it was no big deal, it was just a spare in case the original broke down or something. Marty was such a positive person he would never have thought that things could come to this and that people would actually want to destroy

112

Revelation – and kill its creators!

But Jack laughed as he told Linda how much Marty would have enjoyed revealing the back-up to Jack one day and seeing the surprise on his face. But then all this was nothing but hopeful speculation.

With a copy of Revelation in their hands, if Jack and Linda could get to the right people – not sure who yet and whether anyone could be trusted any more – they might stand a chance of getting the truth out to the world and, not least, save their own skins in the process.

But it was all ifs right now, big ifs.

They had pulled over into a rest area at one point, deliberately chosen as it was small and only really had space for one car. They put their seats back and tried to doze for a while. Thankfully at that time of night there wasn't too much traffic on the road, although a number of heavy trucks thundered past in the opposite direction, heading to stock up stores and supermarkets before the new day began. But the couple managed to get just enough rest to take the edge of their tiredness.

Dawn was beginning to break as they both got out of the car, had a good stretch and took in some fresh air. Back in the car, they drank some water and ate a snack bar and bananas from the supplies Linda had brought from her kitchen the previous evening. A little revitalised, Linda restarted the car and they headed back onto the road.

They drove on, keeping strictly to all speed limits, as the last thing they needed was to be picked up for any indiscretion. At one point Jack spotted a deer wandering along a hillside. *How beautifully free you are*, he thought to himself.

It was Linda who eventually broke the silence, 'You

and Marty were very close. Always seemed to me you had a great friendship.'

Jack spoke quietly as people do when lost in their recollections, 'Yeah, we became almost like brothers. I was the introvert one, solitary life, never married – well except to my work. Had the odd fling but nothing serious. Not to say I wouldn't have wanted it, of course I would, just always seemed too goddam busy, especially once I started getting seconded onto CIA projects and spending time overseas in some godforsaken country or other. But Marty and Jenny, they were so in love, so perfect.

'Sadly they couldn't have kids and I know they would have loved to do all that – you know, kids, the house with the picket fence, apple pie, yeah all that,' he laughed. 'But it was not to be. It was whilst having some medical checks that they first discovered Jenny's cancer. Terrible, so sad, so cruel. Marty was such a gentle soul and Jenny just matched everything about him. Both brilliant physicists. Met at college, as you know. Funny in a way.'

'What makes you say that?' Jenny had been listening intently and enjoying hearing Jack reminisce like this. She couldn't help but also feel a little pleased to hear that Jack was not a player when it came to the opposite sex. She rather liked his shyness and general inexperience.

Jack went on, 'Oh, I think Marty's parents kinda expected him to front a rock and roll band! They were both a bit hippyish and had met at the Woodstock Rock Festival. They used to tease Marty that he was conceived in-between performances by The Who and Jefferson Airplane.'

Linda laughed out loud. She had once cuddled up on a sofa with a past boyfriend to watch a DVD of the film *Woodstock* so she was conjuring up images in her mind of

114

what it must have been like for Marty's parents to experience all that.

'Yeah, well,' Jack continued, 'they even named Marty after the founder of Jefferson Airplane. Bought Marty his first guitar when he was just four. It wasn't that Marty wasn't interested, but he just kept getting straight A's in all his exams, so his future kinda mapped itself out – bit like mine I guess. Marty got a top scholarship to George Washington University.'

'Must've been a huge disappointment to his parents!' Linda quipped sarcastically.

Jack laughed, 'Amen to that. No, I mean they were cool about it all, especially when he did so well and started dating such a lovely girl as Jenny.'

Jack paused for a moment as his train of thought made him take on a more serious tone, 'He was still at college when he was talent-spotted by the CIA. Later, Frank saw we'd make a good team. Frank Caspari, bloody hell, I just can't believe he'd turn on me like that.'

Linda was less surprised as she had always viewed the White House Chief of Staff as akin to a snake oil salesman. 'Oh, don't you know that power corrupts. Nothing would surprise me with that man – sell his own grandmother if it helped his cause. But what about you Jack, what makes you tick?'

Jack looked gently at Linda, inwardly appreciating her interest. 'Oh, I'm just life's great worrier. Even when I've done well in my work, whatever, I worry that it's not enough. And I catastrophise. If I'd have been on The Titanic, I'd have known it would hit an iceberg.'

Linda laughed and playfully slapped Jack's thigh.

'Thing is, I worry about today, worry about tomorrow.

Had therapy once – didn't work, I just worried about why I was having therapy.'

Linda kept laughing and as she gave Jack a loving look, she took one hand off the steering wheel long enough to gently stroke his thigh. Jack wished he had more confidence to tell her exactly how he felt, but it just didn't come naturally to him, and for now it could wait. His first girlfriend had had to ask Jack to kiss her and that was after they'd been going out for a month. At least he'd got to first base with Linda quicker than that, he thought to himself.

They had been driving for a while now and Linda mentioned to Jack that the fuel gauge was getting low. It wasn't too long before they spotted a small filling station and pulled over. Thankfully, being early in the morning, the old man and his wife who ran the place paid little attention to them. They didn't have to, as even a small family-run place like this had CCTV just in case. Jack had noticed the cameras anyway, but it was too late to be overly concerned at this stage. As their pursuers' search grew wider in the next day or so, it would only be a matter of time before the filling stations tapes were viewed by shadowy figures who would also quiz the man and his wife for every detail they might have noticed about Jack and Linda. CCTV is never perfect so they'd want to know what car they were driving, what they were wearing, anything they said, where they might be heading and more.

It was as if two films of their lives were running concurrently, the one slightly ahead of the other. They needed to keep it that way and ensure that they got to a happy ending. For now, time was on their side, but it could all too soon catch up with them.

Having filled up the car and bought more bottled water, they drove off again. After a couple of miles, the road signs started to include Bronxville. Jack told Linda to take a left just in time before they missed the turning towards the village.

Although only some 24 kilometres north of downtown Manhattan, Bronxville felt a world away from the bustling craziness of New York City and still maintained its village feel. The impressive houses, trimmed hedges and manicured lawns immediately told of an area at peace with itself and very much for those with significant dollars in their accounts.

Martha Robinson had been able to afford her more modest bungalow as a result of the payouts from her husband Burt's life insurance policies, as well as the fruits of both of them having worked and saved hard all their lives. She had been attracted to the village by the architectural and cultural legacy left behind by an arts colony that had been prominent there in the early 20th century. And she sought out the more bohemian residents, rather than mixing with the conservative cocktail party set who bored her with their talk of the stock market, horses and little else.

Martha had certainly lived a very full life, immersing herself in the seismic rock 'n roll cultural changes that had defined her early years and forged a new society. Once arrested on an anti-Vietnam War protest that had turned violent, now all she wanted to do was look after her cat, Woodstock, and pursue the quiet life, spending her days painting. Not that the inner rebel in her wasn't still very much alive and well and given to swearing profusely at the television when some politician was, in her view, clearly spouting what she perceived to be horseshit.

It was still relatively early in the morning and Martha peered out of her kitchen window to see if she could spot the paper boy arriving. She didn't notice the small car about one hundred yards away and neatly parked by the curbside. Jack had made Linda pull over as soon as Martha's white bungalow was in sight, but still not so close as to be seen as obvious visitors. Jack had told Linda to park up so he could take a look around and check for any signs of them having been followed.

'Would they come here?' Linda had innocently asked.

'Linda, they'll visit my barber,' Jack replied to emphasise the scale of the search that would no doubt be going on.

'Don't blame them,' Linda replied jokingly, trying to lighten the mood a little.

'Yeah, yeah, funny,' Jack enjoyed the ribbing, 'well let's not pretend we're not shitting ourselves. There are clearly going to be some seriously tough guys on our tail. But Martha's house looks clear from here. Let's go.'

Jack was about to get out of the car when Linda suddenly burst into tears. She put her head in her hands and gently sobbed, the tears freely streaming down her face. Jack didn't know what had prompted this or how he should react. He would readily admit that he wasn't great in emotional situations.

He hesitatingly reached out an arm and touched Linda on the shoulder. She gladly let her whole body fall into his own, with her head rested on his upper chest. Jack gently stroked her hair, at the same time enjoying the feint sweet smell of the scent she must have worn from the previous day before they left her apartment.

For a moment, they must have looked to any casual observer like lovers making up after a tiff. Both were enjoying the closeness and comfort of each other's body. 'Linda, what is it?' Jack asked gently, continuing to stroke her hair and try to calm her down.

'Oh Jack, Jack,' Linda spoke through her sobs, 'I don't want to die, especially now I've got you.'

Her words struck Jack like a thunderbolt and brought a large lump to his throat. He was fully aware of the danger they were in, but it was a stark reminder that he had got Linda into this situation. In a way it strengthened his resolve to make sure they would survive and bring the truth of Revelation to the world.

'I know, Linda, I know,' he said feebly but gently, as he kissed the top of her head. At this, she lifted her head fully and the two kissed passionately like star-crossed lovers who might all too soon be parted. The two of them sat in silence for a while as Linda slowly composed herself, 'It's OK, I'm OK, sorry.'

'Nothing to be sorry about,' Jack replied. 'I'm the one who should be sorry for getting you into all this. What the hell was I thinking!'

'Jack it's OK,' Linda reassured him, 'how could I possibly leave you to fight this all on your own. I'm glad you came to me and I'm with you all the way.' She paused and looked intently at him, 'All the way'.

Jack understood exactly what she was saying. Both their fates were now completely intertwined. *My God she's magnificent*, he thought to himself as he gave her a gentle squeeze as they remained in their embrace.

After another brief silence, Linda sat back in her car seat and pulled the sun visor down so she could take a look at herself in the little mirror. 'Do I look like I've been crying?' she asked.

'No, but don't worry – you can relax about Marty's mom,' Jack told her, 'I know you only met her briefly at the funeral, but she's a gem and you've got nothing to worry about on her count, believe me.'

Linda had been fishing in her bag and applied a touch of lipstick. She then said with surprising new-found confidence, 'OK, let's do it.'

Chapter 21

Linda's apartment was a complete mess. That's not to say that the team going through everything weren't being very methodical, but were certainly not in the business of putting things back in drawers again or anything like that. They knew there was no need for any pretence that they hadn't been there.

Some wore gloves and had clearly been focused on gathering fingerprints from the glasses of water that still sat half full on the table. Linda's computer had been bagged up to be taken away so that experts could plunder the hard drive for any information that might be helpful in tracking down the two fugitives. Some items had also been removed from the bathroom for DNA testing just in case a situation arose when it might be needed.

The team were well-trained and had clearly done this many times, although usually with firm instructions not to leave any trace of their intrusion. So they revelled in the freedom to turn everything over as fast as they could.

There were shakes of the head between various operatives as nothing of great significance seemed to have come to light, other than the obvious fact that Jack and Linda had been together in the apartment.

The team leader pressed a button on his comms piece and it was answered immediately by Bob Howard who had been waiting for the call. 'You were right,' he spoke calmly and in complete control, 'he's been here. We're pretty sure we've got his prints to confirm it. Otherwise there's no trace of them and no obvious clues as to where they may have gone. Our birds have flown.'

Bob replied equally calmly, although inwardly he was growing increasingly concerned, 'OK, well at least we now know he's travelling with Linda Wilson. I've already put out an APB on her car and I'll get her photo circulated.'

He then spoke with a measured menace in his tone, 'She clearly now has to be seen as part of this whole thing. So you know what to do when you find them both.'

'Affirmative,' was all the team leader replied as they both ended the call.

Jack and Linda were on the run together and now they could die together.

Chapter 22

Martha's newspaper had been delivered and she was about to make herself a cup of coffee and settle down for a good read. She wondered aloud to her cat, Woodstock, as to what kind of bullshit would be coming out of Capitol Hill today when she heard the knocking at the door.

She furtively pulled an inch aside of the half-height net curtain in a side window of her living room from where she could see her porch and then hurried to open the door.

'Jack, what a lovely surprise,' Martha exclaimed with genuine delight.

'Hello Martha, you remember Linda?' Jack announced.

'Of course, hello again dear,' Martha said and in her natural way, having lovingly embraced Jack, also gave Linda a warm hug.

'Very nice to see you again Mrs Robinson,' Linda said with a big smile, whilst also finding herself moved by seeing some of Marty's sweet features again in his mother's face. Although now in what is colourfully called the autumn of her life, Martha looked good for her years and was dressed in a full-length hippy-style kaftan with beaded tassels that made a soft rustling sound each time she moved.

The three of them went inside as Martha closed the door and ushered them into her living room. The room was dominated by a giant framed picture poster of Jimi Hendrix playing his version of Star-Spangled Banner which only those like Martha and Burt who had stayed behind until the Monday morning at the Woodstock rock festival had witnessed. Right opposite was a giant dreamcatcher mounted on the wall and the whole room was a fusion of 1970s hippy chic and modern ethnic furnishings complete with multicoloured opulent cushions and throws. On a low bookcase, there was a framed photo of Marty at his degree ceremony, two of him with Jenny and one with him standing with a huge smile with his arms around Martha and Burt, his very proud mom and dad. It brought a tear to Linda's eye.

'Sorry we're unannounced like this,' Jack began to explain, 'but I said I'd be coming to see you sometime. Well now it's a whole lot more urgent. I need to talk to you about something very important, something about Marty.'

A furrow of pain crossed Martha's brow. 'Oh my, OK, let's all take a seat. Coffee?'

'No thanks, it's OK, we don't really have much time, as you'll soon understand,' Jack replied and Martha could see he was a little on edge. She was a little perplexed at what Jack was saying and she could tell that Linda also looked worried. 'How are you coping?' Jack continued. Despite time not exactly being on his side, out of respect and care Jack didn't want to go straight for it and ask if The Alamo made any sense to her or whether Marty had stockpiled any equipment anywhere.

Martha briefly looked down before looking straight at Jack. She liked him immensely. After all, he had been best friends with her darling boy. 'Well, it's not easy,' she replied, 'after Burt died, Marty was all I had. His accident has been beyond hard to take in.'

Linda spoke gently to Martha, 'I'm so sorry for your loss, Mrs Robinson. I knew Marty well; he was the best.'

Jack knew this was not the time to tell Martha that Marty's death had been no accident.

'Thank you, dear,' Martha replied, 'and do please call me Martha. I'm only Mrs Robinson to those bandits from the neighbourhood real estate agency who keep trying to persuade me to sell.'

Jack and Linda both laughed, while at the same time Jack had been looking around and spotted two used coffee mugs still left on the side.

Jack cleared his throat, 'Martha, hope you don't mind me asking, but has anybody official-looking been to see you recently?'

Martha had already followed Jack's gaze over to the two cups and complimented him on his observation. 'Very good, Jack. Yes, late last night, damned too late to be calling on folk if you ask me. Two sharp-suited, short-back-and-sides, 'oh no, we don't work for the Government' types. Didn't like them. Showed me some kind of I.D. and wanted to poke around. Didn't even tell me why. No manners.'

'Did you let them?' Linda innocently enquired.

'Didn't think I had much choice,' Martha replied in a tone that couldn't hide her contempt for her recent intruders.

Jack asked Martha if they had found anything or taken anything away, but Martha said no.

'They searched all the rooms but only briefly and hadn't been interested in going through small stuff like papers, photos and the like. So it wasn't obvious what they might be looking for. They actually bothered to say thank you after they finished and gave me a card with a number to call straight away if I ever heard from you, Jack. Are you in some kind of trouble?'

'No nothing like that, just stuff to do with work,' Jack tried to reassure her but she was clearly unconvinced.

'You won't call them will you, Martha?' Linda asked unnecessarily.

Martha looked at her patiently, 'Sweetheart, do I look like some kind of establishment patsy?'

'No you sure don't!' Linda replied with a laugh. But Jack was still worried and pressed Martha, 'Did they search everywhere?'

Martha replied nonchalantly, 'Oh yes, very thorough. Well, everywhere except Marty's private room of course.'

Jack and Linda glanced towards the narrow corridor leading to the two bedrooms in the house. 'Why ever not?' Jack asked incredulously. It seemed unbelievable that the one place that should have been searched had been overlooked.

Martha read their thoughts, 'No, not there, come with me.' She stood up and led Jack and Linda out of the living room and into the kitchen.

As they followed Martha, she explained, 'One of the things that attracted me to this area are its links back to the Prohibition days. Kinda tickled my anti-establishment bones, if you know what I mean.' Jack and Linda smiled at each other, enjoying Martha's rebellious nature as she went on, 'And what attracted me even more to this little house is what you two are about to find out.'

She walked over to where a tall twin-door fridge-freezer stood. 'I'm getting on, Jack can you help me move this to the side will you? It's on little wheels so isn't hard, just like to save my back!'

Jack and Linda's surprise at Martha's request quickly deepened as Jack moved the fridge-freezer to one side to reveal a small old wooden door behind it.

'Welcome to The Alamo!' Martha exclaimed.

'The Alamo? Oh my God!' Jack was stunned.

Martha had meanwhile removed a Mortice key from the back of a drawer and was busy unlocking the door as she spoke calmly to Jack and Linda, 'Yes, this is Marty's workroom. We called it The Alamo as we used to joke that this is where we'd make our last stand if the country ever got invaded,' she laughed, but not entirely ridiculing the idea. 'God knows by who or what though, as there are already plenty enough cockroaches up on Capitol Hill! And anyway, Marty used to love all those Davy Crockett stories when he was a boy. Unusual I know to find a cellar in a bungalow, but as I say, it dates back to Prohibition in the early 1920s. They used to stockpile illegal stuff down here, mainly rum I think. When the original house was completely renovated before I bought it, they kept the cellar for whatever reason – glad they did, I kinda like its piratical history,' she chuckled.

Flicking on a light switch at the top of the bare wooden stairs leading down into the cellar, Martha led the way as Jack and Linda were still coming to terms with the find. When they reached the bottom of the stairs, their amazement grew even more into total astonishment. The cellar virtually mirrored the whole floor space of the bungalow above, so was spacious, although the ceiling was no more than eight foot high. The single switch had turned on a series of lights that flooded the interior. The room was surprisingly warm, unlike most cellars, as hot water pipes wrapped in a silvery insulation material ran around its perimeter almost at floor level.

Jack and Linda looked around at what, to all intents and purposes, looked like a typical 'man cave'. It was full of every kind of tool hanging from the walls and with workbenches around the sides covered in various small machinery like a metal cutter and lathe. But it was what was standing on a low table in the middle of the room that made Jack catch his breath.

'For the love of God, Revelation!' Jack exclaimed. 'Or should I say Revelation Mark II. Hello my old friend! Wow, Marty, you son-of-a-gun, you bloody genius, you sure meant what you said! The back-up, I just can't believe it!'

'Incredible!' Linda joined in, with tears in her eyes, knowing just what this could mean. 'What a guy, amazing!'

Martha took some delight in their surprise and obvious pleasure in finding whatever the contraption was that her son had spent so many weekends working on. 'Well, whatever it is, got a feeling you'll be wanting to take it with you?'

Jack answered with a quiet passion in his voice, 'Martha, this is what Marty and I worked on for all those years. Did he ever mention Revelation to you?'

'Yeah, the name rings bells,' Martha replied nonchalantly, 'said it was something top secret you and he were working on. I told him I didn't want to know as I would probably object to it seeing as how it was some kind of CIA shit.'

Jack spoke more urgently now, 'Martha, I really need to take this with me, is that OK?'

Linda added supportively, 'Believe me, Jack has the best intentions.'

'Don't worry,' Martha replied, 'I don't need you to tell me that. Take it; I get my cellar back.'

Jack couldn't help himself; he leaned over and gave Martha an appreciative peck on the cheeks. Although roughly the size of a small car engine, Revelation was made from light metals, aluminium hydrous silicates, acrylic, crystals, other composites and some rubber, so it wouldn't be too heavy to carry. In fact the crystals were probably the heaviest element – and crystal energy had been one of the most vital things that Jack and Marty had added to the device post-Iraq as part of their continued experimentation. But making it portable had also been part of the original idea when Jack and Marty had been charged with designing something that could easily be deployed in a combat theatre. They often used to giggle amongst themselves like a couple of schoolkids at how they had come up with such a seemingly haphazard collection of materials.

Martha had briefly disappeared upstairs only to emerge with an old blanket to cover up the device. They used some electrical flex off one of the many reels in the cellar to secure the blanket and ensure nothing of the device was showing. Meanwhile, before they covered it, Jack had been at pains to inspect the device to see if it was fully complete, like the one they had got to work up at the cabin. As he did so, he made noises to himself either of approval or indicating some further adjustments or additional parts might be necessary.

'Boy, I wish those prohibition busters had left some rum down here, I could sure do with a tot right now,' he joked.

But Linda was also deep in thought, 'Hang on, Jack,' she interjected, 'if they've already searched this place, wouldn't it be better to leave Revelation down here and bring whoever to it?'

'I can see your thinking,' Jack replied, 'but right now I don't know how all this is going to pan out and I'll feel better if Revelation is with us. Besides, I don't want Martha to be put in any danger.'

Martha feigned mock indignation, 'Don't you go worrying about me, Jack Taylor! I can take care of myself. Showed those two goons a clean pair of heels didn't I!'

'You sure did.' Jack paused to look straight into her eyes. 'Look Martha, there's no time to explain everything, but there are people who will stop at nothing – and I mean nothing – to get hold of this Revelation device.'

'Why, what does it do?' she asked.

Jack continued, 'For your own good, it's best I don't tell you yet. But believe me, when I can, you'll be one of the first to know. Oh hell, what am I talking about, of course you should know. This is going to sound crazy, but Revelation scientifically proves that life after death is a fact.' He stared at Martha expecting some kind of shocked reaction, but didn't get it.

Martha was remarkably matter-of-fact about it and it was her response that surprised him. 'So what's new. I've always held to that anyway. I'm sure I've felt Burt around quite a few times and my mom used to see things. Mark you, mighty impressive if you and my boy have gone and proved it. Yes indeed. That's sure going to shake things up!'

Jack was shaking his head in surprise and admiration at Martha's reaction, 'Yeah, well you got that right – some very powerful people see it as some kind of threat to their status quo and they want it stopped, destroyed.'

'Now why am I not surprised by that!' Martha quipped. 'It hurts me to think you two are now in danger just for searching after the truth. So what you planning on doing?'

Revelation was by now tightly covered and tied by the blanket and flex and ready to be moved.

Jack spoke softly, 'The best thing Linda and I can do is to get Revelation to those who will listen. That's why it has

130

to be with us as I don't think we'll be able to come back here until all this is over one way or another.'

Martha didn't like the implication in what Jack was saying that one way or another could mean something really bad. She gently held his arm, 'Now you listen to me, Jack, I don't know where all this is taking you, but my Marty thought the world of you. You're dear to me too. You look after yourself, you hear?'

'Don't worry, he won't be on his own,' Linda offered, although at the same time thinking to herself that this was scarce comfort given the nature of who was hot on their tail right this minute.

Martha acknowledged her with a simple 'Good,' but then glanced between Jack and Linda in a rather cheeky manner as she repeated 'Good,' in a very knowing way.

Chapter 23

Back in Jack's research labs, everyone had been slightly perplexed about his sudden absence. An official-looking pair of faceless suited men from no-one knew exactly where had visited the team to tell them Jack had been urgently seconded onto some highly secretive project and might not be back for a while. And no, they wouldn't answer any questions or give any further explanation.

Whilst most seemed to accept this at face value – after all, this was reasonably commonplace in their kind of work – it was Alexis and Jermaine, two of Jack's younger lab assistants, who had briefly exchanged questioning glances and had then caught up with each other later on as they walked home after work.

'What do you make of Jack then?' Alexis asked Jermaine as they strolled arm-in-arm along one of the several different routes they had been told to use to walk back to their apartment. Stopping every few minutes to tie up an imaginary loose shoelace or glance in a shop window to check if they were being followed, they were well-trained and this had become second nature to them.

Both in their early twenties, black and blessed with natural good looks, they were popular members of the research team and flagged for bright futures. Tall and athletic,

Jermaine towered over Alexis, who was a foot shorter than him, but to any casual observer they just looked like any other happy young couple. Their casual mode of dress also helped them blend into any crowd, something that had been part of their training, although Alexis was given to wearing colourful head scarves and flamboyant earrings.

'I know, it's kinda weird, isn't it,' replied Jermaine.

'My thinking exactly,' Alexis went on. 'Remember at Marty's funeral? I'd never seen him look so troubled, so distracted and almost – well, just not himself. Of course, it wasn't exactly a great time for him, especially as he and Marty were such good friends, but I just felt it was perhaps something more than that.'

'And there was something about those guys just now. Just a bit creepy. You reckon Jack's in some kind of trouble?'

'Well, never say never,' Alexis responded, 'but Jack Taylor's got to be the least likely guy ever to have broken the law or anything like that. I doubt he's even had a parking ticket!' They both laughed. 'I dunno, it's just a feeling. We've got his cellphone number, let's give him a call when we get to the apartment, see if he's OK.' They had both forgotten for the moment the warning they had been given during their recruitment inductions two years previously that their phones would always be listened to, for their own good as much as anything.

'Good idea,' agreed Jermaine, 'and if a lady with a sexy voice answers, we'll know Jack's hiding a big secret!'

They both laughed as they walked on. Meanwhile, Jack was indeed hiding a big secret, the biggest secret of all.

Chapter 24

At Martha's suggestion, Jack and Linda had gone back to Linda's car and she had driven it up to the back of Martha's bungalow where it was largely hidden from sight under the double car canopy.

It was just as well, as a CIA drone operated from a secret location under instructions from Bob Howard, was making a wide sweep of the area. This had been instigated following satellite images of quite a number of cars similar to Linda's having been seen leaving the Washington D.C. conurbation over the last 24 hours. But it would take a few hours at least for all the images and cars to be assessed and any visible licence plates to be recorded.

Having said a fairly emotional goodbye to Martha where she had hugged Jack as if he were her son, Jack and Linda had taken a good look around before carrying Revelation out to their car. As she opened the trunk, Linda tried to lighten the mood by joking, 'Well done for designing it to fit in the trunk of an old Chevy!'

'Oh believe me, it was our first consideration,' he countered, enjoying the joke. He slammed down the trunk and they both got in the car.

'Wanna drive?' Linda asked.

'Hope your insurance is up-to-date!' he joked, even though he had to be one of the safest drivers on the planet.

She laughed. 'So let me get this straight, we've got a team of highly trained killers on our tail and you're worried about car insurance?'

Jack made a goofy face as if to say yeah, silly me, and took the keys Linda was offering. As they clipped on their seat belts, Linda complimented Jack in confiding in Martha about what Revelation was able to prove. Just maybe it would help for someone else to know about their situation and she could already tell that Martha was someone they could trust totally as she wasn't going to spill the beans to anyone. But it was best they now put some distance between themselves and Martha and get out of the area.

'Where to?' Linda asked, although she was already beginning to form a plan in her mind.

'We need to get to a general store first as soon as we find one that's open,' he replied.

'Bit risky isn't it?' she looked concerned.

'Maybe,' Jack answered, 'but it's vital, you'll see. And then I need to make the most important phone call of my life.'

Linda was perplexed by his reply but could hear in the tone of his voice that this wasn't the time to probe further. As they drove off, she gently stroked his arm reassuringly. 'OK,' she said, 'but let's head back towards D.C., I've got an idea.'

Jack looked at her but decided not to press her any further at this stage, as all he could think about was making that call. 'Well I'm sure glad one of us has,' he said.

Chapter 25

The inner sanctum of dark conspirators – Bob, Sam and the Reverend – had once again joined Frank in his office.

Frank gave his PA strict instructions that they were not to be disturbed under any circumstances before closing the door and joining the others seated around his conference table.

It was Bob who got things started, 'OK, so we know he's travelling with a Linda Wilson, a long-standing friend. She's a top physicist and college lecturer – very well thought of by all accounts. He must have sought her out after the cabin was destroyed.'

'She'll need to be neutralised too,' the Reverend immediately chipped in.

'Hell, Walter,' remarked Frank in genuine shock, 'you don't hold back do you!'

'But you know he's right, Frank,' Sam offered, 'we can't leave any trace. Bob, are your guys close yet? Can't be too hard if you're onto her too.'

Bob cleared his throat. 'Don't worry, I've already instructed my team about Linda Wilson. Just before coming in here I heard what we believe to be Linda's car had been spotted out of town. We're tracking it now and waiting for the right moment when any potential witnesses will be at a minimum. They may have to wait until it's dark but I should have some news very soon. I've also put out discreet feelers with people we've got embedded in the mainstream media, as well as our online watchers. There are no breaking stories or leaks of any kind on any front so far. Should all be clean and done with by the morning.'

Everyone around the table nodded in silent approval, although Frank clearly looked the most uncomfortable about it all. He decided there was no more to be said for now so brought the brief meeting to a close by addressing Bob. 'OK, let me know the minute your team have dealt with everything. And for God's sake make sure they clean up afterwards – no loose ends, OK?'

'Of course,' Bob muttered, a bit put out at being told how to do his job.

The four of them got up and Frank saw them out of his office. He had a meeting with the President scheduled to start in five minutes. She would want an update on the preparations for launching the Scorpion programme. Yes indeed, nothing could be allowed to get in the way of that.

He left his office for the short walk down the corridor to the Oval Office.

Chapter 26

It was late morning and Jack kept driving while Linda dozed off in the passenger seat. Jack thought how beautiful she looked and once again reprimanded himself for dragging her into all this. Then again, he wondered how he would possibly have coped without her amazing support, for which he loved her all the more.

They were now passing through residential areas as they headed back towards the capital. Linda opened her eyes and they both smiled lovingly at each other. Linda sat herself upright in her seat.

'Music?' Jack asked.

'Yeah, why not,' she replied.

Jack asked her if she would mind finding his favourite classic rock station on the car stereo. 'Already ahead of you there,' she said as she switched on the radio only for the digital display to show it was already tuned to that station. They both smiled at each other, as if a further bond had been found between them and as the poignant lyrics of George Harrison's *My Sweet Lord* filled the car's interior.

Jack had noticed that there were now more shops along the way and spotted a side street ahead which looked quite busy. 'Might find a store down here,' he said, as he turned the car into the street.

They had hardly gone fifty yards when they spotted

three police cars parked sideways up ahead blocking the road, but with just enough space beside them to allow one car to pass. But this was also blocked by armed officers who were clearly only allowing cars to pass once they had been vetted. The police cars' lights were flashing and several armed officers were standing beside the cars.

'Oh shit!' Jack exclaimed.

'Oh dear God no!' Linda added, as both looked ahead in horror at the police roadblock.

There were just two cars ahead of Jack and Linda and both were pulled up. Officers were already talking through the windows of the first car to the occupants. Jack turned to look behind him, thinking of reversing, but a large truck had now stopped right behind them and in the wing mirror Jack could see a taxi also turning into the same street, so there was no chance of reversing. He looked to the front again in time to see the first car being allowed to pass through the gap.

'We could make a run for it,' he suggested, forgetting for a brief moment as his instinctive self-survival took over that this would mean leaving Revelation behind. 'Doubt we'd get far,' Linda replied as she had also spotted several police officers along the sidewalks.

'Yeah,' Jack said resignedly, 'anyway, with Revelation on board, might as well go down with the ship as they say.' He attempted a lame smile and then looked hard at Linda. 'Shit! I'm real sorry.' He couldn't think of anything else to say.

'Surely they won't do it here,' she replied, as they held each other's hands lovingly, 'especially if we don't resist. Too many witnesses.'

'Guess we'll just have to play it out' he replied, trying his best to sound reassuring.

He leaned across and they kissed slowly whilst holding each other's gaze. Linda gave herself totally to Jack and he responded by allowing his hands to pull her tightly into himself, enjoying the closeness of their bodies.

They parted reluctantly like lovers enjoying a final kiss goodbye, which maybe they were. Jack edged the car forwards in response to one police officer beckoning him impatiently to move up. Their car was now first in line and armed police officers approached on both sides. Both Jack and Linda wound down their windows and desperately tried to look as casual and unconcerned as possible. A police chief approached Jack's side and certainly had the air of someone who enjoyed being in charge. Jack addressed him in as relaxed and friendly manner as he could muster, 'Morning officer, everything OK?'

The chief looked at them both impassively. He was in his forties, slightly overweight and clearly a very experienced cop. His roundish face was already lined, with only the slightest wisps of cropped greying hair appearing beneath his hat which was slightly askew on his head. His sleeves were rolled up and he had the demeanour of someone you didn't mess with. He showed Jack a photo. 'We're looking for this guy; armed and dangerous. Was holed up in this neighbourhood and is no doubt right now trying to escape our cordon – you seen him?'

Jack and Linda tried not to make it obvious as to just how relieved they were. Jack responded, 'No sir. Looks a bad 'un.'

'You can say that again,' the chief responded, 'mind if we look in your trunk all the same?'

Jack and Linda's relief had been temporary. The chief's question was of course rhetorical and two officers had already moved to the back of their car with their weapons at the ready just in case. Jack quickly scanned the unfamiliar dashboard with his eyes for the trunk release button. Linda's quick thinking saved the day as she casually leaned across and pressed the right button, casting Jack a reassuring glance as if to say, *Takes a woman*. She had reacted so quickly that the officer didn't register that Jack was unfamiliar with the car.

The officers at the back seemed to take an eternity looking at the contents of the opened trunk and Jack and Linda looked nervously at each other as the officers gestured their chief to take a look. One of the officers had undone some of the ties around the blanket covering Revelation to reveal enough of the device to give it a good look over.

The chief returned from the back of the car to talk to Jack. 'Helluva contraption you got in there – what in God's name is it?'

With his question, Jack and Linda realised they were in no immediate danger. 'Oh sure,' Jack tried to sound as nonchalant as possible, 'we're on our way to a sci-fi convention. It's just this crazy invention of ours that'll completely change the world.'

His reply was at first met with an incredulous silence, but when the chief stated to laugh, his officers joined in as they slammed the trunk shut again. The chief was now smiling broadly at Jack and Linda. 'Get outta here. Oh yeah, and give my regards to any little green men you come across!'

He laughed at his own very feeble joke, while all his officers began laughing a bit too hard as they joined in their chief's joke. They all stood aside to allow the car to pass through the gap. Jack muttered to himself just loud enough for Linda to hear, 'If only we just had little green men to deal with!'

****

The high-tech control centre was mostly in darkness, but illuminated by multiple surveillance screens. One giant central screen kept changing its view and splitting into multiple screens, some with grids and cross-hairs laid over them. Several operators were sitting at desks in front of the monitors. Other staff were walking between the operators and interacting with them, depending upon what was on their screens at any given moment.

Bob Howard was present, drumming his fingers nervously over his pursed lips. He would normally have expected an operation like this to have been executed by now. The head operator was a woman in her early thirties with a ramrod straight posture and manner that gave away the fact she was ex-military. Bob often liked to recruit from the military as they came, as he liked to put it, 'ready cooked'. She had a very efficient, professional manner and was clearly respected by her colleagues.

Bob already knew the answer, but as she passed him, he enquired, 'Anything yet?'

'Nothing definite yet, sir,' she replied, 'a few false leads. We've now got four drones up and are doing a thorough sweep.' She caught Bob's expression and could read his mind as she continued, 'Not something you can rush, but I'm confident.'

Bob nodded but was clearly frustrated, 'Got you. Just call me the minute you've got anything.' He turned to leave without waiting for any reply.

Chapter 27

As they drove on, Linda had confided in Jack about the plan she had secretly been mulling over in her mind and he was genuinely impressed. She had definitely pulled an ace from the pack and now was the right time to play it. It meant going back into the lion's den as their destination was in the Washington suburbs, but right now time was not on their side and they needed to go for broke or risk losing everything, especially their lives.

Jack had found the kind of general store he was looking for and had parked in the small car park behind it. But he had been at pains to park the car right up against the building's back wall as he had already worked out that there would be aerial surveillance of some kind looking for them. A car parked right up against a wall would be much harder to spot and identify from a casual overhead pass.

A drone did indeed fly over the store while Jack and Linda were inside and safely out of sight. After it had long passed, they emerged from the store carrying take-out snacks and coffees. Jack was also carrying a small box with a burner phone in it.

Their take-out snacks were delicious-looking tacos overflowing with tasty fillings and sauces. The snacks were wrapped at the end and both Jack and Linda were munching hungrily at the ends, nodding to each other and smiling in approval at the taste, whilst wiping the sides of their mouths with their fingers and paper napkins, trying not to let the ample fillings drop out onto the sidewalk.

They both made exaggerated 'mmm' noises at each other which made them giggle. The street was quite busy with people passing and crossing in front of them as they made their way round the back of the store to the car park. Jack helped Linda get in whilst they giggled some more at trying to balance everything they were carrying. Linda took a couple more bites of her taco and a sip of coffee before putting both down beside her in the storage well to finish later. She had agreed to drive the next stage of their journey, so she started the car and drove off.

As Linda tried to exit the car park a dishevelled looking man in a well-worn overcoat ambled very slowly across the exit in front of her as though deliberately causing an obstruction. She raised her hands at him with frustration, but he merely responded by giving her the middle finger. Jack shook his head whilst he continued to eat his taco.

'Charming!' she commented. Jack held her taco towards her and she gratefully took another large bite while eventually exiting the car park. 'Boy that's some tasty taco,' she said approvingly, 'shit coffee though.'

Jack laughed. 'Well, as my hero Abe Lincoln once said, "If this is coffee..."' Linda joined him in measured unison, '"Please bring me some tea; but if this is tea, please bring me some coffee".'

They both laughed and gave each other a high five. 'Hey, didn't think you'd know that one.' Jack smiled at Linda.

'Hate to burst your bubble, my friend,' she responded,

'but I read somewhere the quote's been attributed to someone else altogether.'

'Man you sure know how to hurt a guy,' he joked. 'You know, back there in the store, each time that guy in the corner looked at me I couldn't help thinking he'd seen me on a Wanted poster or something. What do you think, Butch Cassidy or the Sundance Kid?' He cocked his head to one side and adopted a gangster-ish face.

Linda laughed, as Jack was the least gangster person she could imagine. 'Good question,' she said, quickly bringing them back to reality as she continued, 'Doubt they'll have put us on TV or anything like that. Reckon they'll want to keep it all hush hush until they have to.'

They both fell silent, as Jack fed her the last of her taco and handed her the coffee so she could take another sip. As much as they were both doing everything they could to keep each other's spirits up, her comment had reminded them both of the danger they were in.

This was immediately reinforced as a black Mercedes overtook them at speed and cut them up, coming to an abrupt halt because of traffic lights. Jack and Linda's first reaction was that it had deliberately stopped to block them in and they quickly looked behind for a potential threat. But the lights changed and the Mercedes just roared off, so the scare was gone. Jack and Linda exchanged glances as if reading one another's thoughts. Linda drove on as they sat in silence for a while.

It was Jack who eventually broke the silence by venting his anger and frustration. 'Fuck this, this is crazy. All my life I've paid my taxes, done the right thing – I've never even gotten a speeding fine and now suddenly I'm some kind of master criminal!'

'Hey, you've done nothing wrong,' Linda reproached him. 'In fact, you've done something amazing. But there must be some who see Revelation as a challenge to their power and control. They won't like that. They'll want people to see the world the way they do, that way they maintain their power.'

'I hear what you're saying,' Jack countered, 'but why the hell can't they see the positives and the broader picture, the hope, the chance to discover so much more.'

Linda nodded her agreement, but continued on her theme, 'They'll see things the way it suits them. Yeah, millions – probably the vast majority of people – believe in an afterlife of some sort, but it's always been too remote. Ends up being a matter of faith. You've come along and are giving people absolute proof.'

Jack was thoughtful for a moment as he considered Linda's supportive words. 'Revelation proves there's a higher form of existence alright. And that it's accessible to everyone.'

'And there's your problem,' Linda interjected. 'You're taking power away from those who want to control that access or make us believe it's somehow wrong to seek it out.'

Jack knew she was right but shook his head in frustration. 'But you've experienced for yourself how the spirit beings come through with total love and compassion. What can possibly be wrong with that? If those in spirit are fine with it, why can't we be?!'

'Amen, Jack.'

He was warming to his theme, 'You know, this isn't even about whether there is or isn't a God. Revelation's not about that. Maybe there is, although religion itself isn't for me.'

Linda started singing John Lennon's *Imagine*. The idealistic lyrics seemed from a distant age, which in many ways they were. And Lennon himself had often been pilloried for his free-thinking anti-establishment views, even making him the subject of an F.B.I. investigation.

Linda's choice of song was rewarded with a loving smile from Jack, 'Yeah, who knows, reckon Revelation's only giving us a glimpse of the many dimensions that may be out there. No heaven, and yeah, no hell, who knows.' He paused for a moment. 'Great voice by the way.'

Linda laughed self-consciously. 'Thanks. You know before all this, my life wasn't exactly full of too much excitement. Was even thinking of getting a cat!'

Jack laughed. They had stopped at some lights and watched as a blind man with a guide dog made his way across the road. There was something Jack had always wanted to ask Linda and he judged this to be a good moment. 'So how come you never married? I mean you're beautiful, intelligent, got a great job...'

She replied teasingly and blushing slightly, 'I'm flattered, sir! But 'got a great job' was probably the thing that got in the way. Oh there have been the odd flings...'

'Yeah,' Jack interrupted, 'what happened to that naval guy? Thought you two were going to get hitched and sail round the world in a dhow or somesuch?'

She laughed, 'Not sure his other 'wives' would have approved! But hey, you can talk – what about that traffic cop you started seeing? Wanted to take you back to her place and try her handcuffs on you?'

They both laughed together. 'Oh yeah, her.' Jack was amused by the reminder. 'Lucky escape in more ways than one.'

As they drove on, it was clear that Jack was slightly distracted and was looking at all the parked cars with unusual interest. He had clearly spotted something and just as they passed an alley he suddenly said to Linda, 'Pull in here, I need to make that call and then we need to do something else which I'll explain after that.'

She trusted Jack completely, so didn't question him, but drove the car into the alley and switched off the ignition.

****

Back in the special operations room, several operators were focusing on individual screens whilst one or two others were taking note of what was being displayed and liaising with others.

The ops room team leader was standing behind one seated operator and both were looking at the giant screen, where they had frozen an image and were zooming in and out of particular sections.

'Play that back again,' the team leader said. She had gained a reputation as a highly skilled tech ops tracker and combined her powers of observation with a clinical intelligence. Some said she could be ruthless and this was certainly not the first time she had been on an operation to track various subjects knowing perfectly well what would happen to them once found.

The drone operator she had been addressing replayed the footage they had both just been watching. It was of the general store where Jack and Linda had bought the tacos and burner phone. 'It's not as clear as we would like, as it's part hidden by a wall, but take a look.,' he said.

They both studied the footage carefully of the images

148

captured by the drone as it had flown over the store, taking in much of the car park at the rear.

'Could well be the one,' the team leader said, 'how long before we can get another drone up and back into that general area?'

'Already working on it,' came the reply, 'should have two scanning a few square miles of that whole area in the next few minutes. With traffic at this time of day, they shouldn't have got too far.'

At that moment Bob Howard entered. It was one of his regular check-ins, but he also enjoyed seeing the way his presence put his team on even higher alert. They knew what he could be like when displeased. But the team leader greeted him with what appeared to be encouraging news as they both looked up at the enlarged image frozen on the screen.

'We reckon there's a pretty good chance this is their car – and if it is, we've got them.'

Bob allowed himself the faintest of smiles. He nodded, 'Good work. Give the ground units the co-ordinates and call them in.'

'Yes sir,' she replied, 'this could be it.'

Chapter 28

They had parked the car halfway down a dead-end alley in a rather run-down area on the outskirts of the city. The alley only had a couple of back doors to restaurants at the very end, with a couple of grime-covered large trash containers against the end wall. One of the containers was already overflowing, scattering what looked like chicken bones and other trash on the filthy concrete. A large rat was impervious to the arrival of the car and kept on gnawing at something on the ground.

Jack and Linda had ignored the sign at the end of the alley stating that access was for deliveries only. After all, they didn't intend to be there for long. Jack reached behind his seat for the carrier bag from the general store and rummaged in it for the burner phone package. He eagerly tore at the packaging to unwrap it. He gave the phone a quick inspection and noted to himself that they usually came with enough juice to make a few calls. He would hopefully only need to make two.

'So who are you calling?' Linda asked.

'An old colleague who right now has suddenly become my very best friend!' he replied. 'He now works at a military academy – though God knows what the cadets will ever learn from him. Should be on his lunch hour around now and believe me, he won't miss that.'

Linda smiled as Jack turned on the phone. As the

display lit up, his face conveyed his delight at finding that it was indeed about half charged. He dialled one of the standard numbers he knew for directory assistance. His call was answered immediately.

Jack spoke quickly, 'Yeah, hi, can you give me the number for the Richmond Military Academy in Virginia?'

He listened as he was given a number. In his line of work, remembering figures and formulas came naturally to Jack, so he didn't feel the need to write the number down as he knew he would remember it. He thanked the operator, ended the call and began to dial the number he'd been given.

At that moment a Chinese kitchen worker wearing grubby overalls and a well-stained apron, emerged from a back door of one of the restaurants to deposit some waste in the large container that still had some space in it. He did so in a very casual manner, so that a few bits slopped onto the ground. He didn't bother to pick them up, opting to just kick them under the container between its wheels where no doubt more hungry rats were lying in wait.

As the worker turned to go back into the restaurant he looked at Jack and Linda and gestured disapprovingly that they shouldn't be parked there. Linda acknowledged by mouthing 'emergency call' and pointing at Jack on the phone. The worker was unimpressed, shrugged as if still displeased, but thankfully went back inside. It was unlikely he would do any more about it, but she still allowed herself a few nervous glances all around.

Meanwhile, Jack had already dialled his number which was answered with the military precision he would expect on the second ring. He spoke clearly, 'Yeah, can you put me through to Jason Thomas please?'

The switchboard operator had come back on the phone

to confirm she would be able to connect Jack shortly. He knew they would have been checking Jason's classification to see if any further checks were necessary before putting Jack through. But Jason was still listed as Requisitions and would have taken many calls every day from military suppliers, so it would be fine to put Jack through without any further delay. Jack knew only too well that the call would probably be recorded. But by the time anyone got onto this particular trail, it probably wouldn't matter – one way or another.

When the desk phone rang in his cubbyhole of an office at the end of a narrow corridor, Jason was indeed on his lunch break. A feast of fast-food snacks and sodas were untidily arrayed in front of him. He often preferred to eat at his desk as the main canteen was a five hundred yard walk across campus. So lunch was often grabbed from the much nearer small café or the multiple vending machines located in every building.

His desk was strewn with papers and there were piles of ring-bound files and documents stacked on the dull grey metallic filing cabinets. A wall-mounted rack of keys was testament to Jason also being custodian of the storerooms, although notably not those housing weaponry of any sort. The giant pinboard on the wall to the left of his desk was covered in notes, bills and sheets of paper, many attached with the same pin. To anyone else, it would have been a nightmare to find anything, but when asked for something that came under his Requisitions remit, Jason could always be relied upon to put his hands immediately on whatever was needed with surprising efficiency.

He answered his desk phone, badly mimicking a voicemail message: 'This is Jason Thomas who's out having

152

a snackalicious lunch. Please leave a…'

Jack wasn't fooled for a moment and cut in before he could get any further, 'Hey Jason, you fat bastard, it's Jack Taylor. How's life in Dixieland?'

Jason spoke with his mouth full, but the banter between the two of them was very warm and well meant. 'Jack, Jack! Great to hear from you, arsehole! What the hell are you calling me for? You spooking the Soviets these days?'

Jack was grinning to himself. 'They haven't been Soviets since 1991, you moron. They're Russians now.'

'But you're still a bigtime top secret laboratorian, yeah?'

'More so than ever, my friend,' Jack replied, 'and that's why I'm calling you. Listen, I need to be quick. I've been given personal authority to give you official top security clearance as I need you to get me some vital items urgently needed for an ultra-secret project.'

Jason was immediately excited at the thought that anyone would consider him for some secret mission as he had always been jealous of Jack and Marty's CIA connections and had secretly harboured fantasies of being some kind of James Bond character himself. He didn't think for a moment to question what Jack was telling him. He put down the huge pastry he was chomping through, wiped his sticky fingers carelessly on his uniform and leaned forward over his desk with great eagerness.

Jack played up to his interest, humouring him without being unkind, as Jason breathlessly announced, 'Count me in, partner. I was born for this. So who we going after?'

'Well, it's not quite like that,' Jack replied, 'but I need someone I can trust. No-one – and I mean no-one – can know. But don't worry, when this is done I'll make sure you get full credit for playing a key part in it. All on the quiet you understand.'

Jason was becoming even more animated, 'Sure, oh yeah, one of those special secret medals only certain people get to wear on Veterans Day, right? Boy, wait 'til I tell my mom. Sorry, sorry, didn't mean that.'

'Oh absolutely. I'll get Bob Howard to pin it on you himself.'

By now Jason was beaming with pride and anticipation. *See pa, who was it who said I'd amount to nothing,* he thought to himself, 'Go for it, buddy, I'm in and my lips are sealed, even if they do send a beautiful busty blonde to torture it out of me.'

'You're one sick dude, Jason,' Jack replied whilst smiling at Linda who could hear the conversation and was stifling her laughter. Jack went on, 'Look there's a few items I urgently need that you're bound to have at the Academy – and I also need to tell you what I want you to do once you've got them…'

Chapter 29

Two blacked-out Jeeps screeched to a halt at the top of the alley where Linda's car was parked, blocking the entrance to anyone else. The team leader turned to his senior team member. 'That's them, it's their car alright. Let's do it.'

The eight attack team members all got out of their Jeeps, while two others stationed themselves at the alley entrance to deter any passers-by. But by now it was mid-afternoon in the lull of the day, so there were few pedestrians about. All attack team members were armed with silenced M16 automatic rifles. One carried a flame-thrower.

The whole scene was being beamed back live from a drone above and watched intensely on the big screen back in the control room. Bob Howard had joined them for what he anticipated would be the end game and was already practising in his head the triumphal coded call he would make to Frank Caspari. Everyone in the control room listened dispassionately on their earphones to the attack team's interchanges.

As the team stealthily began to approach the car from the rear and were still some 20 yards from it, a man's head clearly became visible inside the car as he turned in horror to see the team advancing towards him.

'Sir, there's movement,' one of the team called out.

'Go, go, go!' the team leader barked.

In a well-rehearsed and clinically efficient manner the team sprayed short bursts of gunfire into the car. Even with controlled shooting, at least 100 rounds slammed through the car's metalwork and upholstery, causing complete destruction of anyone and anything inside. They had been told to make sure the car was unidentifiable after their attack, so the team member with the flame-thrower gave no more than a ten second blast of his somewhat antiquated yet deadly efficient flame-thrower, whilst the team kept a safe distance. The whole car burst into flames and the petrol tank exploded which made the car buck and jump.

In an act of great irony, a couple of team members then quickly moved in with fire extinguishers to quench the flames, leaving only some blackened blast damage to the wall nearest to where the car had been parked. A door at the end of the alley opened a fraction and a frightened Chinese man's face peered round it. 'Get the fuck back inside,' the team leader bellowed at him. The man needed no further encouragement.

The team leader and a couple of his aides moved in closer to inspect the damage, noting that the licence plates were now destroyed and completely unreadable. The charred body of a young man, probably no more than eighteen or nineteen years old, was slumped in the front seat with the two bare wires still in his hands where he had been trying to hotwire the car. Although his clothes had mostly been burned off and his body was charred, multiple tattoos were still visible on his forearms.

Meanwhile, just as a final check, another member of the attack team had prised open what remained of the melted trunk of the car; it was empty.

The team leader walked over to a quieter spot and

called Bob on his radio phone, as he knew those in the control room wouldn't have been able to see everything in quite such close detail. 'TPA operation completed,' he called in.

'Thank God,' exclaimed Bob. 'Good work. Need I.D. confirmation on those bodies.'

'Negative to bodies,' came the reply which chilled Bob to the bone. 'Just a kid in his late teens. Looks like he was trying to hotwire the car. Nothing in the trunk either.'

'What! You pissing with me?! You telling me he was on his own?'

'Affirmative,' was all the team leader dared say, noting the anger in Bob's voice.

'Fuck, fuck, fuck, fuck, fuck!' Bob was incandescent and now pacing furiously around the control room whilst he talked, 'right, get it all cleaned up real good and then get the hell out of there! I'll get additional covert support into the area if we're now into a foot search.'

'Roger that,' the team leader replied, but Bob had already switched off and slammed down his radio phone, cracking its casing in the process.

Because Bob didn't know that Jack and Linda had a back-up, he thought they'd be trying to get away on foot and blend into their surroundings rather than have need of a car. But he had to cover all options, which would mean additional teams being called in. Jack and Linda were beginning to get on his nerves.

Chapter 30

Bob's undercover foot team would be wasting their time, because the youth who had died so brutally in Linda's car wasn't the only person to have been hotwiring a car late into that afternoon.

Before turning into the alley, Jack had been scanning the streets nearby for a suitable vehicle that he was confident he could hotwire. He knew that he and Linda needed to change cars fast and he had spotted an old Chevrolet Spark which would also have enough room in the trunk for Revelation.

They had attracted the occasional strange glance from passers-by as the two of them had carried Revelation the hundred yards from the alley to the top of a quiet side street where Jack had spotted the Spark. After a good look around and some surprisingly quick work by Jack with his pocket penknife, it was less than a minute before Linda was slamming down the trunk with Revelation safely stowed inside, while Jack dropped his burner phone down a drain.

Having got into the car and successfully hotwired it, Jack breathed a sigh of relief to see the fuel tank gauge rise to about the halfway mark. They both carefully looked around and exchanged quick glances; they were pretty sure they hadn't been spotted. After all, they must have looked like the least incongruous car thieves in the world.

As Jack steered the car around the block and back onto the main road, it was fortunate that they had also beaten their aerial spotters for now. That's because they had already been on their way for twelve minutes before a drone flown by operators back in the technical ops control room had filmed Linda's car in the alley, it had been correctly identified and the attack team had been given the location.

Linda smiled at Jack as she gently teased him, 'Well Jack Taylor, no prizes for guessing that you're CIA trained. Can't help but say I'm mighty impressed.'

Jack smiled back, enjoying the compliment, albeit for a criminal offence. 'Yeah, well, Marty and I did get a fair bit of collateral training seeing as we were working in a combat theatre. The rest you pick up from guys – you know, people who come from the wrong side of the tracks shall we say. They know the easiest cars to hotwire and tend to like to outboast each other about it!'

'I can imagine. The military's probably the only way some of them can escape poverty and a no hope future.'

'Ain't that the truth.'

Unseen by anyone below, a small drone flew over them, but the images attracted no attention back in the ops room. At this stage they didn't have a clue that their targets were back on the road again.

Linda had adopted a very business-like tone, but was only confirming what Jack knew was their only option now. 'Right Jack, time to go public. We're now committed to my plan to get to my media contact Ed Bishop in Stone Ridge. So we need to get to his place tonight.'

After a pause, she added, as if reading Jack's mind, 'You were still right to go to Frank first and try to take it to the top. Even I couldn't have guessed how he and presumably

159

his inner cabal of rats reacted. Doubt he took it to the President, as I hear she's quite receptive to spirituality in general.'

Jack nodded his agreement, but didn't think he needed to add any more. They drove on mostly in silence, although he reminded Linda that she would need to guide him once they got closer to the smart residential area of Stone Ridge where Ed lived.

They had stopped at some traffic lights and Linda looked out of the window at all the different people on the sidewalks going about their business. She watched an elderly man, poorly dressed in a shabby overcoat and worn-out shoes, shuffling along half bent-over and carrying a plastic carrier bag with clearly very little in it.

'Life can be damned tough at times,' she observed out loud. Jack looked across quizzically at her and noticed the old man on the sidewalk as she continued, 'Does it ever worry you that Revelation could encourage a lot of people to do what Marty did?'

He didn't answer immediately and when he did he was measured and thoughtful. 'Yeah, yeah it does.' He paused. 'Gotta be honest, I've struggled a bit with it. For those who can't find any light in their lives, the assurance of something beyond this existence could be tempting, even though we don't yet know everything that might involve. But surely the flip side is that it's incredibly life-affirming, purposeful…'

'Oh don't worry,' Linda cut in reassuringly, 'I'm with you all the way.'

Jack was still very thoughtful. 'Haven't told you this before, but that day before I came to see you in the lecture hall, I worked Revelation. Was desperate for Marty to show himself. Too soon I guess. But my dad was with me.'

'That's beautiful.' Linda smiled.

'Yeah, well, he sure wasn't a very beautiful person when he was alive. So I was surprised when he came through, but he seemed calmer, more loving, more content. He told me that each and every one of us is here for a reason. That we're all connected. So the way I see it is that the certainty of life after death gives all our lives a wider perspective. Hell, I'm no philosopher, but yeah, live as good a life as you can, try to fulfil your potential whatever that might be, but in the process look after the people, the animals, the planet. Then return to spirit knowing that whatever you did, you did your best.'

He glanced across at Linda for reassurance. She just leaned across and gave him a quick but very loving kiss.

Encouraged, Jack continued, 'Guess what I'm saying is that we, life, everything is part of something so much bigger. And I don't mean in any religious sort of way. But for me at least, that kind of unseen moral code in all of us comes into sharper focus. Hey, I'm gonna sound like Marty's mom and dad now, but yeah, peace, love and happiness, man!'

'Love it!' Linda smiled approvingly.

Jack was well into his stride by now. 'I reckon we've only just scraped the surface of what really may be out there with Revelation. Most religious and political leaders have failed us so badly. They take a position of control not freedom.'

'Oh amen to that!' Linda enthusiastically agreed. 'Jack the revolutionary, who'd have known!' She playfully slapped his arm.

Jack laughed, enjoying the interplay. 'No, you know what I mean. All this has been one hell of an eye-opener for me too, believe me. After Marty and I made the initial breakthrough, I started to read up on it all. Do you know that thousands of people who've had so-called near-death experiences have described it like stepping into another room?'

'Parallel dimensions?'

'I guess so – why not, but I think Revelation has only just given us a glimpse into potentially vast areas that need to be explored. Right now, I can't possibly pretend to have all the answers.'

'Unlike those who are blinkered and are frightened by change. Like the head-in-the-sand robots who are after us now,' Linda added.

'True,' Jack agreed, 'all I know from Revelation is that life after death is a nailed-on reality. And it's probably just the start of discovering what's really out there. Revelation is the beginning, but if we do succeed in getting it into the public domain, who knows who will pick up the challenge and take things even further.'

They both fell silent for a while, allowing themselves to think about the enormity of where Revelation might be taking them.

Linda looked adoringly at Jack, 'I love you, Jack Taylor,' she said.

'And I love you too, Linda,' he replied.

Chapter 31

Once more, Frank Caspari's office in the White House was the scene of a very heated exchange. Frank, Bob, Sam and the Reverend had all been hastily assembled and were having to do their level best to keep their voices under control.

But Frank was incandescent with rage, 'Oh, this just gets better and better! For Christ's sake, Bob, your guys just put on a full scale firework display down some goddam alley and fried some low-life car thief! And now you're telling me you've lost them?!'

Bob tried to remain calm, although inwardly he too was seething, 'It's temporary Frank, we're following up on all kinds of leads. We will find them. We only just missed them in that alley, probably by just a few minutes.'

Uncharacteristically, Sam shifted uncomfortably in his seat as he attempted to strike a conciliatory and encouraging tone. 'Surely they'll come up on surveillance cameras, Motel records or something somewhere. They can't just disappear. How many men you got on this, Bob?'

'That's not the point,' Bob objected to the inference, even if unintended, that he wasn't doing his job properly, 'we still need to keep this under strict control. Don't worry, I've got my very best people on it. We can't let this widen more than we have to.'

Frank had calmed down a little and now spoke in a much more controlled but emphatic tone, 'Think you're all missing something here. If I was in their shoes, I'd figure the best hope of self-preservation would be to go public. Get it into the media somehow or get to someone with influence and start something off that creates its own momentum and before we know it we'll all be in deep shit – worse!'

The others let the impact of Frank's words sink in before the Reverend attempted a note of reassurance, 'But with Revelation destroyed, who will believe them about spirit existence on just say so and no real proof?'

'Well forgive me Reverend,' Frank quickly countered impatiently, 'but isn't that what your entire faith is built upon!'

'I object to that very strongly,' the Reverend replied indignantly. But before he and Frank could take up the argument any further, Sam cut in, 'Look, Frank's right. I would be looking to tell people – newspapers, TV…'

Bob interrupted, 'I've got all my media moles on highest alert. Everywhere's on lockdown. We all just need to stay calm. We will find them. We can deal with any collateral later.'

But Frank wasn't convinced. 'Oh we can, can we? Well you'd better be right, Bob, because right now I'm looking at a whole fucking can of worms.'

Bob tried again to reassure him. 'Frank, as I say, my very best men are on it. These two have got lucky so far, but that won't last and we will find and deal with them.'

'This sure ain't doing my heart any favours,' Sam muttered.

Frank could see there was no point in extending the meeting any further. 'OK, we're adjourned until further news. Shit!'

As the others left his office, Frank gathered up some papers off his desk and made his way into the corridor which, as was usual, was bustling with officials all rushing about on their own agendas. Daniella, the White House Press Secretary, spotted Frank and hurried to catch up with him, handing him a couple of sheets of paper tucked into a buff coloured, open-sided wallet file. 'Hey Frank, here's what I'm aiming to hand out during the press meeting later about the new housing initiative. Can you check it out and get back to me within the hour if you've any comments.'

'Sure, Daniella, happy to.' He tried to raise a smile. Daniella flashed him a much broader smile as she walked off, without either of them having stopped walking during their exchange. This was pretty standard for many of their hurried meetings.

As Frank rounded a corner, he saw the President, Angela Freeman, walking towards him, accompanied by her personal assistant and closest aide Maria. The President was a very striking African American lady who was now in her early sixties. Her hair cascaded in well-cut layers to just above her shoulders and, at just over five foot six and wearing heels, she had a certain stature. She accentuated this by power dressing with excellent taste, mostly in well-tailored trouser suits. She liked to wear distinctive costume jewellery which hinted at her rebellious side, with some splashes of vibrant colour in her other accessories. She was very dignified and had a real presence about her – one of those people that immediately gets noticed in a room. It wasn't long after she had entered politics that she began to make a name for herself.

Maria was of Latin origin and had long dark hair which

she often swept back and tied with a hair band so that it swished behind her as she walked along. She was definitely one of the head-turners in the White House. A very smart, highly educated person with two college degrees, she spoke six different languages and enjoyed the full confidence of the President.

'Ah Frank,' the President greeted him. Although Frank had been her own appointment as White House Chief of Staff, she was wary of him and hadn't entirely turned a deaf ear to the way some of his enemies spoke about his Machiavellian qualities. 'You got a minute?' the question was of course rhetorical. She looked behind them briefly to ensure that, apart from Maria, no-one else was in earshot. 'Thing is, Frank, I'm actually getting a little anxious about progress on Scorpion. You know how much is at stake here. Nothing must deviate us from making it a total success.'

Frank adopted his most positive, reassuring tone. 'Absolutely. Don't worry, Madam President, I've got everyone one hundred per cent focused.'

'Excellent,' she replied, 'good to hear, Frank, knew I could count on you.' She paused. 'Got any exciting plans for the weekend?'

Frank wasn't good at small talk, 'Um, well one or two maybe, yes, nothing fancy, you?'

'Yeah, got another golf lesson would you believe. My husband's really got me into it – well, not as much as him obviously. I'd be a golf widow if he had his way!'

They both laughed in that awkward way people often do when there's no deep warmth between them. 'Well good luck with that,' Frank offered as the two walked on their different ways.

If she had looked back, the President would have seen

Frank pull his personal cellphone out of his pocket to make a very private, coded call.

*****

Back at Linda's college, a phone call had previously been taken by her Faculty Office purporting to be from her brother to say Linda had fallen ill and would be staying with his family for a few days whilst she recuperated.

The caller had correctly banked on the fact that the juniors in the Faculty Office who took the calls wouldn't know Linda well enough to know that she didn't have a brother and they certainly wouldn't have the suspicion or application to check their records for details of her next of kin. So the explanation was accepted and other lecturers and students were duly informed by a standard-worded email. Most of the other academics were far too wrapped up in their own worlds to give it any thought, even the few who might have remembered that Linda had no siblings.

As is often the case, so much can be believed simply by imparting information with enough confidence and not a little bluffing. And the caller was a master at it.

Meanwhile, in one of the student halls of residence, one of Linda's students, Jackson, was making his way down one of the corridors past the students' rooms. The muffled sounds of rock music from one room failed to cover the sound of audible giggling and moaning coming from the next room Jackson passed. He chuckled knowingly to himself.

Jackson was wearing his trademark multicoloured Tibetan style patchwork top loosely over frayed jeans and open-toe sandals. For a change, his hair was neatly braided in dreadlocks and pulled back off his face which invariably

167

was creased into a smile. But his casual appearance and laissez-faire manner hid the sharpest of minds, something that Linda had spotted from their first tutorial together.

Jackson reached another student's door in a quieter area of the corridor and gently knocked.

'Yeah, enter if you dare,' the voice came from within. Jackson entered to see his good friend Nettye rocking gently on the back legs of her chair whilst working on her laptop. The room was typically small as in most modern student halls, but perfectly adequate in terms of the mostly pine furniture, with a single wooden frame bed against one wall, a small wardrobe, chest of drawers, desk and two chairs. There was a large pinboard covered in notes, stickers and flyers and a wipeable whiteboard where Nettye had written her schedule and 'to do' list. The room benefited from good light from a large window beside Nettye's desk.

Originally from New York, Nettye still had the slightly drawn out, rounded vowels in her speech manner which gave her away. She was the same age as Jackson and wore a college sweatshirt with jeans and trainers and could have competed with Jackson for the title of sweetest smile of their class. And it was those smiles that they both flashed warmly at each other now.

Jackson and Nettye had become good friends, although it had never progressed beyond that and never would – they were comfortable with that despite neither currently being in a relationship.

'Hey Nettye,' Jackson greeted her in his happy sing-song voice, 'just wondered how you're doing with that Miss Wilson essay. Chosen your subject yet?'

'Yeah, I'm kind of going with the whole wormholes thing and being able to travel across the universe in seconds.

I'm kinda giving the science on how it could be done and also what it could mean for the future of humankind,' Nettye replied casually, as if it was nothing special.

'Sort of already know a lot about wormholes don't we?' Jackson asked, but not in a challenging way.

'Well yeah,' Nettye countered, 'but I'm adding a lot of my own stuff to it. But what exactly…well, you'll just have to wait and see,' she teased.

'Oh I get it, playing your cards close to your chest. OK, genius, I get it.'

She laughed and asked, 'Coffee?'

Jackson shook his head as he sat himself down on the other chair in the room. 'Nah, I'm good thanks.'

Nettye nodded at the notepad he was holding on his lap. 'So what about you, what are you going with?'

Jackson shuffled a bit self-consciously in his chair, 'OK, so I know everyone's just going to laugh at me…'

'So what's new!' she interjected, affectionately teasing him.

'Yeah, yeah,' Jackson continued, 'well, you know all those grainy, inevitably out-of-focus photos where people think they may have caught an image of a ghost or something in the background of their photo? So, I'm saying what if there really could be a special camera or whatever that actually does capture images of ghosts, if they're real.'

'And there's your problem, *if they're real,*' Nettye said sympathetically.

'Yeah, I know,' Jackson continued, 'but Miss Wilson did tell us to push the boundaries. So OK, the truth is I'm a little stuck and still looking for some inspiration.'

'Hah, so you thought you'd come pick my brains. No, look, go for it! I'm not sure how you're going to build your case, as I can't quite reckon how any camera can see something another can't, but hey, why not.'

Jackson nodded before offering, 'Well maybe it isn't a camera. I dunno, some other device, although right now I'm not sure where to take this. I know Miss Wilson said to keep it as real as possible, substantiate it and not stray into science fiction. But I haven't really thought it all through yet. But it's an idea yeah?' He looked to Nettye for approval.

'Sure, yeah,' she said, trying to sound encouraging. 'I'm just not sure off the top of my head how you're going to bring it back from the realms of fantasy and make it plausible. I mean, yeah, in theory why not, I like the idea, just not sure if it's any more than an idea. Don't you think if it was possible to see so-called ghosts somehow, someone would've invented a camera or something like that already? But at the moment, as far as I'm aware, there's no science anywhere that's even remotely suggesting it's a possibility. But hey, who knows, as I say, go for it!'

'Hmmm, maybe you're right. Have to think about it. Either that or it's back to the drawing board.'

They both smiled at each other before Jackson continued but on a different tack, 'Bit of an enigma isn't she? Miss Wilson. I mean you can see all the other lecturers fancy her like mad, but she seems to kinda hold herself aloof. I don't mean in any superior way and she's really friendly to everyone and all that, just that she manages to keep a distance at the same time. Reckon she must lead a pretty boring life. Right now she's probably tucked up in bed reading The Scientific American.'

Nettye enjoyed the joke. 'Yeah, doubt she gets out much or has any real excitement. I mean, she's never late for lectures or comes in with a hangover or anything like that, unlike one or two other lecturers we could mention!'

They both smiled knowingly at each other, as Jackson stood up. 'Well, gotta go. Catch you later.'

'Yeah, probably see you in the dining hall,' Nettye replied, 'and good luck – you can always hold a séance!'

'Yeah yeah, thanks a bunch,' Jackson chuckled, 'laugh all you like. Boy, why am I so dumb!'

*****

Jack and Linda had dozed as best they could for a few hours in an unlit side street and had now parked just up the road from Ed Bishop's bungalow. It was an impressive-looking neighbourhood, with manicured lawns, tightly trimmed hedges and the kind of immaculate flower beds that gave evidence to the fact that many of the houses were home to retired people with time on their hands. Ed's house was set amidst a cluster of bungalows, although each with large garden areas that no doubt attracted the kind of people who had previously been used to larger houses before selling up to settle into their retirement.

The houses were impeccably kept too, with walls that clearly never went more than three or four years without a fresh coat of paint and woodwork that was lovingly varnished with even greater regularity.

Jack and Linda had quickly eaten a couple of snack bars from the bag Linda had packed back in her kitchen and were taking a swig from their water bottles while keeping their eyes on the streets and sidewalks. By now it was dark and well into the evening, so there were hardly any pedestrians about and this was not the sort of neighbourhood to see too many casual passers-by. The odd cars that passed were mostly family saloons and didn't give the two of them any undue cause for alarm.

'So remind me about this Professor Ed Bishop,' Jack asked Linda, 'lifelong friend of the President eh? Impressive.'

'Oh he's impressive all right,' she replied, 'but you wouldn't know all that when you get to meet him; he's a great bear of a huggy guy, great fun, you'll love him.'

Jack tried to hide his jealousy as Linda spoke so warmly about her friend. As if reading his thoughts, she continued in a more matter-of-fact tone, 'He was a science correspondent for more than thirty years. Took some of my articles and became something of a mentor to me. He was the Science Editor of the Washington Post until he retired last year. Still has great contacts, which is why I immediately thought of him as the most obvious plan B when going to Frank blew up in our face.'

'Unfortunate turn of phrase!' Jack replied wryly.

Linda held up one hand like a sports person accepting their error. 'Yeah, well, Ed has lots of top level media contacts too. And I would trust him with my life.'

'Well let's hope it doesn't come to that!' Jack replied. He suddenly became very thoughtful, 'You know, I wasn't going to tell you this as it sounds kinda weird, but remember when we caught forty winks last night? I had a very vivid dream and it's not really something that happens with me that much – or at least not that I ever recall dreaming. Only the strange thing was it didn't seem like a dream, it felt more real somehow.'

Linda was intrigued. 'Go on.'

'Well, Marty appeared to me. And it was like he was there with me, only I was definitely asleep. I know people have said spirits have appeared to them and inspired them with things during their dreams, but I always discounted it. But haven't musicians, writers and others often said they've been given ideas in dreams? I dunno.'

'Yeah, I've also read or heard about stuff like that. Guess, like you, as a sceptical scientist I never gave it too much thought and just thought typical arty types. Did Marty speak to you?'

'No, well not that I recall, but he just looked so happy, so carefree. He just kept smiling at me and nodding his head. What could that mean?'

'Search me,' Linda said, genuinely perplexed but also intrigued, 'but sounds wonderful. Parking my scepticism for a moment – and now knowing what Revelation proves – I'm willing to believe that was actually Marty and seems to me he was encouraging you and giving you a message that everything's going to be OK.'

Jack was pensive for a moment. 'Oh, I don't know. What if it was just a dream and I only saw him because he's so much in my thoughts'

'Who knows,' Linda replied, 'but what I do know is that you can prove the truth of life after death with Revelation. That's gonna put dreams in the shade don't you think! But don't worry, Jack, your next invention can be a device that records dreams when we're asleep and plays them back to us like a movie when we wake up!'

Jack laughed, enjoying the tease. 'Think some of my madness is rubbing off on you Linda!'

She smiled at him, 'Come on, time to meet a very good friend. It's time to go public and let's face it, you don't have a choice. Just hope Ed has kept up his friendship with the President, otherwise it's the media route with all the risks that carries.' Jack nodded, although he wished the last part of what she had said could have been more reassuring.

They both glanced anxiously up and down the street, while Linda quickly checked her appearance in the sun visor mirror. Content that she looked presentable, they both got out of the car, trying to look as casual as possible, took one last look around and then started to walk towards Ed Bishop's house.

****

One of Bob Howard's covert attack teams were on highest alert in their Jeep as their highly trained driver wove in and out of traffic at speed to try and catch up with a car.

Their control centre had been in overdrive analysing countless images and footage from drones in the aftermath of the destruction of Linda's car in the alley. Believing that Jack and Linda may well have stolen a car, albeit from the testament of a drunk who had told a member of one of the covert foot teams that he had seen them do it with his own eyes, they had identified four different cars that had been stolen in the genera area. Furthermore that all the cars had been stolen within an hour of the attack operation in the alley – a statement in itself on the high level of crime in some of the city's poorer neighbourhoods.

All operatives were now fully focused on a process of elimination of which car it might be, if indeed the drunk had seen something. The Jeep was now in hot pursuit of a car that might match one of the stolen vehicles.

The driver of the Jeep had been nicknamed Crazy Horse by the other team members after the fearless Native American chief. And he was certainly earning his moniker that evening as he accelerated through the traffic, nearly crashing into a car coming in the opposite direction. Later he would tell colleagues it wasn't even close, but at the time even the battle-hardened team members in the back of the Jeep exchanged nervous glances as they tightly clutched the weapons on their laps.

By now, the Jeep had caught up with the targeted car and nose-tailed it for a couple of hundred yards. It was long enough for the team leader to realise that the rather portly, elderly driver of the car didn't remotely resemble the photos he had been shown of Jack, so this was another vehicle that could be taken off the suspected stolen list.

The team leader noted the licence plate in any event and called in to the control centre. 'Negative. Not them. Awaiting your fixes on other vehicles of interest. Ready to rock n' roll. Out.'

Chapter 34

Earlier that same day, as the afternoon light cast giant spindly shadows from the trees across the grassy banks of the cemetery, a solitary figure walked confidently amongst the neat rows of gravestones. There are those who could never be alone in a cemetery, but Martha was not amongst them. Comfortable in her own acceptance that there must be more to life than the crazy meaningless everyday existence that seemed to exemplify most people's lives, she had totally come to accept the reality of life after death long before Jack told her that he and Marty had proved it scientifically beyond any doubt. Mark you, she was sure going to tie Jack down to giving her a demo of his machine once all this nonsense was over.

Martha had amused herself on the longish drive from her bungalow to the cemetery by reminiscing about her exuberant boy Marty. At one point, stuck at traffic lights, she wondered what pedestrians must think of her as she laughed out loud with tears rolling down her cheeks as she recalled his wedding day.

The wedding reception had been at a rather grand country house and as the champagne flowed, Jenny had found a rope swing tied to an old oak tree in the grounds. As the hired video cameraman kept filming, the worn and frayed ropes had broken and Jenny had tumbled to the ground.

Although summer, the well-worn ground underneath the swing had soon dirtied her beautiful ivory wedding dress. But instead of rescuing her, Marty had simply gone to ground himself on top of her in his full morning suit and the two of them had ended up rolling around in fits of squeals and giggles like two naughty children. Martha reminded herself to watch the video again in the morning.

She could never understand this obsession with wearing black to funerals or being overly solemn in graveyards. Of course she had grieved beyond human endurance, first for her beloved husband Burt and now for her dear son Marty. But especially after the pain she had seen Burt suffer with his cancer, Martha saw death as a blessed release and the start of a new adventure.

A man in dirty khaki overalls who was clearly one of the experienced team of gardeners and maintenance personnel charged with looking after the cemetery, was pushing a wheelbarrow which only seemed to have a fork, a spade and a watering can in it. He looked intently at Martha and smiled to himself at the way she was so colourfully and expressively dressed. His attention was particularly drawn to the long, psychedelic-coloured scarf which, due to the moderate breeze that afternoon, was trailing behind her like some great multicoloured sail propelling her forward to some secret destination.

Martha was carrying a large bunch of flowers wrapped in cellophane as she approached Marty's grave. The covering of earth was still bare and the gravestone she had ordered was yet to be laid. Jenny's grave was right next to Marty's and he had been granted permission to have her buried there due to his own status – one thing at least he could thank Frank for. And maybe an unrecognised premonition that he would soon have reason to follow her.

Martha knelt by the grave and carefully unwrapped the cellophane to release the flowers. She removed some dead flowers from the water urns on Jenny's grave and placed them beside her.

She had brought scissors and a bottle of water with her and started to cut the flower stems and place them in both graves' water urns, also pouring in some water. As she did so, she began quietly singing the song *Let the sunshine in* as she went about her task.

Once she had distributed the flowers between the two graves to her satisfaction, she put the scissors down on her right hand side and sat back on her haunches in quiet reflection. She closed her eyes and fell silent for a while, lost in memories and just allowing the gentle breeze to caress her face. She said a quiet prayer, but it wasn't the sort of prayer heard in any church, more an invocation to the universe.

She slowly opened her eyes, briefly squinting at the sudden light as she looked around, taking in the beautiful serenity and tranquillity of the setting. She then calmly gathered up the cellophane, dead flowers, water bottle and cut flower stems and looked down to her right to pick up the scissors, only they were not there anymore. She then noticed that somehow they had moved to be on her left hand side.

She picked them up, smiled knowingly and nodded. As she stood up and took one last loving look at the graves, she began to move away, resuming her singing.

Chapter 35

At the same time as Martha had been visiting the cemetery, a tense meeting had been taking place in the Oval Office, chaired by the President.

As was the custom, six of the attendees, who included Frank, Sam and Bob, were seated on the two long, low-backed sofas ranged opposite each other and separated by an ornate, colourful floor rug that had been a gift from the President of the United Arab Emirates.

The President and her aide Maria sat at the head of the sofas in two matching Queen Anne armchairs. Three other attendees were seated on carved mahogany chairs that usually stood against the walls, but which had been pulled up closer to the inner sanctum that had assembled. The doors to the Oval Office were all closed with security personnel posted outside with strict orders not to let anyone so much as approach until they had been reopened.

'We're agreed then,' the President announced in her usual definitive manner to signal the meeting was done, 'we launch Scorpion two weeks today.' Everyone in the room nodded, with some grunting their agreement. 'And I hope I don't have to stress again the importance of this and the need for total silence until it breaks.'

Once again, murmurs of agreement came from around

the room. It was Frank who officially gave everyone leave to depart and as everyone got up and started to leave the room, Frank was sure to be the last, as if to reinforce his position.

The President approached him. 'You OK, Frank? Only you seem a little distracted of late.'

That's the understatement of the year, Frank thought to himself. 'Sure, absolutely, Madam President, just a lot going on at the moment, you know how it is.'

'That's a fact,' she replied with a smile, although a close look at her eyes would have betrayed the fact that she didn't fully trust the man. 'And don't think I don't appreciate all your support. This sure is going to be pretty demanding on all of us, but for the good of our country and the world, we have to see this Scorpion thing through.'

'Of course, it has my fullest attention,' Frank lied, 'you can count on me.' The two nodded at each other as Frank walked out of the office deep in thought, but not about Scorpion.

The President stood in the middle of the Oval Office watching him depart as Maria came to stand beside her. They had never openly discussed Frank, but she could sense the President's unease which was shared by many in the White House.

'Maria,' the President said, 'can you access Frank's schedule for me – strictly on the quiet you understand, no-one must know.'

'Consider it done,' Maria replied.

Frank had hardly reached his office and gone inside when he was immediately joined by the Reverend who was breathless and looked as white as a sheet. The Reverend quickly closed the door behind him as he produced a copy of that day's Washington Post which he had been carrying tucked under one arm.

'Frank, Frank! Have you seen this?!' he exclaimed, unfurling the newspaper to reveal one of the headlines emblazoned across the page which read: *Is this the final proof of life after death?*

He was amazed at Frank's nonchalant response: 'Yeah, saw it earlier. Why? You read it?'

'Well no, not fully, not yet,' the Reverend admitted, already beginning to feel a little foolish judging from Frank's disinterested tone. 'I just saw the headline and came straight here.'

'You can relax, Walter, it's nothing to do with Revelation. Just some amateur photographer who thinks he's captured the images of a ghost looking out of the window of a derelict building. Think it's already been discounted.'

'Oh right,' the Reverend replied, feeling more than a little sheepish for not reading the full article before rushing in to see Frank as soon as he had read the headline.

'Remember,' Frank added, 'Bob's got media moles everywhere on the highest alert. Nothing like that's going to get through without us being alerted to it first and stopping it – and the source.' He paused for a second before continuing, 'Just goes to show, Walter, you can't believe everything you read.'

There was something in the way Frank said this together with the sardonic look he gave the Reverend which was not appreciated by the man of God.

****

Parked up in a side street, the attack team leader had got out of the Jeep to find a quiet spot where he was making a call on his secure radio phone. It was to Bob Howard.

'Of the cars that had been reported stolen or missing from that area, with the help of tech ops, we've now traced all but one. All our focus is now on that. It's an old Chevrolet Spark and we've got the cops to put out an APB on the plate, but not to approach it and call us in if they find it. The extra men we've now got on the ground are all briefed that it's a TPA, nothing else. All good, shouldn't be long now.'

'Excellent,' Bob replied, 'keep me posted. We're continuing the foot search too just in case, but the Spark sounds like our best bet at the moment.' He allowed himself a wry grin.

Chapter 36

As Linda pressed the doorbell to Ed's house, they both admired the well-kept strips of flower beds along the length of the house, although the climbing roses had long been pruned back at the end of the summer. A host of freshly planted pansies added splashes of colour against the background canvas of the house's neatly painted white walls.

As they waited behind the heavy natural wood door, Jack and Linda could hear the muffled shuffling sound of someone approaching from inside. They could tell that the person had paused behind the door, no doubt to take a peek through the fisheye spyhole to check who was there. Spotting Linda, Ed's booming voice came from behind the door, 'No, no, I told you I'm happy with my energy supplier, go away!' This was immediately followed by mischievous chuckling as he immediately unlocked and opened the door.

Ed was indeed as impressive as Linda had described. Now in his sixties and having been able to take early retirement, Ed was six foot two inches tall, well-built and still a very good-looking man. His now all-white thick head of hair was loosely parted, but well brushed. His lined face framed his hazel eyes which still held an engaging twinkle and he had a neatly trimmed moustache that was also now completely white.

Having suffered problems in both hips, Ed now walked with the use of a thick wooden walking stick, but he managed well for himself. His wife, Susan, had died of a brain haemorrhage not long after they had bought the bungalow – something Ed was convinced had originally been triggered in childhood when her father had accidentally dropped her on her head. He had read that such things can cause delayed problems much later in life.

Susan used to do everything for him, mostly because Ed had enjoyed such a demanding career. But he had since taught himself to cook, even if his repertoire was still a bit limited. And he even quite enjoyed doing the ironing whilst Mahler or Sibelius invariably graced his stereo. Which is partly why he always looked so smart, generally opting for fawn-coloured slacks, brown Hush Puppies and a crisp light blue shirt with the sleeves rolled up past his wrists.

Gregarious, outgoing and with a very engaging personality, he beamed at Jack and Linda with genuine warmth.

Linda laughed at his pretence. 'Ed Bishop you old rogue,' she said as they both embraced and gave each other a kiss on both cheeks. 'Sorry to disturb you like this and so unexpectedly, but it's beyond important.'

Ed raised his bushy white eyebrows. 'Intriguing! Come in, come in.'

As Linda entered followed by Jack, she introduced him. 'Ed, meet my brilliant fellow scientist Jack Taylor who's made a discovery that's about to change the world!'

Ed extended a warm handshake to Jack whilst resting his walking stick against his body so he could also touch Jack's arm with his other hand in a genuinely welcoming gesture. 'Quite an introduction! Good to meet you, Jack. And always a pleasure to see you Linda. Here, come right in and let's sit down – my hips aren't what they used to be!'

As they made their way towards the open plan seating area, Jack admired the way Ed had blended the bright, modern interior with old-style wooden furniture, some of which was clearly antique. The interior was warmly lit by a couple of large table lamps with cream shades and ceramic bases decorated with Chinese dragons. A huge floor-based illuminated globe took centre stage, while the plush twin sofas were in matching pastel hues of blue that perfectly complimented the thick piled oatmeal carpet. Ed had clearly made some good money during his working life and was now enjoying the fruits in his retirement, although sadly now alone. Framed photos of his wife Susan and of the two of them were arranged on a closed mini grand piano at the end of the room. There were also photos of their two daughters as children and at various stages of their lives through to proud graduation poses. The walls boasted framed limited edition prints of beautiful scenery – places that held cherished memories for Ed and Susan.

An armchair draped in a bright tartan throw under an ornate standard lamp was clearly where Ed sat, given away by the presence of a generous measure of whisky in a cut-glass tumbler set beside the chair on an antique walnut side table.

Ed was still processing what Linda had said about Jack as he gestured them both to sit down. 'Loved your recent article on electromagnetic radiation, Linda,' he said, 'a theory I happen to subscribe to myself. Say Jack, your name's kinda familiar – we met before?'

'No, don't think so,' Jack replied, 'though I know you by reputation of course.'

'Don't lie, young man,' Ed responded warmly with a twinkle in his eye. 'Gotta say, you both look kinda harassed. Take it there must be a good reason to pitch up like this out of the blue. Can I fix you both a drink?'

'Can we just talk to you first?' Linda asked, failing to hide the tension in her voice. 'Because after you've heard what we're going to tell you, you may well want us to go away again.'

Ed looked surprised and a little perplexed. 'Would have to be pretty damned serious for me to ever turn you away. You robbed a bank or something? Then again, I'd want to give you a medal for that – bandits!' He laughed, but could see that Jack and Linda could barely raise a smile.

'No no, nothing like that,' Linda came back. 'Ed, I've known you a long time and I trust you implicitly.'

'Thanks,' he said, 'that means a lot.' He had never seen her like this before.

She went on, 'Thing is, there's something we want you to know and it's beyond anything you can imagine.'

'Oh believe me, my imagination is still pretty rampant, even at my age!'

Jack looked at Linda and thought it was probably his turn to add something. 'Linda says you're the guy I really need to speak to about my discovery. More to the point, I need to demonstrate something to you.'

'The mystery deepens,' Ed said with growing interest, 'and you reckon this will change the world eh? Quite some claim. Not sure why me, but, well, let's see it. What you got?'

Jack was becoming increasingly nervous, even though he could already tell that Ed was probably someone he could trust, especially as he had Linda's blessing. 'It's in the trunk of our car just down the road. OK if we bring it in?'

'Sure, let's have some fun. Best you bring your car up and park it in the carport behind the house. Susan and I had that built as we always intended to convert our garage into another bedroom for when both our daughters and partners come to stay. Say, is it heavy? Sorry I can't help but my hips and legs ain't what they were.'

'No, we can manage thanks,' Jack replied. acknowledging Ed's kindness, 'Thing is, it's a copy of the original and not quite complete. It's a long story, but I need to ask a huge favour.'

Linda chipped in supportively, 'You can trust Jack totally. Once you've experienced his invention for yourself – as I have – it will change your life forever.'

Always ready with a quick one-liner, Ed tried to lighten things by joking, 'What, you gonna turn me into a frog or something!?' He laughed, while his guests managed a smile. 'Well, gotta say you've certainly grabbed my interest. So what's this favour you need?'

Jack shifted nervously on the sofa as he knew how strange the first part of his request would sound. 'I could do with borrowing your phone to call a friend in Richmond and then for them to come here tomorrow with some parts I need to complete the device that we've got with us. Then you'll get to experience it for yourself.'

Ed looked kindly at Jack, but it was clear he was not entirely comfortable with his request. 'No problem using my phone but haven't you both got phones? This is all beginning to sound a bit odd.'

Linda came to the rescue. 'Ed, believe me, we'll tell you everything, I promise. But yes, you need to know that Jack and I are in big trouble because of this device and will fully understand if you need us to leave, as we could be putting you in serious jeopardy too.'

This made Ed lean forward, clasping his hands tightly in front of him whilst resting them on the padded arms of his chair. 'That bad eh?' he said, letting the full impact of Linda's words sink in. He paused and his expression had changed from its usual jovial countenance to being more pensive and concerned. He looked both Linda and Jack in their eyes as if searching their souls. At the same time his still sharply analytical mind was quickly weighing things up. 'I've known you long enough, Linda, and to be honest I could already sense you were both in trouble when I opened the door. But like you just said you trust me, well, the feeling's mutual. And if Linda's prepared to vouch for you, Jack, that's good enough for me. You seem an honest, straightforward kinda guy. So my hunch is if I side with you both I'm siding with the good guys.'

They both nodded their appreciation, as Linda continued, 'Ed, I have to warn you that there are risks, big risks. Our lives have been threatened, as we'll explain.'

Ed nodded thoughtfully and took a moment to consider the enormity of what Linda was telling him before responding, 'Can't deny that raises concerns. But don't expect to tell a die-hard scientist who's spent a lifetime breaking down barriers that you've got something that's going to change the world and expect me to turn tail and run. Hell no.' His tone had changed and become more supportive, helping Jack and Linda to relax a little as he went on, 'Look, I'm putting two and two together here and making five pretty damn quick-smart. I'll open the garage and you can put your car in there or under the car port out of sight – take your pick. Then you can make your call and tell me your story.'

They both smiled warmly at him. 'Knew I could count

188

on you Ed,' Linda said as she exchanged encouraging looks with Jack, who chipped in, 'We can't thank you enough, Ed.'

He just gave a wave of his arms as if to say think nothing of it, although inwardly he couldn't deny to himself that he was a little nervous about what he was letting himself in for. But he had the highest regards for Linda, both professionally and as a long-standing friend, and he wasn't the kind of man to let good friends down. The talk of a serious threat had wiped some of the sheen off his naturally jovial manner. He tried to hide his inner concerns as he used his stick to haul himself to his feet and hobbled towards a desk drawer.

As the others watched him, he called back at them, trying to sound as matter-of-fact as he could, 'I'll just get the garage keys and then we're in business.'

****

In her small, terraced house in a quiet street just off the North End Road in Fulham, London where she had lived for many years, Jack's aunt was wondering why he hadn't replied to her email. He usually replied within a few hours or a day at most, so it was very unlike him.

She had decided to pass on the message she had received from the medium just in case it meant anything to him. She decided that if she hadn't heard back from him in the morning, she would give him a call. After all, they were long overdue a catch-up. Perhaps at least they could both have a good laugh about what the medium had said, especially knowing Jack was such a sceptic about those kinds of things.

Chapter 37

Frank was sitting in his office and had at last found a brief moment to himself. He leaned back into his plush, high-backed black leather chair with its studded arms and cushioned upholstery. For a few seconds he allowed himself to close his eyes, but he couldn't relax. *How the hell has it all come to this*, he wondered to himself.

He sat back up and opened one of the top drawers of his desk. He rummaged under some papers and pulled out a framed professional photo of his parents. As with so many portraits, the photographer had opted for black and white and the result perfectly captured the craggy, serious features of the couple as they posed formally in their smartest attire, both well into their sixties at the time. The print had been professionally titled at the bottom: *Edoardo e Sofia Caspari*.

Frank stared at the photo for a few moments. His parents had both died a couple of years ago within a few months of each other. Descended from Italian immigrants, Edoardo and Sofia had worked hard all their lives running a small but very popular café restaurant in Lower Manhattan, New York. Very much a family business, one of Frank's brothers and two of his sisters had also worked there and still ran the place between them, now that the parents were gone.

Whenever in New York, Frank would make a point of

dropping in to catch up with them all and not least for the excellent coffee accompanied by a pastrami on rye sandwich with all the trimmings – one of the house specialities. But other than that, he didn't get to see his siblings too often, although one of his younger sisters who had always been very close to him since childhood and eulogised him, especially now that he was Chief of Staff, never went a week without calling him.

There had been another younger brother, but he had got involved with the wrong sort of people and it was Frank who three years previously had been called to go and identify his bullet-riddled body. Some said the grief had precipitated the rapid demise of his parents and Frank certainly took that view. Already very powerful by then and with all the right contacts to make amends on his own terms, there were three well-known drug dealers at the time who had never made it to court. Instead, they had mysteriously ended up at the bottom of the Hudson River in the very early hours of one early Spring morning when the mist had hung low over the water like a silent cloak of secrecy.

Frank continued to contemplate the photo of his parents whilst lost in his thoughts of his strict Catholic upbringing. He smiled to himself when he remembered how, when aged just seven, his mother had chased him around the kitchen with a wooden spoon when he had dared to question what proof anyone had for the existence of angels. When she had finally caught up with him, she hadn't beat him, but made him recite the Hail Mary prayer out loud ten times while she crossed herself several times as if protecting herself from her son's sinful utterance.

While he still held on to the photo, he looked around the room in a questioning way, wondering to himself if the spirits of his parents were somehow nearby. If this Revelation thing really did do what Jack had claimed, it really would be the greatest scientific breakthrough ever. But, ever the pragmatist, he couldn't allow himself to be distracted. Decisions had been taken and the die had been well and truly cast. He had no choice now but to see this thing through. His career and his whole life depended on it.

He turned the frame over and carefully returned it to the desk drawer. At that moment there was a knock at his door and, without waiting for an answer, the Reverend Walter Cunningham entered and carefully closed the door behind him. Without invitation, the Reverend walked over and sat down in a chair set against the wall next to Frank's desk. Frank turned to face him, noting how troubled the Reverend looked. Perhaps he was there to make amends for his rather ridiculous previous visit to Frank's office after jumping to conclusions about a sub-headline in the Washington Post. The Reverend thought Frank too looked troubled as he opened the conversation. 'You're looking pensive.'

'Yeah, well, lot on my mind at the moment,' he replied, not without some sarcasm about how all his days were full-on, let alone without the secret plot that had now entwined his and the Reverend's fate together.

'Revelation?' the Reverend asked needlessly.

'Guessed that's why you're here,' Frank replied laconically. Frank regretted involving him and hadn't appreciated his firebrand approach to the situation without, of course, having to do the dirty work himself.

'That obvious eh?' the Reverend tried to make light of it. 'So what's happening, what's the latest progress?'

'It's best you don't know the detail,' Frank replied.

The Reverend considered his response for a moment

before pressing the issue. 'Hmmm, but you are close to finding them and shutting all this down, right?'

'Nothing has changed, we're doing what we all agreed. Naturally we'll let you know the minute we get the news we're all waiting for.'

The Reverend realised he wasn't going to get anything else out of the man for now. 'You don't pray do you, Frank?' he asked, almost rhetorically.

'Don't seem to find the time,' Frank replied offhandedly, 'why, you here to save my soul?' He raised a half grin.

This made the Reverend laugh and he came back in similarly jocular fashion, lightening the atmosphere between them a little. 'Ordinarily I'd say you're well past that, but it's never too late for anyone to be saved.'

They both smiled at each other as if to say it's never going to happen. But Frank was inquisitive, 'Level with me, Walter. Why are you so worried about Revelation? I would've thought you of all people would welcome absolute proof of life after death?'

'Already got it in The Bible, it's about having faith.'

Frank looked hard at him, clearly unconvinced before replying, 'Doesn't seem convincing enough for many in these science-based times.'

The Reverend refused to be derailed, 'We've already been over this, you're getting into dangerous territory. Have you thought of all the implications?'

'Oh believe me, I think of little else,' Frank responded truthfully.

There was an awkward pause between them before the Reverend said, 'I just know this whole talk of Revelation and the people behind it need to be stopped. But more than that I don't want to know.'

Once more Frank thought to himself, *that's easy for you to say without being involved in the solution*. As if reading Frank's thoughts, the Reverend stood up and said, 'Well, I must be going.'

The two nodded at each other and as the Reverend walked towards the door he turned briefly to call back, 'God bless you, Frank.'

'Oh I doubt it,' Frank muttered ruefully, but by then the Reverend had left the room.

Chapter 38

The Lear jet touched down at the top secret Military Base on the Colorado-New Mexico border. The base was so secret that it didn't feature on any lists of known bases in the USA and very few even at the top of the armed forces were even aware of its existence.

As the small jet taxied towards the solitary hangar, the man seated in the cream-coloured leather seat towards the back of the plane looked out across the tarmac at the two men and one woman standing outside the hangar waiting to greet him. They were all in civilian dress and wearing aviator sunglasses against the fierce sunlight that seemed to magnify in heat and intensity as it bounced off the concrete.

The man on the plane was also dressed in civilian clothes, but his business at the base was anything but a civilian matter. Although born in America, he was something of a blood cocktail and enjoyed telling people how he could trace family roots in no less than nine countries around the world.

It was his great-grandmother who was ultimately the reason he had become of such interest to the CIA. Born in Palestine and already a widow with children, she had lost her land and house as a result of the 1947 Partition Resolution. Taking advantage of the opportunity at the time, she had taken her children, now in their late teens, and emigrated to

America to try and rebuild their lives.

Her great-grandson had inherited many of her features and had the indeterminate dark looks and olive skin colouring that could pass for a multitude of Middle Eastern and Mediterranean nationalities – the perfect cover in his line of work. As a child he had become fluent in Arabic and many of its dialects. So it was perhaps hardly surprising when, whilst into his second year in Ancient Egyptian Studies at New York University, he had been discreetly approached by a very attractive female who purported to be a lecturer in the Arabic Language faculty.

She had waited until the end of the day to approach him as he was leaving his faculty building. Perfectly practiced, she had pretended to be walking abreast of him in the same direction and then casually looking across had asked, wasn't he the guy she'd heard about who's fluent in various Arabic dialects?

They had got chatting and within half an hour he had found himself sitting in a very nice apartment where they had been joined by two very friendly men who had got straight down to making their pitch. Hell, they had even served him his favourite Turkish coffee, overly sweetened to most people's tastes. Any young person would have been flattered by such attention and he was no exception.

Now highly experienced and with many dangerous missions behind him, this operation was pretty standard for him, although it would again involve huge risks. His welcoming party on the tarmac would escort him to the larger military jet already awaiting take-off. Once he landed at his destination he would be smuggled in the back of a truck across two borders where his drivers would bribe the guards and deliver him to the bomb-damaged house where he would meet the specially trained team who had been embedded there for some months.

As the welcoming party of three outside the hangar had escorted him to his awaiting flight, the woman had handed him a well-worn shirt in his exact size. She had casually explained how a cyanide pill had been sown into the left lapel in case he was captured.

But it was the small, metal, firmly sealed box, no more than six inches square, that he was handed that had focused all their attention. 'Guard it with your life,' he was needlessly reminded, repeating what his CIA controllers had already drummed into him while they had taken him through every detail of his mission so often back in the safe room at Langley.

Once seated on his final flight, he deliberately squeezed his arm against his body to feel the reassuring presence of his Glock pistol. He glanced up the aisle to where the four Special Forces members who were to accompany him were seated, all considerably better armed than himself. They would see him onto the truck and then immediately fly back. From then on he would be on his own until he made his rendezvous.

On the flight he would go over every detail of his mission in his head until it was second nature. And he would remind himself of the particular Arabic dialects that he would need to employ over the next few days and weeks.

The man looked down at the very ordinary-looking, small metal box resting on his lap. *So this is what all the fuss is about*, he thought to himself. *This is Scorpion*.

Chapter 39

As the early evening light highlighted their long shadows, Ed was proudly showing Linda round his beautifully landscaped, walled garden. It was his pride and joy and included an ornate fishpond with koi and other exotic fish and a brightly painted wooden Japanese bridge that added a very stylish, individual touch to what was already a very picturesque setting. There was an abundance of very colourful plants, palms and tropical trees, creating an almost kaleidoscopic effect that changed with the seasons.

Everyone who visited – which these days was mostly just neighbours and his daughters with their partners – couldn't help but be struck by the beauty and tranquillity of the place. This was accentuated by the soothing sound of water gently splashing down a small rock cascade on one side of the pond. A rough-hewn oak bench was set at an angle next to the pond and was framed by a wooden pergola of roses. It made sitting there in the spring and summer a feast for the senses and the perfect place for some quiet meditation. By now many of the blooms had long gone once autumn had arrived.

Ed and his wife Susan had as good as created the garden from scratch and by now it was maturing nicely and very well-maintained. This was confirmed by Ed as he led Linda around the garden, proudly pointing out various features and explaining everything that had been involved in transforming what had largely been overlooked before.

'Took one helluva lot of work. Before my hips began to go on me I did most of the donkey work. It was Susan who really wanted the tropical feel. 'Course I get help with it all now.'

'It's magical,' Linda said.

'Thanks, appreciate it,' he replied.

At that moment there was the sound of something metallic like a spanner falling on a concrete floor as Jack worked on Revelation in the garage.

'Hope he's not about to blow up my garage,' Ed joked. Linda laughed. She and Jack had earlier explained to Ed exactly what Revelation could do and he had been absolutely dumbfounded by it. He could see how earnest the two of them were, so he had no reason not to believe them, but his initial complete amazement had soon turned to excitement when he realised he was now privy to knowing about the greatest ever scientific discovery.

However, his initial excitement had been significantly dampened when they recounted everything that had happened in the aftermath of Jack telling Frank everything. He had sat there shaking his head as he heard about the destruction of the original Revelation and the fact that the two of them had accepted that there would undoubtedly be a frantic search going on for them right now and that it probably wouldn't end well for them.

They had been quite surprised about how readily Ed had accepted that Revelation would challenge the cosy status quo for many in power, especially when it came to the historical complex relationship between church and state. But at that point, all of them had to assume it was Frank largely driving things, presumably with the cooperation of the FBI, CIA, Special Forces or whoever. They were guessing, of course, but they had joined up enough of the dots to know that time was not on their side and they must assume a kill team was hot on their tail.

After they had finished telling Ed everything, he had sat in silence for a while, weighing it all up and letting the sheer enormity sink in of exactly what they were all sitting on. But, true to his word, he wasn't going to let go of the chance to at least play some part in something so incredibly life-changing as this. However, for the moment he didn't know if they would want more from him than just the loan of his garage and to allow a friend to arrive sometime with the spare parts still needed for the back-up device.

As well as his own conviction to always champion the truth, he now felt protective towards Jack and Linda and had made up his mind to square up beside them to whatever and whoever was coming. Realistically he knew they wouldn't have much of a chance, but at least they'd put up one hell of a fight. He had even checked the handgun he kept in the drawer by his bed to confirm it was still fully loaded. At this point he had no idea that they hadn't just come to him for refuge because he was known to Linda, but that she had further plans for him.

Ed was still deep in thought as he and Linda stopped midway on the bridge and leaned over to admire the koi as they seemed to play hide-and-seek with each other under the giant floating water lilies. He spoke softly, 'If this Revelation thing really can prove life after death, wow just doesn't come into it!'

Linda nodded. 'You know, Jack and I were just talking about how people who've had near-death experiences have described it like stepping into another room.'

Ed just nodded. The subject of life after death hadn't occupied his mind too much in the past, although he had loosely wondered about it at times after his wife Susan had died. 'Sounds a whole lot more plausible than the heaven and hell tales I was brought up on.' He paused for a moment. 'Not sure how I'll cope if I see my Susan again.'

Linda reassuringly put her arm through Ed's as they walked on and gave him a gentle squeeze. 'Don't worry, I'll be with you.' They both smiled warmly at each other.

A neighbour's black cat had jumped up on top of one of the walls of Ed's garden, attracting their attention. It sniffed around a bit, gave them a cursory glance, but was clearly preoccupied stalking something.

While looking up at the cat, Ed suddenly announced, 'No such thing as the supernatural anyway.'

Linda gave him a surprised, quizzical look, so he quickly explained his thoughts. 'Strictly from a scientific point of view, of course. Everything works according to natural laws. Nothing is above nature. My God, the arguments I used to have with my sub-editors about that.'

Linda nodded her approval, while complimenting him. 'Not all scientists share your vision. Many don't see the bigger picture like you do and are uncomfortable dealing with these kinds of issues.'

Ed enjoyed the compliment. He gestured towards the cat. 'I mean look at that cat…we know animals experience our world with far more heightened senses than us. Just because we can't always see, hear, taste, touch or smell things with our seriously limited human senses doesn't mean they don't exist or that they've all therefore got to be attributed to some kind of supernatural whatever. Give me a break!' He was warming to his subject. 'Native Americans, Aborigines and countless ancient cultures all understood the natural law in ways we too often seem to ignore today. And that's not good for us or our planet.'

Linda gave his arm another squeeze. 'You are so ready for Revelation, my friend!' she said admiringly.

Ed laughed and instead unlinked their arms so he could put his around her as he guided them both back towards the house. He was a little nervous about doing so, but with the night approaching, felt he needed to probe her relationship with Jack, if only to see if they could both stay in his spare bedroom or whether Jack would need to occupy the couch.

He cleared his throat, 'Um…wasn't sure…but you and Jack…you together?'

Linda instinctively guessed why he would be asking, as she knew Ed wouldn't otherwise pry. In that moment, she had also decided that she and Jack would indeed be sharing the same bed that night. It was their first opportunity and, although she didn't want to dwell on the possibility, it might well be their last.

'Yeah,' she replied confidently, 'we're together.'

'Real happy for you,' Ed said warmly.

'Yeah, thanks,' Linda acknowledged.

'Come on,' Ed said, quickly changing the subject, 'I'll make us some pasta and let's see if I've got a garage left!' Linda laughed, but her mind was already focused on later that night.

Chapter 40

Professor Ed Bishop's name and address were clearly visible on one of the large computer screens being studied by a couple of operators in the control room where Bob Howard was spending increasing amounts of his time.

Thankfully, however, Ed's name was one of over 40 on a list that the operators were now scrolling through. The list had been compiled as the result of exhaustive checking and cross-checking of all Jack and Linda's known contacts and even people remotely linked to them in some way, especially those within a 50 mile radius of Washington D.C. And yes, they had already checked on Jack's barber! Beside each name and address was a brief two line summary of their known current or previous occupation.

Even as the operators were looking at the screen whilst Bob looked over their shoulders, a very surprised Susan Porter was just closing the curtains to one of her upstairs rooms and wondering what two blacked out Jeeps were doing parked up outside one of the houses down the road. But she thought nothing more of it and went back downstairs where she was about to serve dinner to her husband and two young children.

What she couldn't have known is that the occupants of the Jeeps had no interest in the people whose house they were parked directly in front of, but were in fact checking out Susan and her house. Apart from the children returning from school on the bus which stopped outside their house and her husband driving home from work, there had been no other comings and goings.

But before she had married, Susan had once shared an apartment with Linda Wilson and they had become good friends who continued to stay in touch. So she had become what was euphemistically termed 'a person of interest' back in the control room.

Unseen by any of the family, a small drone with penetrating listening capabilities also hovered high above Susan's house. But by the time the family sat down to eat at their kitchen table, Bob had tired of hearing the kids complaining about one of their teachers and especially the husband telling his wife chapter and verse about how the IT department at work just weren't up to it. So Susan was very soon eliminated from being of further interest and the Jeeps were instructed to move on.

At this stage, no house searches had been deemed necessary. Such action would only be carried out as a final resort if the surveillance team were damn sure that the targets were inside. So for now, stealth remained the name of the game.

But Bob hadn't risen to become head of the CIA without having a certain hunch about things and following through on his instincts, often to great advantage. His mind had been working overtime as he scanned the list of names over and over and putting together potential scenarios in his imagination that might make any of them worthy of special interest.

Right now he was focused on three names in particular

who all had some kind of links to the media. What Bob didn't know at that stage was that one of those names had an even better contact than he could have imagined. That person was Professor Ed Bishop.

Chapter 41

A loud screeching of tyres and the sound of a car coming to an abrupt halt immediately outside Ed's house made all those inside jump and look nervously at each other. Each was wondering if this could be their worst nightmare.

Almost immediately the doorbell rang. They had just finished eating a simple but very tasty pasta meal and had been complimenting Ed on his culinary skills. They were completely off their guard.

To save Ed's legs, Jack nodded at him and got up from the table to go and look through the spyhole in the door. As he did so, he put his finger to his lips to gesture to the others to keep quiet. They had closed all the curtains in the house by now, so had not seen the car approaching.

Just as Jack reached the door, the front knocker was hammered loudly, signalling the impatience of whoever was on the other side. The shock caused Jack to momentarily take a step back, while Ed reassuringly reached across the table and grabbed Linda by the hand.

Jack took the briefest of looks through the spyhole and breathed a huge sigh of relief. 'It's OK, it's Jason,' he gladly announced to the others, while sliding back the bolt on the door and unlocking the main lock with the key that was usually left in it.

He opened the door whilst carefully shielding himself

enough to keep himself from view of the road. Jason was biting into a Hershey Bar and carrying an old holdall that was so faded with use that the logo was barely visible.

Ed and Linda both looked their visitor up and down and Linda smiled, remembering his crazy conversation with Jack that she had partly overheard in the alley. Still dressed in his crumpled Army Requisitions uniform with unpolished boots and a missing cuff button, Jason's portly frame, beaming round face and unkempt hair was pretty much what she had imagined he would look like. Meanwhile Ed was simply perplexed at how this very unassuming character could have anything to do with helping them – or more to the point Jack – with Revelation.

Jason was trying to do the impossible by giving Jack a big smile while addressing him with a mouthful of chocolate. 'Code word?'

'What?!' Jack asked in disbelief.

'You didn't give me a code word,' Jason replied, totally unphased.

'God give me strength,' Jack uttered. 'Jason, I know it's you and you know it's me; now get your sorry ass in here!'

Jason entered, dropped his holdall and gave Jack a big hug, as the latter quickly broke it off to close and lock the door again. 'So good to see you again, buddy, this is so cool,' he said to Jack just before noticing the presence of Ed and Linda and completely jumping to the wrong conclusion. 'OK, bit of a cell thing going on, I get it.'

Jack was shaking his head to himself. 'Jason, the only thing I hope you get is what I trust you've brought in that moth-eaten bag of yours. This is Ed and Linda by the way.'

Jason quickly eyed up the two of them whilst still savouring the remains of the chocolate in his mouth. It was already too late to persuade him that this was anything but a top secret cell planning who knows what. But the important thing was that they needed Jason – *you hear that, pa*, he thought to himself, *they need me*! In Quixotic fashion he had completely mistaken Ed for some kind of spy chief as he addressed them: 'Pleasure to meet you both, whatever your real names. And may I say, sir, we're all in your debt for running ops like this and how proud I am…'

'Jason!' Jack interrupted him from behind while giving Ed and Linda a look as if to say just go with it. 'Did you manage to get everything on my list?'

Jason nodded enthusiastically, although his reply was anything but reassuring, 'Yes and no my laboratorian friend. More yes than no, but the yes is a yes and the no I can make a yes.'

By now both Ed and Linda were trying to suppress their laughter. Meanwhile Jack began to rummage through the untidy contents of Jason's holdall.

'Can we get you a coffee Jason or something to eat?' Ed asked as he began to stack the dinner plates and cutlery. 'Got any Dr Pepper?' Jason enquired hopefully.

'Sorry,' Ed replied, 'don't generally tend to keep that kind of thing.'

'Coke? Pepsi? Sprite? Tizer? Fanta? I'm on first name terms with them all,' Jason looked at Ed like a wistful kid asking for candy.

'Got some freshly squeezed orange juice,' Ed offered.

Jason looked as if he'd just been offered a goblet of poison. 'Nah, you're good, think I'll pass, but thank you kindly, sir.'

Jack was kneeling beside Jason's holdall and had carefully laid out most of the contents on the floor next to him after meticulously inspecting each item. Meanwhile Ed gestured Jason and Linda towards the sofas while he sat back in his armchair.

Linda was surprised and touched by the gallant, gentlemanly way Jason gestured with his hand to her to take the seat of her choice. Meanwhile she could see that he was studying Ed.

'Let me guess, ex Seal right?' he addressed Ed, having sat himself near enough to Linda so she caught a faint unmistakable smell of a mixture of metal greases and carbolic soap that was the everyday currency of life in Requisitions.

'Afraid not,' Ed replied, rather enjoying Jason's fantasy, 'closest I've been to a seal is at the zoo.'

It was clear that Jason thought he was bluffing and although he smiled back, his reply of 'sure, sure' couldn't hide his scepticism.

Linda was glancing anxiously across at Jack and hoping upon hope that he now had everything he needed to make the back-up Revelation work so they could carry out the rest of their plan. She tried to hide her anxiety by trying to make light conversation with Jason, as if he were a dinner guest. 'Did it take you long to get here?'

'Nah,' he replied confidently, 'less than two hours. Goes in a flash when you've got Angus for company.' Linda and Ed look bemused and intrigued as to who Angus might be. But Jason had already started imitating the AC/DC lead guitarist Angus Young's crouching, strutting style, looking even more ridiculous in his seated position. Jason started flailing his arms wildly, playing air guitar and howling a couple of lines from *Highway to Hell* making the others laugh.

Jack had to shout to be heard. 'Jason! Jason! What are the 'no' parts?'

Jason stood up and went over to join Jack as they both then knelt beside the holdall. Jason picked out an item which looked a bit like a glass valve in the shape of a candlelight bulb. 'OK, so it's not exactly a no, but here's the culprit, my fiendish friend. It's nearly burnt out and probably only got another thirty minutes in it. I forgot to bring the box of spares on my desk.' He looked sheepishly apologetic over his forgetfulness. 'I know, I know, but fear not, I'll drop them over tomorrow. Got the day off – cadets have got choir practice.'

'You serious?' Linda asked, surprised.

Jason adopted a sing-song voice while imitating exaggerated movements with his arms as if on a Marines route march, 'My Corps, Your Corps, Our Corps, Marine Corps…'

Even Jack had to laugh at Jason's manic mimicry that was more like a demented octopus than anything remotely resembling a hardened Marine recruit on a route march. He quipped to the others, 'Jason used to keep our spirits up in Iraq – you can see how!' He addressed Jason again, 'You have no idea how grateful I am to you for getting this stuff for me.'

Jason cast a furtive sideways glance at Ed – the undoubted 'spy chief' – as he replied to Jack but clearly aiming his remark at Ed, 'Just doing my bit for flag and country.' Ed nodded appreciatively, still enjoying indulging the fantasy.

Meanwhile, Jack had finished rummaging through all the contents of the holdall. 'Great, it's all here. Jason, if you can bring those spare valves here just as damn quick as possible, I'm going to recommend you for the highest honour.'

Jason beamed with pride.

****

No-one in the house could have known that at that moment, someone sat in front of a computer in a large technical ops control room, was punching in the exact co-ordinates of Ed's house onto his screen. These would be used to launch a drone and also to call in ground teams as required, perhaps with helicopter support if the subjects were indeed spotted there and made a run for it.

The web was definitely closing fast and Bob was allowing himself to feel increasingly confident.

Chapter 42

It was getting late and Jack was still tinkering with Revelation in Ed's garage. He was delighted with everything Jason had brought him – the guy may have the outward appearance of being disorganised to say the least, but when it came to Requisitions, Jason had no equal.

Jack remembered in Iraq how he and Marty would sometimes visit Jason in his storerooms and how, whatever obscure item they may be after, he could not only instantly lay his hands on it, but also give them the full spec of the part, where it was manufactured, how many more he held in stock and what alternatives were available. Of course, it was always accompanied by banter and friendly abuse on all sides, so typical of the camaraderie built up between service personnel operating in combat theatres. But it was at times like this that a character like Jason was worth a whole Marine Corps.

Ed had joined Jack in the garage, leaving Linda watching the news channels just in case of any possible breaking stories about them. He watched Jack at work, fascinated by the device and what it supposedly could do.

'Quite a character that Jason,' he said.

'Hmm, you could say that!' Jack confirmed.

Ed's scientific curiosity was getting the better of him as he continued to watch Jack. 'Don't mean to put you off, but how does it work? I don't see any plug.'

Jack gave a little laugh. 'No electricity needed. Creates its own power, but yeah, got to admit it's kinda quirky. Was trial and error a lot of the time. Crystal energy is a really big part of it, that and, dare I say, a bend-the-rules approach to standard physics.'

'Inspired; I'm mighty impressed.'

Jack smiled at him, 'Look, reckon I've got a good hour or so ahead of me. Why don't you get some sleep and I promise I'll give you a knock first thing.'

Ed was certainly ready for bed, so didn't need a second invitation. 'Oh don't worry, I'll be up before the sparrows to see this thing work! Well, good night then...and good luck!'

Jack wished him goodnight in return. He had actually very nearly finished, but didn't want the embarrassment of rejoining Linda in front of Ed and going to their bedroom together.

In fact when Linda had earlier whispered to Jack that they would be sharing a bed that night, he had found it hard to focus on Revelation as his mind raced with the thoughts of what was to come. Not the most experienced of men when it came to the opposite sex, he was both nervous and excited.

Some twenty minutes after Ed had left him, Jack needn't have worried about any embarrassing scene, as when he came back into the kitchen to wash his hands, both Ed and Linda had retired to their rooms.

He still acted like a naughty teenager staying with his girlfriend's parents as he tiptoed down the corridor to Ed's spare bedroom, gently turned the door handle, entered and closed it behind him with all the stealth he could muster.

The room was lit by subdued side lights, giving it a warm, inviting glow. It was tastefully decorated and furnished in traditional style, with natural woods and pastel colours. The king-size bed was made up with large pillows and a quilt with a subtle pattern of spring garden flowers. The quilt was pulled right back to the end of the bed, invitingly exposing the bottom sheet.

Almost at the same time as Jack entered the bedroom, Linda emerged from the bathroom wearing just her loose top and underwear. Her hair was tumbling loosely around her shoulders and Jack thought to himself how sexy she looked. He felt a little apprehensive as they held each other by both hands staring deeply into each other's eyes and smiling tenderly.

Sensing Jack's slight nervousness, Linda took control, unbuttoning his shirt and letting it drop to the floor. He in turn removed her top and bra, excited at the sight of her beautifully pert breasts. They embraced tightly and kissed each other with unrestrained passion. Jack then quickly removed the rest of his clothes as Linda took off her pants and they lay on the bed naked together for the first time. Both felt very aroused and took some time just gently stroking each other's bodies and enjoying their closeness and intimacy.

Although neither of them had been with a sexual partner for a while, they were in no hurry and savoured every moment. They were very sensual in the way they touched and explored each other's bodies for the first time with their fingers, lips and tongues. They entwined passionately in total harmony, lingering over every action and sometimes pausing to just look lovingly at each other. Both felt a slight tension, with the unsaid knowledge that this could not only be the first time they made love to one another, but could also be their last.

Jack did not penetrate Linda for a while, but when he did, it was with great gentleness, care and love. Both couldn't restrain gasping softly with pleasure as they locked their bodies together and began to rock slowly and rhythmically in ecstasy.

As they continued to stroke each other's bodies to accentuate their pleasure, Linda rolled Jack onto his back and quickened the speed of their movements, enjoying the way Jack responded with low moans.

As Jack exploded inside her, it was the final stimulus she needed and she had a deep orgasm that left her whole body shaking with uncontrollable spasms of sheer pleasure.

They clung to each other as one, softly stroking each other's cheeks and kissing gently while they took some time to come back down from the stars. Eventually they disengaged and lay back together whilst holding hands and staring up at the ceiling, each deep in thought.

****

High above Ed's house, a drone was making an initial surveillance pass to check for signs of the car Jack and Linda could be driving and any other obvious signs of their presence. At this stage, it had picked up no clear indicators.

Meanwhile, two other addresses were also being checked out from the sky, although no-one below could have possibly guessed. All the pictures and data were immediately fed back into the tech control room. The next stage would be definitive ground action and would be final.

Chapter 43

It was early morning with the sunrise still in its early stages, as an elderly lady with a flashlight walked past Ed's house with her Golden Retriever held tightly on a lead. Streaks of light were beginning to reveal the shapes of clouds in the eastern sky, while the dawn chorus of birds echoed up and down the street.

The lady knew Ed and thought to herself that he was up unusually early as she could tell the lights were on in his house behind the closed curtains. As she walked on past, briefly admiring the tidy flower beds at the front of his house, she couldn't have known that Ed was right at that moment witnessing the most incredible discovery in the history of humankind.

As soon as they had awoken, still lying naked in each other's arms, Jack and Linda had quickly washed, dressed and gone through the adjoining door from the house into the garage to carry Revelation into the sitting room. Meanwhile Ed had been brewing some fresh coffee for them all.

It was half an hour later when Jack turned off Revelation and stood in silence next to it. The device had worked perfectly, thanks to the requested items Jason had brought, although Jack could tell that the valve Jason had shown him was indeed coming to the end of its life. If Jason didn't get back with those spare valves, it was doubtful if any further demonstrations could be made.

But for now, the demonstration that Ed and Linda had just witnessed had been a great success. They were both sitting transfixed in stunned silence, with traces of tears staining their cheeks. Even though Linda had experienced Revelation before, seeing her mother again and joined by her grandma too, had been incredibly emotional, as well as wonderfully uplifting.

Ed sat riveted to his armchair, staring ahead and slowly and continuously shaking his head in disbelief. He wasn't quite sure what he was expecting when he had sat down for the demo, but what he had just experienced had shaken him to the core. But it had also then given way to feelings of complete elation and euphoria. His initial look of shock had now been replaced by a huge smile that seemed to illuminate all the features of his face and make him look years younger.

Slowly and using his stick for leverage, he stood up and hobbled over to the mini grand piano where he picked up one of the framed photos of his late wife Susan whose spirit he had just seen again with his own eyes. He stared at the photo for a while whilst the others looked at him with sympathy but also happiness at what he now knew to be the truth.

His voice breaking with emotion, he turned towards Jack. 'Thank you, Jack...thank you...' His voice trailed off as Linda joined him and put her arm around him.

As they walked back to sit down again, Jack also sat down as Ed had now gathered his strength again as he looked at Jack with undiminished admiration and speaking slowly in stops and starts, 'Staggering, just staggering...talk about the demo to end all demos...seems like everything I've ever worked on is like nothing compared to this...I'm gonna need a few moments here guys to come down from that – to see and hear Susan again and in her prime, it's just…thank you…my God, this is incredible. Haven't cried like that since I lost her – and now to feel such joy, such love! This is the scientific breakthrough of all breakthroughs. You're a bloody genius, Jack! You and Marty.'

'That's what I keep telling him,' Linda happily agreed.

In his typically self-deprecating way, Jack came back, 'Well, Marty provided the vision and knew where he secretly wanted to steer this whole thing. I was more the nuts and bolts man.'

But Ed wasn't having any of it. 'Hey, don't put yourself down, what you've come up with here is nothing short of mind-blowing. You just hit the ball right out the park buddy!' As he blew his nose on a handkerchief from his trouser pocket, he quipped, 'By the way, before this ever goes live, it's a good time to buy shares in Kleenex!'

Jack and Linda both laughed. 'Well,' Jack remained bashful, 'I'll hold my hands up and admit that the last stages of developing Revelation were as much accidental as anything.'

'Welcome to the history of science,' Ed immediately countered. 'You think Newton deliberately shook the tree to make the apple fall? Just wait until people get to hear about this!'

'Exactly!' Linda agreed and had gauged that this was the moment to broach it to Ed as to why they had come to him, 'Talking about going public with Revelation, we've figured that the only way now is for this to go to the very top and – sorry my good friend – but you're the link. And I'm really sorry to drag you into this, especially in light of everything we've told you that's happened in the last few days. But given all that, we just didn't know where to turn and I thought of you. You see it's as much about survival now as getting the truth about Revelation out there.'

Ed nodded understandingly. 'The very top – you mean Angela Freeman?' His question was largely rhetorical as he was already seeing her logic given what he now knew about Frank Caspari and who was probably on their tail.

'The President, yes,' Linda replied. 'You were her childhood buddy and you told me you've always remained pretty close.'

Ed was thoughtful. 'Sure, but this – I mean phew. I mainly see Angela now when she wheels me out at dinners to sit next to some boring foreign dignitary who happens to have a science background.'

It was Jack's turn to support what Linda had said. 'You understand why we've come to you now and didn't at first trust going direct to the media?'

'Bloody snakepit!' Ed spat. 'They'd sooner make a circus of the whole damn thing. Anyway, Caspari or his cronies will have moles in place in all the mainstream media. You can spot 'em a mile off – reptilian eyes. They'd have people onto you in minutes.'

'I'm almost past caring now,' Jack said, trying to convince himself that that's how he felt. 'I just feel people should know about Revelation – people deserve to know the truth.'

'You bet!' Ed agreed. 'At least now I know for sure I can come back and haunt my bookie!' Jack and Linda laughed as he continued, 'It's still sinking in – not every day you have all your science stood on its head.'

'True, but I've always found when science stands on its head we make the greatest discoveries.'

Ed gave a big nod to show his approval to the truth of Jack's statement.

'Ways and means, Ed; we need a plan,' Linda said.

The three all sat thoughtfully in silence for a while. Ed then got up and made his way over to a beautiful walnut writing desk and lifted up the concertina lid to its front. He took out a writing pad and smart silver rollerball pen and re-joined Jack and Linda. As he sat down he announced triumphantly to them, 'Well now, maybe it's time for me to surprise you both as I may just have a trump up my sleeve – and that's about how we actually get the ear of the President in the first place. So for now, I need to write my friend Angela a letter. And it's going to have to be quite some letter. Something along these lines…'

****

One of Bob's attack teams had surrounded a parked car. Using a special tool that looked like an innocuous kid's penknife, they had opened the trunk and one of the doors and disabled the alarm, all within a matter of a few seconds. As they examined the interior, there were shrugs and grunts between the team members as they didn't find anything of interest.

Their leader called Bob on his secure radio phone. 'Nothing. The car was similar, different plates, but we thought we'd better check it out anyway.'

Bob's reply surprised him: 'It's OK, we think we may have a pretty good reading on where they are. Expect a call from the control room any minute to give you some new co-ordinates. Remember these are dangerous terrorists who've sold our country down the river. When you do find them, they could be armed with detonators; keep it discreet but shoot to kill. And we don't want them taken alive for the bleeding heart liberals to get involved.'

The team leader was used to not questioning his superiors and simply accepted what he was being told as the truth. He hated traitors and would make sure his team didn't hold back. 'Understood. Out,' he replied crisply.

The call from the control room reached him within a minute of ending his call to Bob. *This is it, this is the end game*, he thought to himself as he got back into the Jeep. He had killed for his country before, mainly drug dealers and gang leaders, but there would be a greater satisfaction in dealing with traitors.

Chapter 44

Having not had too much sleep and with Ed's encouragement, Jack and Linda had gently dozed off on Ed's sofa as he composed his letter to the President. He had taken his time and seemed to be going to great lengths to explain absolutely everything. As they cuddled together half asleep, they had heard him talking to someone on his phone from his bedroom but were too tired to think too much of it.

It was nearly an hour later when they were both awoken by the sound of animated voices coming from the open front door. As Jack stood up to get a better look at what was going on, he just caught sight of someone clad head to toe in black leather and wearing a black, darkened visor. There was a throaty roar as the person kicked their motorbike into action and sped off.

Ed closed the door and turned to Jack, clapping his hands together with satisfaction. 'Good, that's all done; the carrier pigeon is on the home flight.'

But Jack was seriously alarmed. 'Whoa, hold up! I thought you'd be delivering the letter yourself. My God, you've just entrusted it to some courier who won't even get past the gates. The letter will be intercepted and then we're all blown. I mean what the…'

Ed gave out a booming laugh and his eyes twinkled

mischievously as Linda joined them and he addressed Jack, 'Hang on in there a minute. My fault, you're right, I should have introduced you both. That was my eldest daughter Claire. Bit of a rebel, took after my Susan. Yeah, our daughters practically grew up with the Freeman kids – always at each other's houses on sleepovers or whatever. Claire's still best friends with Laura, Angela's oldest. Pops round to the White House all the time – she knows the way!'

Ed steered them both back to the sofas as he found it hard to stand for too long. Jack and Linda had relaxed again as he continued, 'Don't worry, Claire's on first name terms with all the security guys – think she even went on a date with one of them. Didn't work out – idiot thought he was some kind of Rambo – soon got emasculated when Claire let him have a taste of her full throttle feminism!' He let out another booming laugh. 'Anyway, rest assured, she'll put the letter right in Laura's hands and I've told her exactly what to say.'

Jack was certainly feeling a lot more relieved at hearing this, but couldn't resist saying, 'You make it all sound so simple.'

'Well you got me there,' Ed replied, 'sure I'm pretty nervous inside, but I know the letter will get to Angela. After that…well, what's worrying going to solve. Didn't someone once say that ninety five per cent of what people worry about never happens.'

'Yeah, well it's the five per cent that happens that worries me!' Jack replied, making the others laugh.

It was Linda's turn to voice some caution: 'Sorry Ed, but I've got to ask, how can we be sure the President isn't in on this with Frank Caspari? After all, he is her Chief of Staff.'

'We can't be…well, not totally,' Ed replied truthfully, although not reassuring the others as much as they would

223

initially have liked. 'But having said that, I would stake my life on it – come to think of it, that's exactly what I'm doing – what we're doing. I've only met Frank briefly on a few occasions at White House functions, but as you know Jack, he's a clandestine Machiavellian figure. Loves working in the shadows. No, he'll be keeping this tight, making sure it's his show, so can't see he'd have told the President. And there's no way on God's earth she would have sanctioned the kind of shitstorm that Frank has stirred up. Nah, if we do get out of this, there's gonna be one helluva day of reckoning for Frank and whoever else he's roped in.'

He paused before continuing, 'By the way, those brave new world speeches you hear Angela make, she truly believes them – writes most of them herself. She's the real deal and is one of life's good ones. Right now, we just have to lie low until we get some kind of answer.'

'What could possibly go wrong,' Jack muttered aloud, as they all fell into a thoughtful silence.

Chapter 45

They had been surprised at just how quickly they had received their answer. It had come in a discreet call from Maria to Ed's cellphone. What was even more surprising had been the invitation to come that same afternoon to the very smart Country Golf Club and Equestrian Centre favoured by the President.

It was the weekend, so for her to make herself available so quickly didn't just impress Jack and Linda in relation to Ed's standing with her, but also made them wonder just what he had put in the letter other than what they had roughly agreed. In fact, the visit to the Club had already been on the President's schedule and was something of a regular ritual at weekends whenever she could spare the time. So things had fallen into place and wouldn't raise any questions with anyone in the same way as a special trip might have done.

Despite his hip problems, Ed could still drive and had brought them all to the Club as arranged in his very comfortable leather-seated C-Class Mercedes. At least this meant that the car Jack had hotwired could stay out of sight in Ed's carport.

They had travelled mostly in silence, with Jack and Linda casting nervous glances at the other traffic on the roads. Even the sound of a car's horn made them all jump and every traffic light seemed to take an eternity before finally changing to green.

Once they had parked in the deserted Club car park, they got out of the car and walked towards the Club House. It was a beautiful afternoon, with the sun casting long shadows so that the three of them walking abreast looked like a dramatic final gunslinger scene from a Western. This wasn't far from Jack's mind as he was thinking to himself it was the perfect place to be ambushed.

There was a gentle breeze, but still quite mild for the time of year. Birds flitted between the trees, but otherwise all was peace and calm. No echoes of ball on rackets came from the empty hardcore tennis courts to their right hand side and no horses could be seen in the large paddock or the adjoining stables where all the doors had been closed and barred. Someone had gone to great lengths to clear the entire place.

Apart from the odd birdsong, the silence was quite eery, accentuating the crunching noise of their shoes as they walked across the gravel leading towards the Club House.

Ed casually kicked a fir cone out of his path, making a loud scuffing noise with his shoe that drew an anxious look from Jack who also took the opportunity to break their silence. 'How do we know she'll come? This has got set-up written all over it.'

'Relax,' Ed returned with surprising calm, 'she's here. Place is empty, their cars will be discreetly out the back. And we wouldn't have made it this far from the car park if this was a set-up. Besides, haven't you noticed the guys on the roof who've been watching us all the way?'

Jack and Linda hadn't. Too intent on looking down and to their sides as if trying to make themselves as invisible as possible, they hadn't raised their eyes much above head level. But now they spotted the armed security detail on the Club House roof who weren't trying to keep out of sight.

But Linda also wanted some further reassurance from Ed. 'You still sure that call you took was genuine and we're not walking into some kind of trap?'

'I'm as sure as I can be,' Ed replied. 'Angela always uses a code word when she gets someone to call me, usually a name from The Wizard of Oz – childhood thing. Yeah, the message was genuine, but if you're asking if my guts are churning a little, you bet!'

'Amen to that,' Jack agreed, 'but why didn't the President just invite us to the White House?'

'Too conspicuous,' Ed replied, 'especially after everything I put in that letter. Plus she'll want some convincing even though I like to think she trusts my word.'

'Makes sense,' Linda agreed. 'Well, whatever happens, we'll handle it,' Jack added, rediscovering his fighting spirit.

Linda smiled at him proudly as they mounted the steps to the Club House entrance at the same time as the double doors abruptly swung open and three security personnel appeared. All dressed in black suits and, perhaps unnecessarily, all wearing aviator sunglasses, they looked unsmilingly at Ed, Jack and Linda as they reached the top of the steps.

One of the older security men who was clearly in charge and recognised Ed from his previous visits to the White House, nodded to him. 'Professor Bishop. Can I ask you all to stand over here and hold your arms out to the side.' It wasn't a question. As they did so, another member of the security team with a hand-held body scanner, moved it expertly over each of them in turn. Unlike airport scanners, this one was sophisticated enough to discount keys, coins and the like and was designed to find much more sinister items.

Ed felt the need to reassure them that they wouldn't give them any trouble, but this was met with a stony silence, as was Jack's question as to whether the President was there. This made them all a little more nervous.

'Right, follow me,' the head security man ordered. As they dutifully followed him, the two other security men fell in behind them. As they went through the Club House main doors and entered the large reception area, they became aware of more security officers standing with their hands lightly clasped in front of their bodies and ready for action should the need arise. They were led briskly towards doors to the side of the main reception desk, leaving little time to appreciate the beautiful teak wood interior with vaulted ceiling, plush leather sofas, generous well-stocked bar area and expensive art on the walls.

Ed, Jack and Linda all exchanged nervous glances, but were now resigned to whatever they would find on the other side of the doors that were about to be opened.

****

Bob Howard had joined Frank in his office and was taking a call from his attack team leader. Bob deliberately spoke so that Frank could follow the conversation, 'Copy that, so you're sure their car was seen in that area? And you're now keeping Professor Bishop's house under surveillance? OK, I understand, they're not there at the moment, but you'll be ready for when they return from wherever they've gone.'

Frank was nodding at Bob, appreciating the way he

was handling the call so that Frank was involved in the exchange. After Bob had hung up, he turned to Frank with clear relief in his voice. 'I reckon this is it. They were seen in the area and Professor Bishop is a long-standing friend of Linda Wilson. He's also extremely well connected to the media. It all adds up. Just hope we're not too late, but I've heard nothing from any of my media moles so we just need to act fast. All units are focused and ready to go.'

'Thank the Lord!' Frank responded with equal relief. 'At last, we've got them!'

Chapter 46

Having been guided through the side door of the reception area, Ed, Jack and Linda found themselves on a wide close-slatted dark wooden veranda set with tables and chairs. The pillared area was covered with a similar vaulted ceiling to the Club House and had beautiful open views looking down the fairway of the 18th hole of the golf course.

The fairway was tree-lined and immaculate on what was generally accepted to be one of the most picturesque golf courses in the whole county – a fact reflected in its hefty membership fees.

But the trio didn't have much time to appreciate it all as they immediately spotted the President and her aide Maria getting up from the table where they had been seated and walking towards them. Further security personnel were also stationed around the edges of the veranda, while Jack also briefly noticed a couple of others positioned on the fairway who were scanning the trees for any activity.

The President was smiling broadly at Ed as she approached them. She was dressed in a very smart dark navy trouser suit with heels that accentuated her height. Her posture was upright and confident, adding to the undoubted presence she had about her. Jack instantly understood why people talked about her charisma as it positively oozed out of her before she had even said a word.

The slightly smaller Maria was wearing a smart black dress and was colourfully accessorised with costume jewellery that gave away her Latino origins. Woe betide anyone who underestimated her fierce intelligence and total loyalty to the President whom she had worked with from back when she had been a State Governor.

As the President approached, she addressed Ed first, having first exchanged kisses with him on both cheeks. 'Good to see you, Ed – I think!'

Ed gave a low laugh, acknowledging the President's jocular hint at her concern as to what this was all about. 'You too, Angela,' he replied warmly.

She feigned mock indignation, 'How many times do I have to tell you, it's Madam President to you!'

This time they all laughed and could feel the tension ease. It was one of Angela Freeman's great skills to help people relax in her company, whether she was with another Head of State or talking to the ordinary working people who had voted for her in their millions.

'I take it you must be Jack and Linda,' she said shaking hands with them. 'I share your pain having this guy as your friend.'

They were both totally disarmed by her charm and pleasant, easy manner. 'Yes ma'am, it's a real honour to meet you' Linda said, while Jack added, 'Sure is, Madam President; and thank you so much for at least agreeing to give us this chance.'

The President flashed them each a winning smile and gestured to them join her and Maria at a table in the middle of the veranda that had already been set for them and had bottled water and a jug of fresh orange juice awaiting them. With a gentle wave of her hand, the security detail all withdrew to a discreet distance out of earshot, leaving the President and Maria alone with their guests.

A Club waiter quickly flitted between them all pouring water and juice for each before hastily withdrawing back inside.

Once it was just the five of them, the President addressed Ed in particular, 'Well, I can't deny this isn't all highly irregular, but your letter couldn't exactly be ignored.' She had adopted a far more serious tone, 'And some of what you wrote is highly disturbing to say the least.' She exchanged glances with Maria as if to confirm that she had fully briefed Maria on the contents of Ed's letter.

She continued, 'Right now I need to know a whole lot more about this matter of the utmost world importance you mentioned. Change the whole world you said. I know I can trust you Ed, and what you wrote has got me here, but it had better be good.'

Ed looked straight into her eyes and she could feel the same sincerity and integrity that had always made him one of her most trusted friends. 'Angela,' he began, 'I've known you for over fifty years. You have my absolute word as your lifelong friend that what we're about to tell you is a matter of the greatest world importance. You can trust me on this. This is big, massive, it will blow your mind.'

Both the President and Maria were now looking at Ed with rapt attention. The President nodded, confirming the mutual trust and admiration she and Ed shared for one another. He continued, 'Please just hear Jack and Linda out, Angela. I promise you this is beyond amazing.'

'Amazing is pretty good these days,' she replied, exchanging a knowing smile with Maria. 'OK, let's hear what you got.'

232

Jack and Linda shifted in their seats and then began to make the pitch of their lives, with Jack doing most of the talking while Linda chipped in supportively.

Watching the scene from the fairway, it appeared to the security detail as if the President was having a pleasant afternoon with friends. They could have no idea of the extraordinary chain of events that was being set in motion.

A surprisingly tame squirrel calmly ran past them and disappeared into the trees. The gentle breeze made the autumn leaves rustle a little, but otherwise all was tranquil and calm.

Chapter 47

There was certainly no peace and quiet outside Ed's house as the roar of a car driven at speed broke the suburban calm. The noise was augmented by the sound of the car stereo playing at full volume that made the beaten up old Mustang shake, rattle and roll as Jason steered it without slowing onto the slightly sloping drive at the front of Ed's house, only braking at the last moment.

With the driver's window half down, the symphonic heavy metal song *Wish I Had an Angel* by Nightwish echoed down the street, with Jason bellowing along to the provocative lyrics of the chorus. It was just as well that most residents were still indoors, or the cardiac ward would have been busier that day!

Jason switched off the ignition and the Mustang came to a reluctant throaty halt, but not before the exhaust had given a final noisy blow that suggested a service was well overdue. Jason was oblivious to it all.

As he opened the door to get out of his car, had anyone been passing they would have recoiled at the mess inside. The interior was strewn with all the fast food detritus of sandwich and chocolate bar wrappers, half empty soda bottles and burger cartons with the odd wisp of stale lettuce garnish still clinging forlornly to the sides like seaweed left behind on a sea wall after the tide had retreated. It was on Jason's list to give his car a good clean, but it had clearly been on his list for some weeks!

He slammed his car door shut as a gentle push wouldn't have succeeded and went to the front door to ring the bell. What he hadn't noticed, was that his every move was being watched by the occupants of a blacked out Jeep parked some hundred yards down the road. Or that another Jeep was discreetly parked a little further on beside an open area where it would attract less attention form the occupants of the houses.

Having got no answer to the doorbell, Jason hammered the door knocker loudly. After a few seconds, he walked to the side to peer through a window whilst trampling on a flower in the bed underneath. Seeing no obvious sign of life inside, he returned to his car whilst looking up at the sky as if to confirm it was a nice dry day. Opening the door, he took out a white bread sandwich bought from a gas station, a large half-finished pack of potato chips and one of the half-drunk bottles of soda lying on the floor in front of the passenger seat.

Leaving the car door open, he sauntered over to an area of the well cut grass in front of Ed's house and sat himself down to enjoy his snack while waiting for the others to return.

Bob Howard was once again in Frank Caspari's office when he took the call from his incredulous attack team leader. 'Yeah, we've had a positive I.D. It's come from a neighbour that a man and woman fitting their description were seen going inside the house. We were just setting up to enter, but there's a problem.'

'What d'ya mean – what problem?' Bob came back impatiently.

'There's some guy just turned up and he's military,' the team leader replied while one of his team was using a scope to get a better look at Jason and try to identify anything from his uniform that would give them a better fix on where he was from.

'Shit!' Bob exclaimed. 'what's he doing there?'

The team leader knew his answer wasn't going to be received too kindly. 'Well, er…he's sitting on the front lawn having a picnic.'

'He's what?' Bob exploded. 'Hold on…' he turned to Frank whilst cupping his mouthpiece with his hand, 'You're not gonna believe this…they've found where they've been holed up, but some military guy has just turned up and decided to have a bloody picnic in full view on the front lawn!'

'What the fuck!' Frank couldn't quite believe what he was hearing. 'We can't involve him, just leaves too many ends to tie up, plus he's in plain sight of anyone passing. Get them to I.D. him, but you'll have to stand them down for now.'

Bob nodded, having already come to the same conclusion. He took his hand away from the mouthpiece to speak to the team leader again. 'OK, roger that, stand down for now, but keep watching. I.D. him and let me know the minute that bozo disappears.'

'Affirmative,' the team leader responded, ending the call. But Jason was savouring every mouthful of his picnic and wasn't planning on going anywhere anytime soon.

He didn't have to. Three black Audis suddenly arrived at speed and parked up near both Jeeps. Everyone inside the Jeeps instinctively unlocked their weapons in case this could be a threat.

It was only now that Jason first noticed the various vehicles parked at different points down the road from Ed's house, but, unperturbed, he continued to tuck into his snacks. It was only as the drama began to unfold that he became slightly more intrigued as to what might be going on.

A sharply dressed man in a dark suit and in his forties with tightly cropped hair, got out of one of the Audis and was soon flanked by two others. Although all were armed, their pistols were still hidden beneath their jackets in their straps.

It was clear that the suited man knew exactly who he wanted to speak to. The three approached the Jeep with the attack team leader in it and approached the passenger side where he was sitting with his weapon cocked just out of sight below window level, but pointing in their direction. He lowered the window to find out who the hell these people were and why they were approaching an undercover team in such a brazen fashion.

From Jason's viewpoint, it seemed that a very animated conversation was taking place between the two men, although they were too far away for him to hear anything. He could see the man in the suit showing whoever it was in the Jeep what looked like a badge and some kind of I.D. which clearly impressed the team leader. The latter seemed to be nodding his head a lot but also gesticulating with his hands in the way people do when they've just been told something completely contradictory to everything that had gone before.

Jason couldn't make it out from that distance, but the man was now clearly resigned to whatever he had just been told, had wound down his window fully and was resting one elbow on the door in a relaxed way. Whoever was in the Audis had clearly just pulled rank in a really big way.

The team leader had reached for his comms piece. Had Jason been in earshot, he would have heard him say into it, 'All units stand down and return to base. I say again, all units stand down. Acknowledge, out.'

Jason watched intrigued but not too fussed as both Jeeps turned in the road and headed off, followed in turn by two of the Audis. The remaining Audi parked up where the Jeep nearest to Ed's house had been, switched off the ignition and stayed put. Jason hadn't put two and two together yet, otherwise he might have guessed that the occupants were now keeping Ed's house under close observation.

Jason shrugged and took a big swig from his soda. *Not a bad way to spend an afternoon*, he thought to himself.

Chapter 48

It wasn't much later before another black Audi car pulled up, but this time right outside Ed's house. It was immediately followed by Ed's car carrying Jack, Linda and the head of the security detail, special agent Mike Spencer, who had shadowed them at the Club House.

Jason hurried over to greet them, leaving a small pile of rubbish on Ed's perfectly manicured front lawn. They were all delighted to see Jason had made it back and hearing that he had brought the spare valves with him. But seeing Ed looking disapprovingly over his shoulder, Jason hurried back, quickly picked up all his rubbish, opened his car door and threw it all into the passenger well whilst retrieving the box of spare valves.

Little did he know that just his presence at Ed's house had saved the back-up Revelation from being destroyed. He truly was a hero, but knew nothing about it.

Ed opened the door to his house and they all entered, followed by Agent Spencer who had accompanied them in their car, together with two more security men who had by now joined them from the other Audi parked nearby.

Mike Spencer clearly had some authority as he ordered the other two to make a search of the property just in case of anyone else having gained entry whilst they had been away. He addressed Jack, 'OK, as soon as my team have done a quick check, we'll leave you to it. But my orders are to get you back to the White House as quickly as possible.' 'Sure thing,' Jack replied, 'we shouldn't be too long here.'

Agent Spencer turned to Jason, 'Can you show me some details so I can get clearance for you too?'

Jason put the box of valves down by his feet and started to rummage among the many pockets in his uniform to find some I.D. As he did so, he started handing the special agent whatever was coming out of the pockets in his search, including candy wrappers, crumpled receipts and various notes to himself as memory joggers. Mike Spencer was not in the slightest impressed at being used as a human shelf but said nothing. Eventually Jason produced his I.D. from the Military Academy which seemed to satisfy the man. After taking a photo of it with his cellphone, Agent Spencer gladly handed all the rubbish back to Jason who put each item in different pockets as if they each had a place.

Ed, Jack and Linda had been watching all this in bemused silence, as the other members of the security detail returned from their brief search of the house and nodded to their leader.

This time Mike Spencer addressed Ed. 'OK, we'll wait outside and then escort you.'

'Thank you, sir,' Ed replied.

As the security team started to leave the house, Jason saluted them, but it was not returned. He was unphased as he was far more excited at the realisation that he would be going to the White House. 'Hey, did someone say we're going to the White House? Somebody pinch me,' he blurted to no-one in particular.

'Are those the valves?' Jack asked, pointing to the box Jason was carrying, adding, 'sorry though, I'm not sure we can take you with us.'

'Aw go on, what harm can he do?' Linda asked Jack playfully.

'Plenty,' he replied half-caustically but also with genuine warmth towards Jason.

Jason handed Jack the box of valves with misplaced pride, 'There you go, buddy, six brand spanking new valves at your service.'

Jack opened the box only to find it was half empty – something Jason had only just noticed himself as he too peered inside, 'OK, three, but that's still OK right?' he looked at Jack like a kid at school seeking their teacher's approval.

'How fortunate you checked before setting off,' Jack observed sarcastically, although it was completely lost on Jason.

Ed was walking over to his desk, 'I'll just get the garage key – Linda, you OK to stay and entertain Jason?'

'Reckon that's more likely to be the other way round,' she quipped, 'anyway Jason may need to be with Jack with those spares.'

But Jason was lost in his own world and muttering aloud, 'The White House, that's quite something, man, wonder if we'll bump into Laura Freeman whilst we're there!'

The thought of meeting one of the President's beautiful daughters had clearly energised him. He licked his fingers and started to push back his hair into some kind of unkempt shape. 'Say Ed, can I use the washroom?'

'Sure, it's down there,' he replied. All three watched Jason disappear, Linda shaking her head but with a big smile on her face.

A few minutes later, Ed steered Jason into the garage

where Jack was already tinkering with the Revelation back-up device. Jason stopped dead in his tracks at his first sight of it and stared at it in amazement. It wasn't so much that it was impressive to look at – although its crystals certainly gave it an out-of-space feel – but more how quirky it was and unlike anything else he had ever seen.

'Wow man, what the hell is that?' he exclaimed before jumping again to his own conclusion. 'Oh I get it, this is some kind of space wars programme yeah?'

'Right now it's nothing,' Jack muttered, 'unless these new valves work. Don't quite look like the last ones which worries me a bit. Let's see…' He had taken one of the new valves from the box and began trying to fit it where the previous valve had been. But no matter which way he turned it, the new valve didn't seem to fit. 'Shit, I don't believe it!' he said angrily. 'These are new, right?'

'Newer than new, my friend,' Jason replied in such a relaxed way that it actually annoyed Jack even more.

'Well they don't seem to fit,' Jack retorted with mounting frustration. 'This is a fucking disaster.'

Jason remained calm and relaxed and spoke to Jack in the matter-of-fact way a car mechanic would in replacing a spark plug, 'New valves, new specs, new contacts. These are the new multi-use valves – we use them on practically everything. With these new babies – you see the longer stem, well you have to push down and twist first – releases a spring in them and supposedly makes them a tighter fit. Was on the updated instructions.'

'Which weren't in the box,' Jack chided, although also hopeful that all was now not lost.

'Sorry,' Jason apologised sheepishly.

Jack did as Jason had instructed with the new valve

and switched on Revelation. To his immense relief and delight, it began to warm up and everything was clearly working perfectly. He couldn't help but let out an elated cry as he switched it off again. 'Thank God! Jason you son-of-a-bitch, you've saved the day, my friend!'

Jason beamed and the two embraced.

'So what the hell does it do?' Jason asked. They both sat down on the garage's concrete floor whilst Jack explained everything, including about Marty. Jason sat open-mouthed in complete astonishment followed by huge respect for his friend. He kept shaking his head partly in disbelief and partly at the sheer magnitude of what he was hearing.

When Jack told him that the reason for going back to the White House was to give the President a demonstration of Revelation, Jason was literally speechless with excitement and with the dawning realisation of quite what was at stake here.

As Jack also told him about certain people who would stop at nothing to destroy his invention, Jason began to put two and two together about the Jeeps he had seen and the security team who had come to the house. But he wasn't frightened. Instead, he put his arm around Jack and said, 'Fear not, my secret laboratorian friend, they've now got me to deal with too.'

Jack just looked at him and smiled.

Chapter 49

The President very rarely found herself alone in the Oval Office, but she had asked for complete privacy whilst she made a couple of extremely confidential phone calls.

She had given the security on the doors strict instructions that only Maria was to be allowed in for the moment and it was indeed Maria who had now entered.

'Madam President, they're here and they're just setting up in the Ballroom as agreed. We've also got extra security on the doors for when we go in.'

'Excellent, thank you Maria,' the President answered warmly as she closed down her laptop computer and put it in a drawer. She was in one of the safest locations in the country, but was in the habit of always clearing her desk. 'We'll go together. That is of course unless you'd rather not. After all, if this thing really works, you can imagine the kind of things that might happen.'

'No way, count me in!' Maria quickly retorted. 'Did you hear that Barbara said she thought she saw Lincoln again in the East Wing just recently?'

'Hadn't heard, no,' the President replied, 'but there's a whole load of people who've made the same claim over the years – and I include past Presidents in that.'

Maria nodded, 'Yeah, Barbara's not one to exaggerate

– don't think she normally even believes in these kinds of things, so for her to say that is quite something. Did you know that Lincoln had vivid dreams of being assassinated three nights in a row before going to the theatre?'

'Yeah, think I may have read that somewhere. Say Maria, you're sure up for this aren't you! What was it Shakespeare wrote – there are more things in heaven and earth, Horatio, than are dreamed of in your philosophy.'

'Very good, Madam President,' Maria complimented her.

The President laughed. 'Guess most of us are too damned busy these days with our everyday lives to give these things too much thought.'

'So true,' Maria agreed as they both made their way out of the Oval Office.

****

The various people who needed to be told thought nothing strange about the official explanations they were being given, especially as they came from the President's inner circle. And they certainly would have no obvious reason to link the four people in question together.

Reverend Walter Cunningham was apparently on compassionate leave, although no-one knew exactly which of his relatives had passed away. General Sam Collins was reportedly on a flying tour of some of the USA's military bases in the Far East, although again no-one could be too specific about which bases he was visiting, and anyway that would be classified information.

Bob Howard was supposedly in Finland personally supervising the defection of one of the highest ranking operatives in Russia's Foreign Intelligence Service (the SVR), whom people were told Bob had groomed himself from way back when he had been a field officer. Naturally no-one could provide any details as to whether Bob was staying at the U.S. Embassy in Helsinki or in a secret safe house somewhere. And no-one could say when he might be back.

Meanwhile Frank Caspari had allegedly been called to New York on a family emergency concerning what was being termed a life-and-death matter with one of his sisters. Knowing that Frank's family ran an Italian restaurant in an area of New York with a certain reputation, no-one was inclined to ask any deeper questions.

Of course, the actual whereabouts of all four were unknown – for now.

Chapter 50

As the President and Maria entered the White House ballroom, the security detail outside closed the doors and stood guard. Others were already standing guard outside the other doors to the ballroom with the somewhat perplexing instructions not to disturb those inside no matter what they might hear.

On the way there, the President and Maria had confided in each other that they were a little nervous. Maria had admitted that she had once been to see a Tarot card reader many years ago who had also claimed to give her messages from her dead grandma, but that was the closest she had ever got to anything like this.

Not quite sure what to expect, the sight of the Revelation device sitting on a low table in the middle of the room was quite a surprise and very impressive in a very unexpected way. Later they would both admit that it was smaller than they might have thought and definitely didn't look like any contraption they had seen before.

The different coloured crystals that were literally at its heart were visible and certainly gave it a distinctive look. But so too did the various strange looking interlocking pieces that resembled nothing recognisable, yet had some similarities to telescopic camera lenses, digital recording equipment and no doubt the kind of apparatus that would not look out of place in a NASA laboratory. Yet they were none of those too.

The heavy gold-coloured curtains had all been drawn across the room's symmetrical deep windows. The magnificent chandeliers had been switched off, with the only light coming from the dimmed wall lights to one side of the room, giving only a subdued light in the main large space. Two huge ornate but by no means garishly designed rugs covered a large central part of the highly polished wood floor. The only furniture in the room was the central table on which Revelation had been placed together with a horseshoe of traditional mahogany Queen Anne chairs with cream upholstered seats.

Jack, Linda and Ed were waiting to greet the President and Maria, while Jason was busy saluting a large oil painting of George Washington that was hanging on the wall opposite to where the others had entered.

The President greeted them all with a warm smile, 'Lucky I know you so well Ed, or I'd have you locked up in a madhouse – still might!' Everyone laughed as she continued, 'And thanks in advance for the sleepless nights I'm gonna have thinking out all the implications – always assuming your thing does what you say it does. Hope you won't mind me saying, but it looks kinda weird.'

'No denying that,' Jack readily agreed.

At this point Jason had joined them and stammered, 'Mrs President, it's an absolute honour…' But she cut him off with a disarming smile and big wave of the hand.

'It doesn't matter where you choose to sit, so shall we get started?' Jack asked, trying desperately to hide his own nerves. This demonstration had to succeed, otherwise it would have all been for nothing. His stomach was in knots,

248

his mouth dry and he even noticed his hands were shaking a little. No-one else had noticed.

Everyone apart from Jack sat down, while he stood beside Revelation. The President glanced across at him. 'Can't deny I'm a little apprehensive about all this, but if what you've told me is true, this is history in the making. So, let's see what you got.'

Linda had sat herself down in a chair next to Revelation. She reached out and squeezed Jack's hand. 'Jack, this is for Marty.'

'I know,' he replied, giving her a loving look, 'just wish he was here.'

'Maybe he is,' she answered encouragingly. 'Go for it Galileo!'

Jack turned and adjusted some dials. Powered entirely by itself with no need for electricity or any other external fuel, Revelation's crystals began to glow and the whole device seemed to be bathed in a bright glowing white light, tinged with the most stunningly vivid colours of the rainbow. There was no sound, but the soft light slowly seemed to filter out and fill the entire room, like the early morning mist on a secluded, tree-shaded lake.

To those seated in the ballroom it seemed as if all substance, including the walls, floor and ceiling, had become a gently vibrating sea of vibrant shimmering colours. But no-one found it disturbing. On the contrary, the sheer beauty of it combined with feelings of complete peace and harmony, made everyone relax into the moment. They were still aware of being seated on solid chairs and there was enough of their recognisable surroundings still visible to make them accept that they hadn't slipped into some parallel dimension, however much the somewhat altered state of reality might suggest such a possibility.

There were one or two gasps at the sight of the first spirit being who seemed to float into view, as if hovering in some way just above floor height but still walking with the same actions as a 'living' person. It was in such a natural way that it didn't seem strange at all. Both the President and Maria had clasped their hands to their mouths in the way people do when shocked or surprised. They were wide-eyed in complete astonishment.

More spirit beings had come into view and it was as if some had passed through the walls of the room, with the solid substance having no effect on them. All appeared to look as they must have done in their prime during their earthly lives. And all had the most benign, peaceful and loving look on their faces.

Although clearly distinguishable as human forms, they did not look as solid as the people seated in the room and had an almost transparent shimmering appearance that seemed to pulsate in rhythmic harmony with the gently vibrating sea of colours all around them. It was as if everything was as one. Although they appeared clothed, it would have been hard to describe exactly what that clothing was as it was indeterminate in the softly pulsing light. It gave more of a sense of colour and shape, but very much similar to the style of clothing they would have worn in their prime years.

By now it was clear that there were spirit beings in the room who were known individually to all those present. The softest voices could be heard conversing with each person, smiling at them and making them feel totally loved and reassured. Inevitably, tears of joy were freely shed by the President and Maria, for whom this was their first experience of Revelation. Jason too was completely staggered and open-mouthed as he clasped his hands to his head in disbelief and pure emotion as he quietly talked to a military best friend he had lost in combat in Iraq.

It all seemed so natural – and indeed it was, just as Ed had spoken with Linda about in his garden. Only he too was sobbing gently to be reunited again with his beloved wife Susan.

Linda's mother and two of her grandparents were reminding her of some childhood memories and telling her they would always walk beside her through the rest of her earthly journey before she too was ready to join them. She determined that she would never fear death again.

The President's face was heavily tear-stained, but she was also laughing at the spirit lady who was reminding her about how she had put on heart-shaped earrings that morning and then had second thoughts and changed them to the more subtle gold hoops she now wore. The lady was reassuring the President that they would never come to intrude, but that they would always be there for her and walk beside her whenever she wanted them to.

The lady had gently said how very proud they were of her, calling her by her childhood nickname, Chi-chi. The President had begun to cry freely at hearing her nickname, known only to a very few, and reached in her pocket for a handkerchief she had brought along with great foresight.

For Maria, probably the only one present who had any particularly strong religious beliefs, the whole experience shook her to her core. This was what she had always liked to think heaven might be like, only this was reality right here, right now. A man with the kindliest face was telling her about all the people she knew who were now with him 'on the other side' and how simple and easy their passing over had been.

He was reminding her of some childhood memories that no-one else could have possibly known. Maria sat in dumbstruck silence, tears freely flowing, but also with a huge smile on her face.

Meanwhile Jack had taken it upon himself to walk behind them all to check if they were alright, whilst also keeping an eye on Revelation. He allowed himself a moment of pride that the device was working perfectly. If only Marty had been there to see the President experiencing their invention.

With huge exchanges of love, the spirits each began to fade and retire from sight, although two or three spirit beings were still visible – mostly people who had worked at the White House and had remained close to its energetic vibration. These were sometimes seen as so-called 'ghosts' by living people, often in the early hours when everything in the building was a little more still and peaceful.

Jack had left Revelation still running when, having given them quite a few minutes to compose themselves, everyone said goodbye to the President and Maria as the two of them prepared to leave the room. Like everyone else, they had clearly been profoundly affected by their experience and they knew their lives had changed forever. The President was already trying to clear her head and think beyond. She thanked Jack and tried to find the words to compliment him on making the greatest discovery in scientific history, but for once the words didn't come as naturally as she would have liked. Maria stood by her side simply looking at Jack with complete wonder.

The President told Ed she needed to think it all through and that she would very shortly be back in touch. They embraced warmly, before she and Maria then left the room, the door closing behind them.

A sense of calm amazement was shared by everyone in the room. It was Jack who broke the silence. 'Well, that was something else, even if I do say so myself. Everyone OK?'

Nobody spoke but just nodded, still too wrapped up in their thoughts at what had just happened. Jason looked at Jack with complete hero worship.

Jack continued, 'Well, I guess I'd better close this thing down.' Ed and Jason exchanged glances and shook their heads at each other as if in silent agreement that there was no need for words. Linda was now standing to the side of Revelation and was looking down the length of the ballroom as Jack bent down, ready to turn off all the dials. He couldn't see from his position, but Linda's face had suddenly frozen; her mouth dropped open in total astonishment.

Her face then broke into the broadest of smiles as tears filled her eyes. 'Jack!' she cried out with breathless elation. 'Jack!'

Hearing the sudden excitement in her voice, Jack stopped himself from switching off Revelation and slowly raised himself up, then turned to follow the direction of Linda's gaze. There, standing in front of them, were the spirits of Marty and Jenny. They were smiling at Jack and Linda and exuded pure love. Marty spoke quietly: 'Well done, Jack, my wonderful friend, well done!'

Chapter 51

When Ed took the call the next day, he might have been more excited. After all, his friend the President of the United States had just told him that she had given everything a lot of thought and would be making a special statement in her next weekly address to the nation. This was set for tomorrow.

However, whether he was imagining it or not due to his own anxiety, he felt there had been a certain ambiguity in her tone. Her reassurance that Frank Caspari and his co-conspirators had all been taken care of didn't sound too convincing either, but he didn't want to probe too far.

So he triumphantly announced the news to the others, holding back any doubts he may have had. No, Angela was the real deal he kept telling himself, everything was going to be fine.

Deprived of their cellphones and not yet having had time to replace them, Jack and Linda had made use of Ed's laptop computer to catch up on their emails. Jack was delighted to find one from his aunt in England but somewhat bemused as to why she was making such forthright and seemingly concerned enquiries about his health and wellbeing. He had written back a loving reply saying everything was good and that he would call her later in the week as he was expecting some very big, exciting news to do with his work. He also replied to a couple of cheeky emails from Jermaine and Alexis – boy, were they soon in for the shock of their lives when they found out what their boss had been up to!

Linda had also taken a turn on the computer to reassure her students that all was well and that she would soon be back at college. Privately, she knew her destiny had changed forever and that she may never be able to go back to her previous life in quite the same way.

Following Ed's announcement that the President was going to make a special statement in her address to the nation, Jack had phoned Marty's mother, Martha, to tell her to watch the address, although he said he couldn't say any more for now. But yes, he and Linda were fine.

Martha had taken the call just as she was putting down some food for her cat. As if on cue, Woodstock came bounding through the catflap in the front door and started tucking in happily to his bowl of food.

'Woodstock, now where you been?' Martha asked her cat lovingly. Like so many people who live on their own, she was given to talking with her pet. 'That lovely man Jack, you know, Marty's friend, he just called me; told me to watch the President's address. Said it might be interesting and, if it was, that he and Linda would call me afterwards. I didn't like to ask too much, but he said it was to do with that thing he worked on with Marty. You remember my beautiful Marty, don't you, Woodstock? You always used to keep him company when he was working on that crazy contraption downstairs.'

She went to the window and looked out, noticing how the leaves on the trees had mostly all turned now. Guess it would just be another ordinary day in another ordinary week. She couldn't have been more wrong.

Chapter 52

Everyone in Ed's house was trying to relieve the tension as best they could. Jason was probably the most relaxed, engrossed in playing a mind-numbing game on his handheld games console. Jack couldn't help himself and was pacing nervously around like a caged tiger. Ed was in his favourite armchair, while Linda sat near him on one of the sofas.

Jack walked over to the front window for what seemed to the others like the hundredth time. He took another look at the black Audi parked a little down the road. It was unobtrusive enough not to draw much attention from the neighbours, although anyone walking past might have found it strange why a smartly dressed man and woman would have parked up there just to read the paper.

What no-one noticed, including Jack, were the four innocuous looking pedestrians who were walking past at regular intervals. One middle-aged, rather plump and ordinary-looking lady carried shopping bags, followed a while later by a younger woman who jogged past in her dark navy tracksuit while she supposedly kept checking her time and distance on her wrist piece. An elderly man in a raincoat looked as if he was enjoying an unhurried autumnal walk, while later on, a much younger man sauntered past carrying a sports bag and tennis racket as if on his way to a club. None would have merited a second glance, yet all were armed and on the same payroll.

Jack spoke as he continued to keep the car in view, 'Well, there's at least two of them in that car. Guess they're here to keep us in more than to keep others out.'

Ed and Linda smiled at him, accepting the probable truth of what he was saying. Linda got up and walked over to him, gently stroking his back to try and calm his nerves. He put his arm around her waist and they kissed.

Ed was in a reflective mood. 'Safe houses I have known. Mark you, never thought my own home would become one!'

Without breaking off from playing his game, Jason's ears pricked up at hearing this as it simply confirmed in his mind what he already believed about Ed. 'So you've done covert work before then, like my secretive laboratorian friend over there?' he probed.

Ed tried to make light of it, although he enjoyed teasing Jason. 'Oh a bit of this, bit of that. Guess the spooks saw me being a Science Editor as a handy cover. Once helped a professor from Kiev to… actually, best not say, think that's still classified.'

Jason was delighted to have his suspicions fully confirmed, or so he thought.

There was a pause as they all continued to be lost in their thoughts. Linda had returned to perch on the arm of the sofa near Ed and asked him plaintively, 'Do you think she'll do it?'

Ed glanced across at her and decided to be perfectly honest, 'You mean say something in her address to the nation? After the demonstration I was sure. Now? I just dunno.'

This didn't help calm Jack and Linda's nerves. If Jason heard what Ed had said, he didn't show any reaction as he was too busy trying to achieve level four on his game.

They could rely on Jack to see the downside. 'What if they're now seeing things Frank's way or whatever. Let's face it, this whole thing could just as easily go the other way. And I mean it's the Presidential address, that's big.'

'So's what you've done with Revelation, Jack,' Ed countered. 'I'll level with you, reckon it'll come down to who Angela shares it with and what influence they have over her.'

'Do many people get to see what's in the Presidential address?' Linda asked.

'More than a few would be my guess,' Ed replied, 'but hey, Angela's a strong woman – more than that, she knows her own mind. Can be stubborn as a mule too if she thinks she has right on her side. She's bound to confide in the First Gentleman, her husband, for sure and he's got a wise old head on him. Then she'll have her most trusted inner circle. She'll also know that her address to the nation is the only real option to breaking something of this magnitude. But look, I'm only guessing, who knows, we can only hope.'

Jack nodded, 'Well, I'm not sure what the hell I'd say and I helped build the damn thing!' Linda joined in, 'Wonder how she'll do it – if she does.'

Jack addressed the room, 'Well, mark my words, if she gets to the God bless America bit and still hasn't said anything, we're toast. Maybe that's the whole reason they've got us holed up in here.'

'Let's stay optimistic,' Ed chimed in, while secretly sharing many of Jack's fears.

Surprisingly Jason came to life to lighten the mood by cracking what he thought was a great joke, 'It's OK Captain

Smith, it was only an iceberg.'

Ed enjoyed the Titanic reference. He had warmed to Jason immensely and knew a good heart when he met one. He smiled at him while shaking his head at the jokey riposte, but Jason had already immersed himself back in his game. Level four was surely there for the taking now.

Jack resumed his theme, 'Well all I'm saying is if we get to God bless America and still nothing, we're finished.'

****

Flanked on both sides by a security detail, the President and Maria walked along the White House corridors towards the Oval Office. Both were deep in thought, with the President glancing across at Maria a couple of times. Even the strongest sometimes need a little reassurance. Maria smiled back confidently, which was exactly what was needed.

They were greeted by people as they passed them in the corridors, but the President was too focused to give them much more than a quick smile.

Inside the Oval Office, the TV cameras were already set up with the usual security-cleared crew in attendance. As the President entered the room she acknowledged them all and smiled at the director. As she sat down behind her desk, her favourite hair and make-up assistant immediately moved in to give her the lightest of touches just to ensure she looked as soft and natural as possible.

Her team had given the director her speech just 15 minutes beforehand and this had hastily been added to the autocue. But there was no mention of Revelation.

Chapter 53

The large television was turned up loud in Ed's sitting room area while he, Jack, Linda and Jason all watched in rapt attention as the President made her address to the nation.

There had been no special trailers for it, other than the usual ones, and no hint that there would be anything of particular note in it to encourage people to watch. In fact, so far the speech had been nothing out of the ordinary and mainly just updates on some new environmental programmes, as well as the latest progress on foreign policy initiatives.

Jack stood up and began pacing around in his usual manner when anxious. The President had been talking for a while and he felt that time was running out.

He addressed the room with helpless resignation, 'That's it, she's not going to do it is she. It's nearly over – and we're toast.'

Ed tried to calm him down, 'Yeah, but it isn't over 'til it's over, let's hang fire here.'

'Appreciate your optimism Ed, but…' Jack countered but was cut off by Linda, 'Quiet Jack, let me hear.'

But he had made up his mind. 'What's to hear? You can tell she's beginning to wind up already!'

However, he dutifully sat back down with the others,

as all four sat forward in hopeful hunched anticipation of something, anything.

The President was continuing on her themes, 'These are some of the most pressing challenges we face today. But we will prevail. Thank you. And God bless…'

'Shit!' The collective unrestrained exclamation came from all four of them as they reacted in horror and disappointment to what they believed to be the President's usual wrapping up statement of God bless America.

Only the President hadn't finished. Not by a long way. She continued, '… all those who are working so selflessly towards making this happen.'

The President paused to collect her thoughts. The main camera in front of her had now zoomed in so that just her head and shoulders filled the screen. She looked intently into the camera lens and began to speak in a very measured, sincere and friendly manner, 'My friends and compatriots, people of America, people of the world. There is one more thing of the most extraordinary importance that I need to share with you…'

There are moments in everyone's life when you hear something so incredible, so staggering, so beyond anything imaginable that you can only meet it with a shocked silence. Time and motion seem to stand still while the brain races to process the information before any reaction can follow.

As the President confidently continued to make the most mind-blowing statement the world had ever heard about the scientific proof of the reality of life after death, people would later share with each other where they had been and what they were doing at the time and how they reacted. Some wondered at first if it had been some kind of a joke, many just shook their heads in disbelief and wonder, while others danced with joy once the initial shock had subsumed. Some were even not surprised and welcomed the proof about something they had always accepted to be true.

Jack, Linda, Ed and Jason exploded almost as one from their seats, leaping into the air and shrieking with unbridled elation. They all hugged each other while the tears and laughter flowed. Jason began doing a weird jig, whirling his arms in the air, while Ed clapped rhythmically as if keeping time to some unheard music to accompany him. Jack and Linda embraced tightly, looking deep into each other's tear-stained eyes. No words were necessary before they kissed passionately and continued to hold each other close.

Dressed in a rainbow-coloured kaftan, Martha was hugging Woodstock, crying and saying the name of her son Marty out loud over and over again. Maria Gonzales, the clairvoyant Jack had briefly met, was allowing herself a told you so moment, while the SAGB in London had needed to lock its doors due to the number of excited people trying to get in. Jermaine and Alexis just stared in complete shock at the small TV in their apartment – hadn't they just heard Jack and Marty's names mentioned by the President of the United States whilst she had made the most staggering statement possible? And Jackson and Nettye helped the news spread like wildfire around Linda's college that she had somehow been involved in all this. Over the next few days, all would have to come to terms with the fact that they personally knew the very people involved in the greatest discovery yet made in the history of humankind.

Apart from the few million in America and around the world who had actually seen the President's address as it went out, it took a few hours for the news to filter throughout the world.

But all news channels and most TV and radio stations had cleared their schedules to focus solely on the announcement about Revelation. The internet and digital media had gone into virtual meltdown, while newspapers began to write their entire issues around Revelation.

Although the White House press secretary was being bombarded with calls from around the world, thankfully the identity of Revelation's creators and its whereabouts were being withheld for the moment for security reasons. So it would be some days before news teams began to camp out in front of Ed's house. Thankfully by then, Revelation had been moved to a secure, secret location.

In advance of her address, the President had in fact authorised brief highly confidential messages to be sent to a number of world leaders, informing them that there would be some big news of world importance in her address. Normally subordinates of these leaders would be tasked with watching the address to spot any particular items of interest for their country that might need immediate attention. But this time Presidents, Prime Ministers, Chancellors and more had sat in their private offices in stunned silence as they listened to the announcement that would mean the world would never be the same again.

Most people heard the news in their homes, in pubs and bars, on their car radios or on their cellphones. As the announcement rapidly began to filter around the world, the effect was beginning to show. The President had asked for calm and a period of quiet reflection while the enormity of Revelation could sink in. But inevitably there were some immediate consequences. There was indeed a spike in suicides, although interestingly this was more marked in the more affluent Western countries.

A number of religious leaders expressed outrage and trotted out their standard accusations of dabbling with the occult, inviting in the devil, or whatever other fears they could strike into people's hearts, much as they had done throughout the centuries. But more enlightened religious leaders took a more measured approach and tried to find ways to shoehorn Revelation's discovery into their individual philosophies.

However, as the days went by and further announcements were made from the White House, it was clear that a profound change in mindset was taking place around the world across the entire political, religious, spiritual and material spectrum.

A homeless man camped opposite an electrical shop wondered why the empty paper coffee cup he placed on the sidewalk in front of him kept filling up with coins in no time at all from passers-by who also stopped to wish him well. It was all a puzzle to him. He had watched with curiosity at the large TV in the electrical shop's front window.

Over the next few days, the man watched in wonder as he saw on the screen what looked like tribal fighters shaking hands with U.S. military men and both sides laying down their arms in huge piles. He saw world leaders signing and exchanging new treaties with each other, rough-looking leather-clad bikers relaxing by their bikes and enjoying a joke with police officers who obviously had little else to do, Buddhist monks chatting on the sidewalk with business executives and many more scenes of friendship and togetherness. He had also noticed that he was seldom now disturbed during the night by endless police sirens.

The television was permanently set to a major news channel and the man began to understand that something very big must have happened in the world as he read the tickertape announcements that were running across the bottom of the screen:

>>> *Crime rates plummet in all major world cities* >>> *Timetable for unilateral nuclear disarmament to be agreed* >>> *Regional centres for the even distribution of food to be set up* >>> *New global currency to be announced* >>> *United Nations to be reformed* >>>

The man watched transfixed as reports seemed to be coming in from all corners of the globe. In one scene a camera crew had managed to film a beautiful black Jaguar cat watching from the edge of a clearing in the rainforest as tree fellers all dumped their chainsaws as junk in a skip before making their way onto a bus to leave the area. It was as if the magnificent animal knew it would be getting back its natural habitat.

What the homeless man didn't see were the four people who had once held very high office who were now locked away in a secret top security location before the time would be right to bring them to trial. And he didn't see the man boarding a secret private jet to fly back from the Middle East with the Scorpion container once more on his lap on its way back to the States where it would be safely destroyed. Nor did he know anything about Jack supervising the construction of further Revelation devices at a top secret location where, at Jack's insistence, the Site Manager was a certain Jason Thomas. Global locations for demonstrations of Revelation were already being arranged.

It was a few weeks later when the homeless man had sat back on the sidewalk for what may have been the last time. The previous day, a very kind man and woman had approached him to tell him a place was being prepared for him nearby that he would be able to call his home. They would take him there tomorrow by which time it would be stocked with food, he would be given a regular income and they would explain everything to him.

The man wondered if his new home would have a television as he glanced at the tickertape news on the screen opposite again

>>> *Suicide helplines report significant decrease after initial peak* >>> *A new Worldwide Institute for Psychic Research has been announced* >>> *All Native American tribal rights to be fully recognised* >>>

Later he watched as a man and woman, clearly very much in love with each other, were shown smiling broadly while being interviewed. He couldn't hear what Jack and Linda were saying, but there were people around them clapping and cheering. The tickertape news kept running on a continuous feed on the one lead story

>>> *Jack Taylor and Marty Robinson (posthumously) are jointly awarded the Nobel Peace Prize. Jack's wife Linda has announced they are expecting their first child* >>>

The man looked on with tears in his eyes as all he could see was scene after scene of the birth of a new world where people were happy, smiling, embracing one another and exuding pure joy. Everything he could see was an expression of peace, toleration, love, goodwill and happiness.

--- The End ---

From the author

The footsteps always started in the very early hours of the morning. They began in the attic room at the top of our house. They would then come down the bare wooden staircase and walk along the corridor leading to our bedrooms. The footsteps were unmistakably human and perfectly normal, just as if you or I were walking along the same landing. But everyone in the house was asleep in their rooms, so who could it possibly be?

Aged just six at the time, I didn't understand why the footsteps would carry on past my parents' bedroom and past my younger brother's bedroom until entering my room and standing by my bed. Why me? I was completely terrified. But so began my early realisation that, to paraphrase Shakespeare, there are more things in heaven and earth than are dreamt of in conventional philosophy! The 'ghost' was a young teenage seamstress who would have occupied the attic room but was believed to have passed in the house many years before.

As I grew up, I embarked on a questioning journey that saw me get a degree in Philosophy and take a keen interest in the struggle between religious teachings and scientific developments. I sat in circle at the Spiritualist Association of Great Britain (SAGB) in London and developed as a spiritual medium while pursuing a busy career in advertising. But I don't like to call myself a spiritualist as such, as I believe labels already cause too many divisions in our world. So I prefer to remain a free thinker, still searching for many more answers whilst recognising my own imperfections!

I studied Philosophy – a sceptical, forensic analysis of the nature of human existence and perceived knowledge – precisely because I didn't just want to accept the way the world was presenting itself to me; I wanted to question it rigorously and find my own truths. When it comes to life after death, I fully encourage people to be sceptical until you have either experienced spirit beings for yourself or have been given incontrovertible evidence in some way. But just think about this for a moment. Of all the millions of encounters with 'ghosts' recounted every year by people from all walks of life – most with no interest in spirituality and many downright sceptical or even hostile to the concept – just one of these experiences, just one, has to be true to prove that life after death is a reality!

The empirical approach in Philosophy examines the way we come to understand our world through our five senses. What we can see, hear, touch, taste and smell gives us our experience of the world. Anything outside this, closed minds like to call the supernatural, i.e. above or outside our normal sensory perception and therefore somehow strange, inexplicable, or even dangerous!

But just because we don't comprehend the full workings of nature doesn't make things beyond our limited senses 'supernatural'. There is no such thing as the supernatural, it's simply that the full extent of nature's laws are beyond our experience and comprehension. For example, dogs are estimated to have a sense of smell thousands of times greater than humans – we can't even conceive what that must be like. An eagle flying way up high in the sky has panoramic vision, yet can also pinpoint a hare on the ground. Bats have a kind of in-built, advanced radar that allows them to fly about in their thousands in dark caves. Whales can navigate around the oceans and return to the very same bay every year. I could cite countless more examples.

So there are many more heightened ways of sensing and interacting with our physical world than we possess. Why is it then such a leap to accept sensing other energetic dimensions – indeed, like many animals do? Ancient cultures right around the world understood and embraced the natural reality of spirit existence as part of their everyday lives, until so many of them literally had it beaten out of them.

We are part of something absolutely vast – and I firmly believe we are only at the very start of this incredible adventure. This is another reason why it's so vital that we address and find solutions now to the huge environmental issues that face us, before all else becomes superfluous. I believe that to understand and be able to explore the reality of life after death free from man-made restrictions, helps us put our physical existence into better perspective and gives it greater meaning and purpose. Your life is important, whatever your circumstances, and is a vital part of the universal energy that connects us all.

I very much hope you have enjoyed this book and that you continue to find your own enlightened path in life in your own wonderfully individual way.

Wishing you peace, love and happiness, Nick

CPSIA information can be obtained
at www.ICGtesting.com
Printed in the USA
LVHW030324110322
712944LV00001B/2